MORTAL
ECHOES

MORTAL ECHOES

Encounters with the End

edited by
GREG BUZWELL

First published in 2018 by
The British Library
96 Euston Road
London NW1 2DB

Introduction and notes copyright © Greg Buzwell 2018

'Kecksies' reproduced by permission of the Estate of Marjorie Bowen.

'A Little Place off the Edgware Road' reproduced by permission of
David Higham Associates on behalf of the Estate of Graham Greene.

'Your Tiny Hand is Frozen' reproduced by permission of Artellus
Limited. Copyright © The Estate of Robert Aickman.

'Kiss Me Again, Stranger' reproduced with permission of
Curtis Brown Group Ltd, London, on behalf of The Chichester
Partnership. Copyright © The Chichester Partnership, 1952.

'The School' from AMATEURS by Donald Barthelme. Copyright © 1977,
Donald Barthelme, used by permission of The Wylie Agency (UK) Limited.

'Death by Scrabble' reproduced by permission of the author.

Dates attributed to each story relate to first publication.

Cataloguing in Publication Data
A catalogue record for this publication is available from the British Library

ISBN 978 0 7123 5281 9
eISBN 978 0 7123 6454 6

Frontispiece illustration by Enrique Bernardou, 2018

Typeset by Tetragon, London
Printed and bound by CPI Group (UK) Ltd, Croydon CR0 4YY

CONTENTS

INTRODUCTION

There are, in Benjamin Franklin's memorable phrase, only two certainties in life—death and taxes. Of the two only the former has inspired a wealth of great literature. Taxes can be regarded as an unfortunate necessity, something to be grudgingly waved away with a shrug of the shoulders, but death is an altogether more troubling prospect. Death is also, for all its seeming certainty and finality, infinitely more mysterious. For a subject so universal it is remarkable just how many different responses an encounter with The Grim Reaper can inspire. The poet John Keats wished 'To cease upon the midnight with no pain'. The novelist Henry James lying on what he believed to be his deathbed uttered the words 'So here it is at last, the distinguished thing'. Lytton Strachey meanwhile, as his final moments approached, commented 'If this is dying, then I don't think much of it'. Whether we regard it with reverence, awe or just as a crashing bore bringing a premature end to a wonderful party there's no getting away from the fact that death is always there, the dark shadow waiting for us all at the end of the line.

When it comes to Gothic fiction, however, death opens up a whole new world of terrors, doubts and possibilities. Gothic fiction is obsessed with death. Within the pages of novels such as *The Castle of Otranto* (1764), *The Monk* (1796), *Frankenstein* (1818), *Wuthering Heights* (1847), *Dracula* (1897) and *The Woman in Black* (1983) there are deaths foretold, unnatural deaths, hauntings and things that should be dead and yet which continue to walk above ground. Part of Gothic fiction's fascination with mortality and with what might occur should death not provide the definitive conclusion we expect stems from its unknowability. Particularly in the Victorian era, when so much progress was made in explaining the natural world, the impossibility of knowing with certainty what (if anything) lay beyond the veil allowed the imagination to run riot. Even technological inventions such as the telephone hinted at fascinating new prospects. If it was possible to converse with someone on the far side of town, or even on the far side of the world would it also one day be possible to converse with someone separated by the greatest distance of all, that between life and death? It is no surprise that the ghost story, in which the boundaries between the living and the dead are broken, reached such a height of popularity during the 19th century.

Each of the fifteen stories contained in this volume addresses a particular fear associated with mortality. Each one touches upon death in a distinct way. There are stories about death's inevitability, such as Edgar Allan Poe's 'The Masque of the Red Death' in which wealth, status, arrogance and a fortified abbey prove of little use in halting the arrival of a particularly unwelcome guest. There are tales of what might lie ahead in the afterlife such as May Sinclair's 'Where Their Fire is not Quenched' and Mary Coleridge's 'The King is Dead, Long Live the King'. Then there are the stories in which the dead seem reluctant to remain in their graves such as Marjorie Bowen's 'Kecksies'. Humour is also present. H. H. Munro's tale 'Laura' focuses upon a young woman who believes that after death she will be reincarnated as 'a nice animal, something elegant and lively, with a love of fun. An otter, perhaps'. On such a basis perhaps dying wouldn't be too great an ordeal after all. Charlie Fish's story explores a particularly murderous game of Scrabble where it isn't always clear which of the two players has the upper hand. Donald

Barthelme's 'The School' meanwhile is a riot of unfortunate deaths that ultimately ends in a surreal and life-affirming fashion.

Then, finally there are the stories that are plain macabre. No collection of Gothic tales would be complete without a selection of disturbing tales. These include Daphne du Maurier's 'Kiss Me Again, Stranger' with its mysterious and troubled femme fatale; Joseph Sheridan Le Fanu's 'Schalken the Painter' with its queasy mingling of sex and death, and Robert Aickman's 'Your Tiny Hand is Frozen' in which a mysterious voice at the end of a telephone line causes very real problems for the person taking the calls. Like several of the stories in this volume Aickman's enigmatic tale explores the very fine line between madness and sanity. After all if you see someone whom you believe to be dead, or hear their voice, which is the more likely explanation: a ghost or a disturbance in the balance of one's mind? Graham Greene's 'A Little Place off the Edgware Road' is a particularly fine example of the shadowy ground between the barely explicable and the completely unhinged.

Although these tales have mortality as their subject their overall effect is always thrilling, chilling or eerie rather than gloomy. The unknown inevitably inspires fear, wonder and awe. Whatever else, it is never dull. I hope you enjoy reading these stories as much as I enjoyed selecting them. So here it is at last, the distinguished thing...

GREG BUZWELL

Curator of Contemporary Literary Archives at the British Library

STRANGE EVENT IN THE LIFE OF SCHALKEN THE PAINTER (1839)

Joseph Thomas Sheridan Le Fanu

Born in Dublin, Joseph Sheridan Le Fanu (1814–73) came from a family with an impressive literary heritage. His grandmother, Alicia Sheridan Le Fanu, and his great uncle, Richard Brinsley Sheridan, were both playwrights. His niece, Rhoda Broughton, would become a successful novelist. Although his literary output covered a range of subjects he is best known today for his horror fiction. His novel *Uncle Silas* (1864) was a chilling addition to the genre of sensation fiction popularized by authors such as Wilkie Collins and Mary Elizabeth Braddon while his novella *Carmilla* (1871), with its predatory female vampire, was an influence on Bram Stoker's *Dracula* (1897), not to mention any number of racy horror films from the late 1960s and 1970s such as *The Vampire Lovers* and *Lust for a Vampire*.

'Strange Event in the Life of Schalken the Painter' tells of the mysterious suitor, Minheer Vanderhausen of Rotterdam, for the hand in marriage of the beautiful Rose Velderkaust. Vanderhausen is wealthy and persuasive but with each successive appearance in the house of Rose's guardian, the painter Gerard Douw, his presence becomes more loathsome. The story was an important influence on the ghost story writer M. R. James who admired its subtlety and its ability to defy easy categorization. Just as with James' own fiction much of the tale's power to horrify lies in what is implied, rather than overtly stated.

YOU WILL, NO DOUBT, BE SURPRISED, MY DEAR FRIEND, AT THE subject of the following narrative. What had I to do with Schalken, or Schalken with me? He had returned to his native land, and was probably dead and buried before I was born; I never visited Holland nor spoke with a native of that country. So much I believe you already know. I must, then, give you my authority, and state to you frankly the ground upon which rests the credibility of the strange story which I am about to lay before you. I was acquainted, in my early days, with a Captain Vandael, whose father had served King William in the Low Countries, and also in my own unhappy land during the Irish campaigns. I know not how it happened that I liked this man's society spite of his politics and religion: but so it was; and it was by means of the free intercourse to which our intimacy gave rise that I became possessed of the curious tale which you are about to hear. I had often been struck, while visiting Vandael, by a remarkable picture, in which, though no *connoisseur* myself, I could not fail to discern some very strong peculiarities, particularly in the distribution of light and shade, as also a certain oddity in the design itself, which interested my curiosity. It represented the interior of what might be a chamber in some antique religious building—the fore-ground was occupied by a female figure, arrayed in a species of white robe, part of which is arranged so as to form a veil. The dress, however, is not strictly that of any religious order. In its hand the figure bears a lamp, by whose light alone the form and face are illuminated; the features are marked by an arch smile, such as pretty women wear when engaged in successfully practising some roguish trick; in the back-ground, and, excepting where the dim red light of an expiring fire serves to define the form, totally in the shade, stands the figure of a man equipped in the old fashion, with doublet and so forth, in an attitude of alarm, his hand being placed upon the hilt of his sword, which he appears to be in the act of drawing.

"There are some pictures," said I to my friend, "which impress one, I know not how, with a conviction that they represent not the mere ideal shapes and combinations which have floated through the imagination of the artist, but scenes, faces, and situations which have actually existed. When I look upon that picture, something assures me that I behold the representation of a reality."

Vandael smiled, and, fixing his eyes upon the painting musingly, he said—

"Your fancy has not deceived you, my good friend, for that picture is the record, and I believe a faithful one, of a remarkable and mysterious occurrence. It was painted by Schalken, and contains, in the face of the female figure, which occupies the most prominent place in the design, an accurate portrait of Rose Velderkaust, the niece of Gerard Douw, the first, and, I believe, the only love of Godfrey Schalken. My father knew the painter well, and from Schalken himself he learned the story of the mysterious drama, one scene of which the picture has embodied. This painting, which is accounted a fine specimen of Schalken's style, was bequeathed to my father by the artist's will, and, as you have observed, is a very striking and interesting production."

I had only to request Vandael to tell the story of the painting in order to be gratified; and thus it is that I am enabled to submit to you a faithful recital of what I heard myself, leaving you to reject or to allow the evidence upon which the truth of the tradition depends, with this one assurance, that Schalken was an honest, blunt Dutchman, and, I believe, wholly incapable of committing a flight of imagination; and further, that Vandael, from whom I heard the story, appeared firmly convinced of its truth.

There are few forms upon which the mantle of mystery and romance could seem to hang more ungracefully than upon that of the uncouth and clownish Schalken—the Dutch boor—the rude and dogged, but most cunning worker of oils, whose pieces delight the initiated of the present day almost as much as his manners disgusted the refined of his own; and yet this man, so rude, so dogged, so slovenly, I had almost said so savage, in mien and manner, during his after successes, had been selected by the capricious goddess, in his early life, to figure as the hero of a romance by no means devoid of interest or of mystery. Who can tell how meet he may have been in his young days to play the part of the lover or of the hero—who can say that in early life he had been the same harsh, *unlicked*, and rugged boor which, in his maturer age, he proved—or how far the neglected rudeness which afterwards marked his air, and garb, and manners, may not have been the growth of that reckless apathy not unfrequently produced by bitter misfortunes and disappointments in early life? These questions can never now be answered. We must content ourselves, then, with a plain statement of facts, or what have been received and transmitted as such, leaving matters of speculation to those who like them.

When Schalken studied under the immortal Gerard Douw, he was a young man; and in spite of the phlegmatic constitution and unexcitable manner which he shared (we believe) with his countrymen, he was not incapable of deep and vivid impressions, for it is an established fact that the young painter looked with considerable interest upon the beautiful niece of his wealthy master. Rose Velderkaust was very young, having, at the period of which we speak, not yet attained her seventeenth year, and, if tradition speaks truth, possessed all the soft dimpling charms of the fair, light-haired Flemish maidens. Schalken had not studied long in the school of Gerard Douw, when he felt this interest deepening into something of a keener and

intenser feeling than was quite consistent with the tranquillity of his
honest Dutch heart; and at the same time he perceived, or thought
he perceived, flattering symptoms of a reciprocity of liking, and this
was quite sufficient to determine whatever indecision he might have
heretofore experienced, and to lead him to devote exclusively to her
every hope and feeling of his heart. In short, he was as much in love
as a Dutchman could be. He was not long in making his passion
known to the pretty maiden herself, and his declaration was followed
by a corresponding confession upon her part. Schalken, however, was
a poor man, and he possessed no counterbalancing advantages of
birth or otherwise to induce the old man to consent to a union which
must involve his niece and ward in the strugglings and difficulties
of a young and nearly friendless artist. He was, therefore, to wait
until time had furnished him with opportunity and accident with
success; and then, if his labours were found sufficiently lucrative, it
was to be hoped that his proposals might at least be listened to by
her jealous guardian. Months passed away, and, cheered by the smiles
of the little Rose, Schalken's labours were redoubled, and with such
effect and improvement as reasonably to promise the realization of
his hopes, and no contemptible eminence in his art, before many
years should have elapsed.

The even course of this cheering prosperity was, however, destined to experience a sudden and formidable interruption, and that,
too, in a manner so strange and mysterious as to baffle all investigation, and throw upon the events themselves a shadow of almost
supernatural horror.

Schalken had one evening remained in the master's studio considerably longer than his more volatile companions, who had gladly
availed themselves of the excuse which the dusk of evening afforded,
to withdraw from their several tasks, in order to finish a day of
labour in the jollity and conviviality of the tavern. But Schalken

worked for improvement, or rather for love. Besides, he was now engaged merely in sketching a design, an operation which, unlike that of colouring, might be continued as long as there was light sufficient to distinguish between canvas and charcoal. He had not then, nor, indeed, until long after, discovered the peculiar powers of his pencil, and he was engaged in composing a group of extremely roguish-looking and grotesque imps and demons, who were inflicting various ingenious torments upon a perspiring and pot-bellied St. Anthony, who reclined in the midst of them, apparently in the last stage of drunkenness. The young artist, however, though incapable of executing, or even of appreciating, any thing of true sublimity, had, nevertheless, discernment enough to prevent his being by any means satisfied with his work; and many were the patient erasures and corrections which the limbs and features of saint and devil underwent, yet all without producing in their new arrangement any thing of improvement or increased effect: The large, old-fashioned room was silent, and, with the exception of himself, quite deserted by its usual inmates. An hour had passed—nearly two—without any improved result. Daylight had already declined, and twilight was fast giving way to the darkness of night. The patience of the young man was exhausted, and he stood before his unfinished production, absorbed in no very pleasing ruminations, one hand buried in the folds of his long dark hair, and the other holding the piece of charcoal which had so ill executed its office, and which he now rubbed, without much regard to the sable streaks which it produced, with irritable pressure upon his ample Flemish inexpressibles.—"Pshaw!" said the young man aloud, "would that picture, devils, saint, and all, were where they should be—in hell!" A short, sudden laugh, uttered startlingly close to his ear, instantly responded to the ejaculation. The artist turned sharply round, and now for the first time became aware that his labours had been overlooked by a stranger. Within about a yard and half, and rather behind him, there stood what was, or appeared to be, the figure of an elderly man: he wore a short cloak, and broad-brimmed hat, with a conical crown, and in his hand, which was protected with a heavy, gauntlet-shaped glove, he carried a long ebony walking-stick, surmounted with what appeared, as it glittered dimly in the twilight, to be a massive head of gold, and upon the breast, through the folds of the cloak, there shone what appeared to be the links of a rich chain of the same metal. The room was so obscure that nothing further of the appearance of the figure could be ascertained, and the face was altogether overshadowed by the heavy flap of the beaver which overhung it, so that not a feature could be discerned. A quantity of dark hair escaped from beneath this sombre hat, a circumstance which, connected with the firm, upright carriage of the intruder, proved that his years could not yet exceed threescore or thereabouts. There was an air of gravity and importance about the garb of this person, and something indescribably odd, I might say awful, in the perfect, stone-like movelessness of the figure, that effectually checked the testy comment which had at once risen to the lips of the irritated artist. He, therefore, as soon as he had sufficiently recovered the surprise, asked the stranger, civilly, to be seated, and desired to know if he had any message to leave for his master.

"Tell Gerard Douw," said the unknown, without altering his attitude in the smallest degree, "that Minheer Vanderhausen, of Rotterdam, desires to speak with him on tomorrow evening at this hour, and, if he please, in this room, upon matters of weight—that is all—good night."

The stranger, having finished this message, turned abruptly, and, with a quick but silent step quitted the room, before Schalken had time to say a word in reply. The young man felt a curiosity to see in what direction the burgher of Rotterdam would turn on quitting the studio, and for that purpose he went directly to the window which commanded the door. A lobby of considerable extent intervened between the inner door of the painter's room and the street entrance, so that Schalken occupied the post of observation before the old man could possibly have reached the street. He watched in vain, however. There was no other mode of exit. Had the old man vanished, or was he lurking about the recesses of the lobby for some bad purpose? This last suggestion filled the mind of Schalken with a vague horror, which was so unaccountably intense as to make him alike afraid to remain in the room alone and reluctant to pass through the lobby. However, with an effort which appeared very disproportioned to the occasion, he summoned resolution to leave the room, and, having double-locked the door and thrust the key in his pocket, without looking to the right or left, he traversed the passage which had so recently, perhaps still, contained the person of his mysterious visitant, scarcely venturing to breathe till he had arrived in the open street.

"Minheer Vanderhausen," said Gerard Douw within himself, as the appointed hour approached, "Minheer Vanderhausen of Rotterdam! I never heard of the man till yesterday. What can he want of me? A portrait, perhaps, to be painted; or a younger son or a poor relation to be apprenticed; or a collection to be valued; or—pshaw, there's no one in Rotterdam to leave me a legacy. Well, whatever the business may be, we shall soon know it all."

It was now the close of day, and every easel, except that of Schalken, was deserted. Gerard Douw was pacing the apartment with the restless step of impatient expectation, every now and then humming a passage from a piece of music which he was himself composing; for, though no great proficient, he admired the art; sometimes pausing to glance over the work of one of his absent pupils, but more frequently placing himself at the window, from whence he might observe the passengers who threaded the obscure by-street in which his studio was placed.

"Said you not, Godfrey," exclaimed Douw, after a long and fruitless gaze from his post of observation, and turning to Schalken—"said you not the hour of appointment was at about seven by the clock of the Stadhouse?"

"It had just told seven when I first saw him, sir," answered the student.

"The hour is close at hand, then," said the master, consulting a horologe as large and as round as a full-grown orange. "Minheer Vanderhausen from Rotterdam—is it not so?"

"Such was the name."

"And an elderly man, richly clad?" continued Douw.

"As well as I might see," replied his pupil; "he could not be young, nor yet very old neither, and his dress was rich and grave, as might become a citizen of wealth and consideration."

At this moment the sonorous boom of the Stadhouse clock told, stroke after stroke, the hour of seven; the eyes of both master and student were directed to the door; and it was not until the last peal of the old bell had ceased to vibrate, that Douw exclaimed—

"So, so; we shall have his worship presently—that is, if he means to keep his hour; if not, thou may'st wait for him, Godfrey, if you court the acquaintance of a capricious burgomaster; as for me, I think our old Leyden contains a sufficiency of such commodities, without an importation from Rotterdam."

Schalken laughed, as in duty bound; and after a pause of some minutes, Douw suddenly exclaimed—

"What if it should all prove a jest, a piece of mummery got up by Vankarp, or some such worthy. I wish you had run all risks, and cudgelled the old burgomaster, stadholder, or whatever else he may be, soundly. I would wager a dozen of Rhenish, his worship would have pleaded old acquaintance before the third application."

"Here he comes, sir," said Schalken, in a low admonitory tone; and instantly upon turning towards the door, Gerard Douw observed the same figure which had, on the day before, so unexpectedly greeted the vision of his pupil Schalken.

There was something in the air and mien of the figure which at once satisfied the painter that there was no *mummery* in the case, and that he really stood in the presence of a man of worship; and so, without hesitation, he doffed his cap, and, courteously saluting the stranger, requested him to be seated. The visitor waved his hand slightly, as if in acknowledgment of the courtesy, but remained standing.

"I have the honour to see Minheer Vanderhausen of Rotterdam?" said Gerard Douw.

"The same," was the laconic reply of his visitant.

"I understand your worship desires to speak with me," continued Douw, "and I am here by appointment to wait your commands."

"Is that a man of trust?" said Vanderhausen, turning towards Schalken, who stood at a little distance behind his master.

"Certainly," replied Gerard.

"Then let him take this box and get the nearest jeweller or goldsmith to value its contents, and let him return hither with a certificate of the valuation."

At the same time, he placed a small case about nine inches square in the hands of Gerard Douw, who was as much amazed at its weight as at the strange abruptness with which it was handed to him. In accordance with the wishes of the stranger, he delivered it into the hands of Schalken, and repeating *his* directions, despatched him upon the mission.

Schalken disposed his precious charge securely beneath the folds of his cloak, and rapidly traversing two or three narrow streets, he stopped at a corner house, the lower part of which was then occupied by the shop of a Jewish goldsmith. Schalken entered the shop, and calling the little Hebrew into the obscurity of its back recesses, he proceeded to lay before him Vanderhausen's packet. On being examined by the light of a lamp, it appeared entirely cased with lead, the outer surface of which was much scraped and soiled, and nearly white with age. This was with difficulty partially removed, and disclosed beneath a box of some dark and singularly hard wood; this, too was forced, and after the removal of two or three folds of linen, its contents proved to be a mass of golden ingots, closely packed, and, as the Jew declared, of the most perfect quality. Every ingot underwent the scrutiny of the little Jew, who seemed to feel an epicurean delight in touching and testing these morsels of the glorious metal; and each one of them was replaced in its birth with the exclamation: "*Mein Gott* how very perfect! not one grain of alloy—beautiful, beautiful." The task was at length finished, and the Jew certified under his hand the value of the ingots submitted to his examination, to amount to many thousand rix-dollars. With the desired document in his bosom, and the rich box of gold carefully pressed under his arm, and concealed by his cloak, he retraced his way, and entering the studio, found his master and the stranger in close conference. Schalken had no sooner left the room, in order to execute the commission he had taken in charge, than Vanderhausen addressed Gerard Douw in the following terms—

"I may not tarry with you tonight more than a few minutes, and so I shall briefly tell you the matter upon which I come. You visited the town of Rotterdam some four months ago, and then I saw in the church of St. Lawrence your niece, Rose Velderkaust. I desire to marry her, and if I satisfy you as to the fact that I am very wealthy, more wealthy than any husband you could dream of for her, I expect that you will forward my views to the utmost of your authority. If you approve my proposal, you must close with it at once, for I cannot command time enough to wait for calculations and delays."

Gerard Douw was, perhaps, as much astonished as any one could be, by the very unexpected nature of Minheer Vanderhausen's communication, but he did not give vent to any unseemly expression of surprise, for besides the motives supplied by prudence and politeness, the painter experienced a kind of chill and oppressive sensation, something like that which is supposed to affect a man who is placed unconsciously in immediate contact with something to which he has a natural antipathy—an undefined horror and dread while standing in the presence of the eccentric stranger, which made him very unwilling to say any thing which might reasonably prove offensive.

"I have no doubt," said Gerard, after two or three prefatory hems, "that the connection which you propose would prove alike advantageous and honourable to my niece; but you must be aware that she has a will of her own, and may not acquiesce in what *we* may design for her advantage."

"Do not seek to deceive me, sir painter," said Vanderhausen; "you are her guardian—she is your ward—she is mine if *you* like to make her so."

The man of Rotterdam moved forward a little as he spoke, and Gerard Douw, he scarce knew why, inwardly prayed for the speedy return of Schalken.

"I desire," said the mysterious gentleman, "to place in your hands at once an evidence of my wealth, and a security for my liberal dealing with your niece. The lad will return in a minute or two with a sum in value five times the fortune which she has a right to expect from a husband. This shall lie in your hands, together with her dowry, and you may apply the united sum as suits her interest best; it shall be all exclusively hers while she lives—is that liberal?"

Douw assented, and inwardly thought that fortune had been extraordinarily kind to his niece; the stranger, he thought, must be both wealthy and generous, and such an offer was not to be despised,

though made by a humorist, and one of no very prepossessing presence. Rose had no very high pretensions; for she was almost without
dowry; indeed altogether so, excepting so far as the deficiency had
been supplied by the generosity of her uncle; neither had she any
right to raise any scruples against the match on the score of birth,
for her own origin was by no means elevated, and as to other objections, Gerard resolved, and, indeed, by the usages of the time, was
warranted in resolving not to listen to them for a moment.

"Sir," said he, addressing the stranger, "your offer is most liberal,
and whatever hesitation I may feel in closing with it immediately,
arises solely from my not having the honour of knowing any thing
of your family or station. Upon these points you can, of course,
satisfy me without difficulty?"

"As to my respectability," said the stranger, drily, "you must take
that for granted at present; pester me with no inquiries; you can
discover nothing more about me than I choose to make known. You
shall have sufficient security for my respectability—my word, if you
are honourable: if you are sordid, my gold."

"A testy old gentleman," thought Douw, "he must have his own
way; but, all things considered, I am justified in giving my niece to
him; were she my own daughter, I would do the like by her. I will
not pledge myself unnecessarily however."

"You will not pledge yourself unnecessarily," said Vanderhausen,
strangely uttering the very words which had just floated through
the mind of his companion; "but you will do so if it is necessary, I
presume; and I will show you that I consider it indispensable. If the
gold I mean to leave in your hands satisfy you, and if you desire that
my proposal shall not be at once withdrawn, you must, before I leave
this room, write your name to this engagement."

Having thus spoken, he placed a paper in the hands of Gerard, the
contents of which expressed an engagement entered into by Gerard

Douw, to give to Wilken Vanderhausen of Rotterdam, in marriage, Rose Velderkaust, and so forth, within one week of the date hereof. While the painter was employed in reading this covenant, Schalken, as we have stated, entered the studio, and having delivered the box and the valuation of the Jew, into the hands of the stranger, he was about to retire, when Vanderhausen called to him to wait; and, presenting the case and the certificate to Gerard Douw, he waited in silence until he had satisfied himself by an inspection of both as to the value of the pledge left in his hands. At length he said—

"Are you content?"

The painter said he would fain have another day to consider.

"Not an hour," said the suitor coolly.

"Well then," said Douw, "I am content—it is a bargain."

"Then sign at once," said Vanderhausen, "I am weary."

At the same time he produced a small case of writing materials, and Gerard signed the important document.

"Let this youth witness the covenant," said the old man; and Godfrey Schalken unconsciously signed the instrument which bestowed upon another that hand which he had so long regarded as the object and reward of all his labours. The compact being thus completed, the strange visitor folded up the paper, and stowed it safely in an inner pocket.

"I will visit you tomorrow night at nine of the clock, at your house, Gerard Douw, and will see the subject of our contract—farewell;" and so saying, Wilken Vanderhausen moved stiffly, but rapidly out of the room.

Schalken, eager to resolve his doubts, had placed himself by the window, in order to watch the street entrance; but the experiment served only to support his suspicions, for the old man did not issue from the door. This was very strange, very odd, very fearful; he and his master returned together, and talked but little on the way, for each had his own subjects of reflection, of anxiety, and of hope. Schalken, however, did not know the ruin which threatened his cherished schemes.

Gerard Douw knew nothing of the attachment which had sprung up between his pupil and his niece; and even if he had, it is doubtful whether he would have regarded its existence as any serious obstruction to the wishes of Minheer Vanderhausen. Marriages were then and there matters of traffic and calculation; and it would have appeared as absurd in the eyes of the guardian to make a mutual attachment an essential element in a contract of marriage, as it would have been to draw up his bonds and receipts in the language of chivalrous romance. The painter, however, did not communicate to his niece the important step which he had taken in her behalf, and his resolution arose not from any anticipation of opposition on her part, but solely from a ludicrous consciousness that if his ward were, as she very naturally might do, to ask him to describe the appearance of the bridegroom whom he destined for her, he would be forced to confess that he had not seen his face, and if called upon, would find it impossible to identify him. Upon the next day, Gerard Douw having dined, called his niece to him, and having scanned her person with an air of satisfaction, he took her hand, and looking upon her pretty, innocent face with a smile of kindness, he said—

"Rose, my girl, that face of yours will make your fortune." Rose blushed and smiled. "Such faces and such tempers seldom go together, and when they do, the compound is a love potion, which few heads or hearts can resist; trust me, thou wilt soon be a bride, girl; but this is trifling, and I am pressed for time, so make ready the large room by eight o'clock tonight, and give directions for supper at nine. I expect a friend tonight; and observe me, child, do thou trick thyself out handsomely. I would not have him think us poor or sluttish."

With these words he left the chamber, and took his way to the room to which we have already had occasion to introduce our readers—that in which his pupils worked.

When the evening closed in, Gerard called Schalken, who was about to take his departure to his obscure and comfortless lodgings, and asked him to come home and sup with Rose and Vanderhausen. The invitation was, of course, accepted, and Gerard Douw and his pupil soon found themselves in the handsome and somewhat antique-looking room which had been prepared for the reception of the stranger. A cheerful wood fire blazed in the capacious hearth; a little at one side an old-fashioned table, with richly carved legs, was placed—destined, no doubt, to receive the supper, for which preparations were going forward; and ranged with exact regularity, stood the tall-backed chairs, whose ungracefulness was more than counterbalanced by their comfort. The little party, consisting of Rose, her uncle, and the artist, awaited the arrival of the expected visitor with considerable impatience. Nine o'clock at length came, and with it a summons at the street door, which being speedily answered, was followed by a slow and emphatic tread upon the staircase; the steps moved heavily across the lobby, the door of the room in which the party which we have described were assembled slowly opened, and there entered a figure which startled, almost appalled, the phlegmatic Dutchmen, and nearly made Rose scream with affright; it was the form, and arrayed in the garb of Minheer Vanderhausen; the air, the gait, the height was the same, but the features had never been seen by any of the party before. The stranger stopped at the door of the room, and displayed his form and face completely. He wore a dark-coloured cloth cloak, which was short and full, not falling quite to the knees; his legs were cased in dark purple silk stockings, and his shoes were adorned with roses of the same colour. The opening of the cloak in front showed the under-suit to consist of some very dark, perhaps sable material, and his hands were enclosed in a pair of heavy leather gloves, which ran up considerably above the wrist, in the manner of a gauntlet. In one hand he carried his walking-stick and his hat, which he had removed, and the other hung heavily by his side. A quantity of grizzled hair descended in long tresses from his head, and its folds rested upon the plaits of a stiff ruff, which effectually concealed his neck. So far all was well; but the face!—all the flesh of the face was coloured with the bluish leaden hue, which is sometimes produced by the operation of metallic medicines, administered in excessive quantities; the eyes were enormous, and the white appeared both above and below the iris, which gave to them an expression of insanity, which was heightened by their glassy fixedness; the nose was well enough, but the mouth was writhed considerably to one side, where it opened in order to give egress to two long, discoloured fangs, which projected from the upper jaw, far below the lower lip—the hue of the lips themselves bore the usual relation to that of the face, and was, consequently, nearly black; the character of the face was malignant, even satanic, to the last degree; and, indeed, such a combination of horror could hardly be accounted for, except by supposing the corpse of some atrocious malefactor which had long hung blackening upon the gibbet to have at length become the habitation of a demon—the frightful sport of satanic possession. It was remarkable that the worshipful stranger suffered as little as possible of his flesh to appear, and that during his visit he did not once remove his gloves. Having stood for some moments at the door, Gerard Douw at length found breath and collectedness to bid him welcome, and with a mute inclination of the head, the stranger stepped forward into the room. There was something indescribably odd, even horrible, about all his motions, something undefinable, that was unnatural, unhuman—it was as if the limbs were guided and directed by a spirit unused to the management of bodily machinery. The stranger said hardly any thing during his visit, which did not exceed half an hour; and the host himself could scarcely muster courage enough to utter the few necessary salutations and courtesies; and, indeed, such was the nervous terror which the presence of Vanderhausen inspired, that very little would have made all his entertainers fly bellowing from the room. They had not so far lost all self-possession, however, as to fail to observe two strange peculiarities of their visitor. During his stay he did not once suffer his eyelids to close, nor even to move in the slightest degree; and farther, there was a death-like stillness in his whole person, owing to the total absence of the heaving motion of the chest, caused by the process of respiration. These two peculiarities, though when told they may appear trifling, produced a very striking and unpleasant effect when seen and observed. Vanderhausen at length relieved the painter of Leyden of his inauspicious presence; and with no small gratification the little party heard the street door close after him.

"Dear uncle," said Rose, "what a frightful man! I would not see him again for the wealth of the States."

"Tush, foolish girl," said Douw, whose sensations were any thing but comfortable. "A man may be as ugly as the devil, and yet if his heart and actions are good, he is worth all the pretty-faced, perfumed puppies that walk the Mall. Rose, my girl, it is very true he has not thy pretty face, but I know him to be wealthy and liberal; and were he ten times more ugly"—("which is inconceivable," observed Rose)—"these two virtues would be sufficient," continued her uncle, "to counterbalance all his deformity, and if not of power sufficient actually to alter the shape of the features, at least of efficacy enough to prevent one thinking them amiss."

"Do you know, uncle," said Rose, "when I saw him standing at the door, I could not get it out of my head that I saw the old, painted, wooden figure that used to frighten me so much in the church of St. Laurence of Rotterdam."

Gerard laughed, though he could not help inwardly acknowledging the justness of the comparison. He was resolved, however, as far as he could, to check his niece's inclination to ridicule the ugliness of her intended bridegroom, although he was not a little pleased to observe that she appeared totally exempt from that mysterious dread of the stranger, which he could not disguise it from himself, considerably affected him, as also his pupil Godfrey Schalken.

Early on the next day there arrived from various quarters of the town, rich presents of silks, velvets, jewellery, and so forth, for Rose; and also a packet directed to Gerard Douw, which, on being opened, was found to contain a contract of marriage, formally drawn up, between Wilken Vanderhausen of the *Boom-quay*, in Rotterdam, and Rose Velderkaust of Leyden, niece to Gerard Douw, master in the art of painting, also of the same city; and containing engagements on the part of Vanderhausen to make settlements upon his bride, far more splendid than he had before led her guardian to believe likely, and which were to be secured to her use in the most unexceptionable manner possible—the money being placed in the hands of Gerard Douw himself.

I have no sentimental scenes to describe, no cruelty of guardians, or magnanimity of wards, or agonies of lovers. The record I have to make is one of sordidness, levity, and interest. In less than a week after the first interview which we have just described, the contract of marriage was fulfilled, and Schalken saw the prize which he would have risked any thing to secure, carried off triumphantly by his attractive rival. For two or three days he absented himself from the school; he then returned and worked, if with less cheerfulness, with far more dogged resolution than before—the slumbers of love had given place to that of ambition. Months passed away, and, contrary to his expectation, and, indeed, to the direct promise of the parties, Gerard Douw heard nothing of his niece or her worshipful spouse. The interest of the money which was to have been demanded in quarterly sums, lay unclaimed in his hands. He began to grow extremely uneasy. Minheer Vanderhausen's direction in Rotterdam he was fully possessed of; after some irresolution he finally determined to journey thither—a trifling undertaking, and easily accomplished—and thus to satisfy himself of the safety and comfort of his ward, for whom he entertained an honest and strong affection. His search was in vain, however; no one in Rotterdam had ever heard of Minheer Vanderhausen. Gerard Douw left not a house in the Boom-quay untried; but all in vain—no one could give him any information whatever touching the object of his inquiry; and he was obliged to return to Leyden nothing wiser than when he had left it. On his arrival he hastened to the establishment from which Vanderhausen had hired the lumbering, though, considering the times, most luxurious vehicle, which the bridal party had employed to convey them to Rotterdam. From the driver of this machine he learned, that having proceeded by slow stages, they had late in the evening approached Rotterdam; but that before they entered the city, and while yet nearly a mile from it, a small party of men, soberly clad, and after the old fashion, with peaked beards and moustaches, standing in the centre of the road, obstructed the further progress of the carriage. The driver reined in his horses, much fearing, from the obscurity of the hour, and the loneliness of the road, that some mischief was intended. His fears were, however, somewhat allayed by his observing that these strange men carried a large litter, of an antique shape, and which they immediately set down upon the pavement, whereupon the bridegroom, having opened the coach-door from within, descended, and having assisted his bride to do likewise, led her, weeping bitterly and wringing her hands, to the litter, which they both entered. It was then raised by the men who surrounded it, and speedily carried towards the city, and before it had proceeded many yards, the darkness concealed it from the view of the Dutch charioteer. In the inside of the vehicle he found a purse, whose contents more than thrice paid the hire of the carriage and man. He saw and could tell nothing more of Minheer Vanderhausen and his beautiful lady. This mystery was a source of deep anxiety and almost of grief to Gerard Douw. There was evidently fraud in the dealing of Vanderhausen with him, though for what purpose committed he could not imagine. He greatly doubted how far it was possible for a man possessing in his countenance so strong an evidence of the presence of the most demoniac feelings, to be in reality any thing but a villain, and every day that passed without his hearing from or of his niece, instead of inducing him to forget his fears, on the contrary tended more and more to exasperate them. The loss of his niece's cheerful society tended also to depress his spirits; and in order to dispel this despondency, which often crept upon his mind after his daily employment was over, he was wont frequently to prevail upon Schalken to accompany him home, and by his presence to dispel, in some degree, the gloom of his otherwise solitary supper. One evening, the painter and his pupil were sitting by the fire, having accomplished a comfortable supper, and had yielded to that silent pensiveness sometimes induced by the process of digestion, when their reflections were disturbed by a loud sound at the street door, as if occasioned by some person rushing forcibly and repeatedly against it. A domestic had run without delay to ascertain the cause of the disturbance, and they heard him twice or thrice interrogate the applicant for admission, but without producing an answer or any cessation of the sounds. They heard him then open the hall-door, and immediately there followed a light and rapid tread upon the staircase. Schalken laid his hand on his sword, and advanced towards the door. It opened before he reached it, and Rose rushed into the room. She looked wild and haggard, and pale with exhaustion and terror, but her dress surprised them as much even as her unexpected appearance. It consisted of a kind of white woollen wrapper, made close about the neck, and descending to the very ground. It was much deranged and travel-soiled. The poor creature had hardly entered the chamber when she fell senseless on the floor. With some difficulty they succeeded in reviving her, and on recovering her senses, she instantly exclaimed, in a tone of eager, terrified impatience—

"Wine, wine, quickly, or I'm lost."

Much alarmed at the strange agitation in which the call was made, they at once administered to her wishes, and she drank some wine with a haste and eagerness which surprised them. She had hardly swallowed it, when she exclaimed, with the same urgency,

"Food, food, at once, or I perish."

A considerable fragment of a roast joint was upon the table, and Schalken immediately proceeded to cut some, but he was anticipated, for no sooner had she become aware of its presence, than she darted at it with the rapacity of a vulture, and, seizing it in her hands, she tore off the flesh with her teeth, and swallowed it. When the paroxysm of hunger had been a little appeased, she appeared suddenly to become aware how strange her conduct had been, or it may have been that other more agitating thoughts recurred to her mind, for she began to weep bitterly and to wring her hands.

"Oh send for a minister of God," said she; "I am not safe till he comes; send for him speedily."

Gerard Douw despatched a messenger instantly, and prevailed on his niece to allow him to surrender his bedchamber to her use; he also persuaded her to retire to it at once and to rest; her consent was extorted upon the condition that they would not leave her for a moment.

"Oh that the holy man were here," she said; "he can deliver me— the dead and the living can never be one—God has forbidden it."

With these mysterious words she surrendered herself to their guidance, and they proceeded to the chamber which Gerard Douw had assigned to her use.

"Do not, do not leave me for a moment," said she; "I am lost for ever if you do."

Gerard Douw's chamber was approached through a spacious apartment, which they were now about to enter. Gerard Douw and Schalken each carried a wax candle, so that a sufficient degree of light was cast upon all surrounding objects. They were now entering the large chamber, which, as I have said, communicated with Douw's apartment, when Rose suddenly stopped, and, in a whisper which seemed to thrill with horror, she said—

"Oh, God! he is here, he is here; see, see, there he goes."

She pointed towards the door of the inner room, and Schalken thought he saw a shadowy and ill-defined form gliding into that apartment. He drew his sword, and, raising the candle so as to throw its light with increased distinctness upon the objects in the room, he entered the chamber into which the shadow had glided. No figure was there—nothing but the furniture which belonged to the room, and yet he could not be deceived as to the fact that something had moved before them into the chamber. A sickening dread came upon him, and the cold perspiration broke out in heavy drops upon his forehead; nor was he more composed, when he heard the increased urgency, the agony of entreaty, with which Rose implored them not to leave her for a moment.

"I saw him," said she; "he's here. I cannot be deceived—I know him—he's by me—he is with me—he's in the room; then, for God's sake, as you would save me, do not stir from beside me."

They at length prevailed upon her to lie down upon the bed, where she continued to urge them to stay by her. She frequently uttered incoherent sentences, repeating, again and again, "the dead and the living cannot be one—God has forbidden it;" and then again, "rest to the wakeful—sleep to the sleep-walkers." These and such mysterious and broken sentences, she continued to utter until the clergyman arrived. Gerard Douw began to fear, naturally enough, that the poor girl, owing to terror or ill-treatment, had become deranged, and he half suspected, by the suddenness of her appearance, and the unseasonableness of the hour, and, above all, from the wildness and terror of her manner, that she had made her escape from some place of confinement for lunatics, and was in immediate fear of pursuit. He resolved to summon medical advice, as soon as the mind of his niece had been in some measure set at rest by the offices of the clergyman whose attendance she had so earnestly desired; and until this object had been attained, he did not venture to put any questions to her, which might possibly, by reviving painful or horrible recollections, increase her agitation. The clergyman soon arrived—a man of ascetic countenance and venerable age—one whom Gerard Douw respected much, forasmuch as he was a veteran polemic, though one, perhaps, more dreaded as a combatant than beloved as a Christian—of pure morality, subtle brain, and frozen heart. He entered the chamber which communicated with that in which Rose reclined, and immediately on his arrival, she requested him to pray for her, as for one who lay in the hands of Satan, and who could hope for deliverance—only from heaven.

That our readers may distinctly understand all the circumstances of the event which we are about imperfectly to describe, it is necessary to state the relative position of the parties who were engaged in it. The old clergyman and Schalken were in the anti-room of which we have already spoken; Rose lay in the inner chamber, the door of which was open; and by the side of the bed, at her urgent desire, stood her guardian; a candle burned in the bedchamber, and three were lighted in the outer apartment. The old man now cleared his voice,

as if about to commence, but before he had time to begin, a sudden
gust of air blew out the candle which served to illuminate the room
in which the poor girl lay, and she, with hurried alarm, exclaimed—

"Godfrey, bring in another candle; the darkness is unsafe."

Gerard Douw, forgetting for the moment her repeated injunc-
tions, in the immediate impulse, stepped from the bedchamber into
the other, in order to supply what she desired.

"Oh God! do not go, dear uncle," shrieked the unhappy girl—and
at the same time she sprung from the bed, and darted after him, in
order, by her grasp, to detain him. But the warning came too late,
for scarcely had he passed the threshold, and hardly had his niece
had time to utter the startling exclamation, when the door which
divided the two rooms closed violently after him, as if swung to by
a strong blast of wind. Schalken and he both rushed to the door,
but their united and desperate efforts could not avail so much as to
shake it. Shriek after shriek burst from the inner chamber, with all the
piercing loudness of despairing terror. Schalken and Douw applied
every energy and strained every nerve to force open the door; but
all in vain. There was no sound of struggling from within, but the
screams seemed to increase in loudness, and at the same time they
heard the bolts of the latticed window withdrawn, and the window
itself grated upon the sill as if thrown open. One *last* shriek, so long
and piercing and agonized as to be scarcely human, swelled from
the room, and suddenly there followed a death-like silence. A light
step was heard crossing the floor, as if from the bed to the window;
and almost at the same instant the door gave way, and, yielding to
the pressure of the external applicants, they were nearly precipitated
into the room. It was empty. The window was open, and Schalken
sprung to a chair and gazed out upon the street and canal below.
He saw no form, but he beheld, or thought he beheld, the waters
of the broad canal beneath settling ring after ring in heavy circular

ripples, as if a moment before disturbed by the immersion of some large and heavy mass.

No trace of Rose was ever after discovered, nor was any thing certain respecting her mysterious wooer detected or even suspected—no clue whereby to trace the intricacies of the labyrinth and to arrive at a distinct conclusion was to be found. But an incident occurred, which, though it will not be received by our rational readers as at all approaching to evidence upon the matter, nevertheless produced a strong and a lasting impression upon the mind of Schalken. Many years after the events which we have detailed, Schalken, then remotely situated, received an intimation of his father's death, and of his intended burial upon a fixed day in the church of Rotterdam. It was necessary that a very considerable journey should be performed by the funeral procession, which, as it will readily be believed, was not very numerously attended. Schalken with difficulty arrived in Rotterdam late in the day upon which the funeral was appointed to take place. It had not then arrived. Evening closed in, and still it did not appear.

Schalken strolled down to the church—he found it open—notice of the arrival of the funeral had been given, and the vault in which the body was to be laid had been opened. The officer, who is analogous to our sexton, on seeing a well-dressed gentleman, whose object was to attend the expected funeral, pacing the aisle of the church, hospitably invited him to share with him the comforts of a blazing wood fire, which, as was his custom in winter time upon such occasions, he had kindled in the hearth of a chamber which communicated, by a flight of steps, with the vault below. In this chamber Schalken and his entertainer seated themselves, and the sexton, after some fruitless attempts to engage his guest in conversation, was obliged to apply himself to his tobacco-pipe and can, to solace his solitude. In spite of his grief and cares, the fatigues of a rapid journey of nearly forty hours gradually overcame the mind and body of Godfrey Schalken, and he sank into a deep sleep, from which he was awakened by some one's shaking him gently by the shoulder. He first thought that the old sexton had called him, but *he* was no longer in the room. He roused himself, and as soon as he could clearly see what was around him, he perceived a female form, clothed in a kind of light robe of muslin, part of which was so disposed as to act as a veil, and in her hand she carried a lamp. She was moving rather away from him, and towards the flight of steps which conducted towards the vaults. Schalken felt a vague alarm at the sight of this figure, and at the same time an irresistible impulse to follow its guidance. He followed it towards the vaults, but when it reached the head of the stairs, he paused—the figure paused also, and, turning gently round, displayed, by the light of the lamp it carried, the face and features of his first love, Rose Velderkaust. There was nothing horrible, or even sad, in the countenance. On the contrary, it wore the same arch smile which used to enchant the artist long before in his happy days. A feeling of awe and of interest, too intense to be resisted, prompted him to follow the spectre, if spectre it were. She descended the stairs—he followed—and, turning to the left, through a narrow passage, she led him, to his infinite surprise, into what appeared to be an old-fashioned Dutch apartment, such as the pictures of Gerard Douw have served to immortalize. Abundance of costly antique furniture was disposed about the room, and in one corner stood a four-post bed, with heavy black cloth curtains around it; the figure frequently turned towards him with the same arch smile; and when she came to the side of the bed, she drew the curtains, and, by the light of the lamp, which she held towards its contents, she disclosed to the horror-stricken painter, sitting bolt upright in the bed, the livid and demoniac form of Vanderhausen. Schalken had hardly seen him, when he fell senseless upon the floor, where he lay until discovered, on the next morning, by persons employed in closing the passages into the vaults. He was lying in a cell of considerable size, which had not been disturbed for a long time, and he had fallen beside a large coffin, which was supported upon small stone pillars, a security against the attacks of vermin.

To his dying day Schalken was satisfied of the reality of the vision which he had witnessed, and he has left behind him a curious evidence of the impression which it wrought upon his fancy, in a painting executed shortly after the event we have narrated, and which is valuable as exhibiting not only the peculiarities which have made Schalken's pictures sought after, but even more so as presenting a portrait as close and faithful as one taken from memory can be, of his early love, Rose Velderkaust, whose mysterious fate must ever remain matter of speculation. The picture represents a chamber of antique masonry, such as might be found in most old cathedrals, and is lighted faintly by a lamp carried in the hand of a female figure, such as we have above attempted to describe; and in the back-ground, and to the left of him who examines the painting, there stands the form of a man apparently aroused from sleep, and by his attitude, his hand being laid upon his sword, exhibiting considerable alarm: this last figure is illuminated only by the expiring glare of a wood or charcoal fire. The whole production exhibits a beautiful specimen of that artful and singular distribution of light and shade which has rendered the name of Schalken immortal among the artists of his country. This tale is traditionary, and the reader will easily perceive, by our studiously omitting to heighten many points of the narrative, when a little additional colouring might have added effect to the recital, that we have desired to lay before him, not a figment of the brain, but a curious tradition connected with, and belonging to, the biography of a famous artist.

THE MASQUE OF THE RED DEATH (1842)

Edgar Allan Poe

Edgar Allan Poe (1809–49), born in Boston, Massachusetts, was the son of itinerant actors. His father abandoned the family in 1810 and his mother died the following year setting the tone for the run of ill fortune that dogged Poe throughout his short life. Although tragedy was never far behind Poe did achieve success as a poet and author, publishing such classic tales of the macabre as 'The Pit and the Pendulum' (1842), 'The Fall of the House of Usher' (1839) and 'The Tell-Tale Heart' (1843) along with poems such as 'The Raven' (1845) and 'Annabel Lee' (1849).

First published in *Graham's Lady's and Gentleman's Magazine* in May 1842 'The Masque of the Red Death' is amongst Poe's finest stories. The action takes place within a castellated abbey, the property of the sadistic Prince Prospero, while outside the fortified walls a plague ravages the landscape. The story can be read as an allegory for the inevitability of death, with neither wealth nor status providing any protection, but on another level the story is also a reflection on mortality. Even the most debauched of Prospero's guests is given cause to pause in their revels by the hourly chimes of the ebony clock within the darkest chamber of the abbey.

THE "RED DEATH" HAD LONG DEVASTATED THE COUNTRY. NO pestilence had ever been so fatal, or so hideous. Blood was its Avatar and its seal—the redness and the horror of blood. There were sharp pains, and sudden dizziness, and then profuse bleeding at the pores, with dissolution. The scarlet stains upon the body and especially upon the face of the victim, were the pest ban which shut him out from the aid and from the sympathy of his fellow-men. And the whole seizure, progress and termination of the disease, were the incidents of half an hour.

But the Prince Prospero was happy and dauntless and sagacious. When his dominions were half depopulated, he summoned to his presence a thousand hale and light-hearted friends from among the knights and dames of his court, and with these retired to the deep seclusion of one of his castellated abbeys. This was an extensive and magnificent structure, the creation of the prince's own eccentric yet august taste. A strong and lofty wall girdled it in. This wall had gates of iron. The courtiers, having entered, brought furnaces and massy hammers and welded the bolts. They resolved to leave means neither of ingress or egress to the sudden impulses of despair or of frenzy from within. The abbey was amply provisioned. With such precautions the courtiers might bid defiance to contagion. The external world could take care of itself. In the meantime it was folly to grieve, or to think. The prince had provided all the appliances of pleasure. There were buffoons, there were improvisatori, there were ballet-dancers, there were musicians, there was Beauty, there was wine. All these and security were within. Without was the "Red Death."

It was toward the close of the fifth or sixth month of his seclusion, and while the pestilence raged most furiously abroad, that the Prince Prospero entertained his thousand friends at a masked ball of the most unusual magnificence.

It was a voluptuous scene, that masquerade. But first let me tell of the rooms in which it was held. There were seven—an imperial suite. In many palaces, however, such suites form a long and straight vista, while the folding doors slide back nearly to the walls on either hand, so that the view of the whole extent is scarcely impeded. Here the case was very different; as might have been expected from the duke's love of the *bizarre*. The apartments were so irregularly disposed that the vision embraced but little more than one at a time. There was a sharp turn at every twenty or thirty yards, and at each turn a novel effect. To the right and left, in the middle of each wall, a tall and narrow Gothic window looked out upon a closed corridor which pursued the windings of the suite. These windows were of stained glass whose colour varied in accordance with the prevailing hue of the decorations of the chamber into which it opened. That at the eastern extremity was hung, for example, in blue—and vividly blue were its windows. The second chamber was purple in its ornaments and tapestries, and here the panes were purple. The third was green throughout, and so were the casements. The fourth was furnished and lighted with orange—the fifth with white—the sixth with violet. The seventh apartment was closely shrouded in black velvet tapestries that hung all over the ceiling and down the walls, falling in heavy folds upon a carpet of the same material and hue. But in this chamber only, the colour of the windows failed to correspond with the decorations. The panes here were scarlet—a deep blood colour. Now in no one of the seven apartments was there any lamp or candelabrum, amid the profusion of golden ornaments that lay scattered to and fro or depended from the roof. There was no light of any kind emanating from lamp or candle within the suite of chambers. But in the corridors that followed the suite, there stood, opposite to each window, a heavy tripod, bearing a brazier of fire that projected its rays through the tinted glass and so glaringly illumined the room. And thus were produced a multitude of gaudy and fantastic appearances. But in the western or black chamber the effect of the fire-light that streamed upon the dark hangings through the blood-tinted panes, was ghastly in the extreme, and produced so wild a look upon the countenances of those who entered, that there were few of the company bold enough to set foot within its precincts at all.

It was in this apartment, also, that there stood against the western wall, a gigantic clock of ebony. Its pendulum swung to and fro with a dull, heavy, monotonous clang; and when the minute-hand made the circuit of the face, and the hour was to be stricken, there came from the brazen lungs of the clock a sound which was clear and loud and deep and exceedingly musical, but of so peculiar a note and emphasis that, at each lapse of an hour, the musicians of the orchestra were constrained to pause, momentarily, in their performance, to harken to the sound; and thus the waltzers perforce ceased their evolutions; and there was a brief disconcert of the whole gay company; and, while the chimes of the clock yet rang, it was observed that the giddiest grew pale, and the more aged and sedate passed their hands over their brows as if in confused reverie or meditation. But when the echoes had fully ceased, a light laughter at once pervaded the assembly; the musicians looked at each other and smiled as if at their own nervousness and folly, and made whispering vows, each to the other, that the next chiming of the clock should produce in them no similar emotion; and then, after the lapse of sixty minutes, (which embrace three thousand and six hundred seconds of the Time that flies,) there came yet another chiming of the clock, and then were the same disconcert and tremulousness and meditation as before.

But, in spite of these things, it was a gay and magnificent revel. The tastes of the duke were peculiar. He had a fine eye for colours and effects. He disregarded the *decora* of mere fashion. His plans were bold and fiery, and his conceptions glowed with barbaric lustre. There are some who would have thought him mad. His followers felt that he was not. It was necessary to hear and see and touch him to be *sure* that he was not.

He had directed, in great part, the moveable embellishments of the seven chambers, upon occasion of this great *fête*; and it was his own guiding taste which had given character to the masqueraders. Be sure they were grotesque. There were much glare and glitter and piquancy and phantasm—much of what has been since seen in "Hernani." There were arabesque figures with unsuited limbs and appointments. There were delirious fancies such as the madman fashions. There was much of the beautiful, much of the wanton, much of the *bizarre*, something of the terrible, and not a little of that which might have excited disgust. To and fro in the seven chambers there stalked, in fact, a multitude of dreams. And these—the dreams—writhed in and about, taking hue from the rooms, and causing the wild music of the orchestra to seem as the echo of their steps. And, anon, there strikes the ebony clock which stands in the hall of the velvet. And then, for a moment, all is still, and all is silent save the voice of the clock. The dreams are stiff-frozen as they stand. But the echoes of the chime die away—they have endured but an instant—and a light, half-subdued laughter floats after them as they depart. And now again the music swells, and the dreams live, and writhe to and fro more merrily than ever, taking hue from the many tinted windows through which stream the rays from the tripods. But to the chamber which lies most westwardly of the seven, there are now none of the maskers who venture: for the night is waning away; and there flows a ruddier light through the blood-coloured panes; and the blackness of the sable drapery appals; and to him whose foot falls upon the sable carpet, there comes from the near clock of ebony a muffled peal more solemnly emphatic than any which reaches *their* ears who indulge in the more remote gaieties of the other apartments.

But these other apartments were densely crowded, and in them beat feverishly the heart of life. And the revel went whirlingly on, until at length there commenced the sounding of midnight upon the clock. And then the music ceased, as I have told; and the evolutions of the waltzers were quieted; and there was an uneasy cessation of all things as before. But now there were twelve strokes to be sounded by the bell of the clock; and thus it happened, perhaps, that more of thought crept, with more of time, into the meditations of the thoughtful among those who revelled. And thus, too, it happened, perhaps, that before the last echoes of the last chime had utterly sunk into silence, there were many individuals in the crowd who had found leisure to become aware of the presence of a masked figure which had arrested the attention of no single individual before. And the rumour of this new presence having spread itself whisperingly around, there arose at length from the whole company a buzz, or murmur, expressive of disapprobation and surprise—then, finally, of terror, of horror, and of disgust.

In an assembly of phantasms such as I have painted, it may well be supposed that no ordinary appearance could have excited such sensation. In truth the masquerade license of the night was nearly unlimited; but the figure in question had out-Heroded Herod, and gone beyond the bounds of even the prince's indefinite decorum. There are chords in the hearts of the most reckless which cannot be touched without emotion. Even with the utterly lost, to whom life and death are equally jests, there are matters of which no jest can be made. The whole company, indeed, seemed now deeply to feel that in the costume and bearing of the stranger neither wit nor propriety existed. The figure was tall and gaunt, and shrouded from head to foot in the habiliments of the grave. The mask which concealed the visage was made so nearly to resemble the countenance of a stiffened corpse that the closest scrutiny must have had difficulty in detecting the cheat. And yet all this might have been endured, if not approved, by the mad revellers around. But the mummer had gone so far as to assume the type of the Red Death. His vesture was dabbled in *blood*—and his broad brow, with all the features of the face, was besprinkled with the scarlet horror.

When the eyes of Prince Prospero fell upon this spectral image (which with a slow and solemn movement, as if more fully to sustain its *rôle*, stalked to and fro among the waltzers) he was seen to be convulsed, in the first moment with a strong shudder either of terror or distaste; but, in the next, his brow reddened with rage.

"Who dares?" he demanded hoarsely of the courtiers who stood near him—"who dares insult us with this blasphemous mockery? Seize him and unmask him—that we may know whom we have to hang at sunrise, from the battlements!"

It was in the eastern or blue chamber in which stood the Prince Prospero as he uttered these words. They rang throughout the seven rooms loudly and clearly—for the prince was a bold and robust man, and the music had become hushed at the waving of his hand.

It was in the blue room where stood the prince, with a group of pale courtiers by his side. At first, as he spoke, there was a slight rushing movement of this group in the direction of the intruder, who at the moment was also near at hand, and now, with deliberate and stately step, made closer approach to the speaker. But from a certain nameless awe with which the mad assumptions of the mummer had inspired the whole party, there were found none who put forth hand to seize him; so that, unimpeded, he passed within a yard of the prince's person; and, while the vast assembly, as if with one impulse, shrank from the centres of the rooms to the walls, he made his way uninterruptedly, but with the same solemn and measured step which had distinguished him from the first, through the blue chamber to the purple—through the purple to the green—through the green to the orange—through this again to the white—and even thence to the violet, ere a decided movement had been made to arrest him. It was then, however, that the Prince Prospero, maddening with rage and the shame of his own momentary cowardice, rushed hurriedly through the six chambers, while none followed him on account of a deadly terror that had seized upon all. He bore aloft a drawn dagger, and had approached, in rapid impetuosity, to within three or four feet of the retreating figure, when the latter, having attained the extremity of the velvet apartment, turned suddenly and confronted his pursuer. There was a sharp cry—and the dagger dropped gleaming upon the sable carpet, upon which, instantly afterwards, fell prostrate in death the Prince Prospero. Then, summoning the wild courage of despair, a throng of the revellers at once threw themselves into the black apartment, and, seizing the mummer, whose tall figure stood erect and motionless within the shadow of the ebony clock, gasped in unutterable horror at finding the grave-cerements and corpse-like mask which they handled with so violent a rudeness, untenanted by any tangible form.

And now was acknowledged the presence of the Red Death. He had come like a thief in the night. And one by one dropped the revellers in the blood-bedewed halls of their revel, and died each in the despairing posture of his fall. And the life of the ebony clock went out with that of the last of the gay. And the flames of the tripods expired. And Darkness and Decay and the Red Death held illimitable dominion over all.

RAPPACCINI'S DAUGHTER (1844)

Nathaniel Hawthorne

Nathaniel Hawthorne (1804–64) was born in Salem, Massachusetts, where his ancestors included John Hathorne, the only judge involved in the Salem Witch Trials who never repented of his actions. Hawthorne's four great dark romances—*The Scarlet Letter* (1850), *The House of Seven Gables* (1851), *The Blithedale Romance* (1852) and *The Marble Faun* (1860)—are amongst the finest and most influential works of 19th-century American fiction. Hawthorne also wrote many short stories including 'Young Goodman Brown' (1835), 'Dr Heidegger's Experiment' (1837), 'The Birth-Mark' (1843) and 'The Artist of the Beautiful' (1846), all of which fall within the Gothic tradition.

'Rappaccini's Daughter' was first published in the December 1844 issue of *The United States Magazine and Democratic Review*. The story is set in an 'eden of poisonous flowers', tended by Beatrice Rappaccini, the beautiful daughter of Signor Giacomo Rappaccini. Into this beautiful but toxic landscape comes Giovanni Guasconti who, inevitably, falls for the lovely Beatrice. As ever with Hawthorne the imagery is lush and sensuous and the garden with its gorgeous but deadly plants is exquisitely described. 'Rappaccini's Daughter' was also possibly an influence on Ian Fleming's novel *You Only Live Twice* (1964) in which James Bond's nemesis, Ernst Stavro Blofeld, acquires his own garden of toxic blooms.

A YOUNG MAN, NAMED GIOVANNI GUASCONTI, CAME, VERY LONG ago, from the more southern region of Italy, to pursue his studies at the University of Padua. Giovanni, who had but a scanty supply of gold ducats in his pocket, took lodgings in a high and gloomy chamber of an old edifice, which looked not unworthy to have been the palace of a Paduan noble, and which, in fact, exhibited over its entrance the armorial bearings of a family long since extinct. The young stranger, who was not unstudied in the great poem of his country, recollected that one of the ancestors of this family, and perhaps an occupant of this very mansion, had been pictured by Dante as a partaker of the immortal agonies of his Inferno. These reminiscences and associations, together with the tendency to heart-break natural to a young man for the first time out of his native sphere, caused Giovanni to sigh heavily, as he looked around the desolate and ill-furnished apartment.

"Holy Virgin, signor," cried old dame Lisabetta, who, won by the youth's remarkable beauty of person, was kindly endeavouring to give the chamber a habitable air, "what a sigh was that to come out of a young man's heart! Do you find this old mansion gloomy? For the love of heaven, then, put your head out of the window, and you will see as bright sunshine as you have left in Naples."

Guasconti mechanically did as the old woman advised, but could not quite agree with her that the Lombard sunshine was as cheerful as that of southern Italy. Such as it was, however, it fell upon a garden beneath the window, and expended its fostering influences on a variety of plants, which seemed to have been cultivated with exceeding care.

"Does this garden belong to the house?" asked Giovanni.

"Heaven forbid, signor!—unless it were fruitful of better potherbs than any that grow there now," answered old Lisabetta. "No: that garden is cultivated by the own hands of Signor Giacomo Rappaccini, the famous Doctor, who, I warrant him, has been heard of as far as Naples. It is said that he distils these plants into medicines that are as potent as a charm. Oftentimes you may see the signor Doctor at work, and perchance the signora his daughter, too, gathering the strange flowers that grow in the garden."

The old woman had now done what she could for the aspect of the chamber, and, commending the young man to the protection of the saints, took her departure.

Giovanni still found no better occupation than to look down into the garden beneath his window. From its appearance, he judged it to be one of those botanic gardens, which were of earlier date in Padua than elsewhere in Italy, or in the world. Or, not improbably, it might once have been the pleasure-place of an opulent family; for there was the ruin of a marble fountain in the centre, sculptured with rare art, but so wofully shattered that it was impossible to trace the original design from the chaos of remaining fragments. The water, however, continued to gush and sparkle into the sunbeams as cheerfully as ever. A little gurgling sound ascended to the young man's window, and made him feel as if a fountain were an immortal spirit, that sung its song unceasingly, and without heeding the vicissitudes around it; while one century embodied it in marble, and another scattered the perishable garniture on the soil. All about the pool into which the water subsided grew various plants, that seemed to require a plentiful supply of moisture for the nourishment of gigantic leaves, and, in some instances, flowers gorgeously magnificent. There was one shrub in particular, set in a marble vase in the midst of the pool, that bore a profusion of purple blossoms, each of which had the lustre and

richness of a gem; and the whole together made a show so resplend-
ent that it seemed enough to illuminate the garden, even had there
been no sunshine. Every portion of the soil was peopled with plants
and herbs, which, if less beautiful, still bore tokens of assiduous care;
as if all had their individual virtues, known to the scientific mind
that fostered them. Some were placed in urns, rich with old carving,
and others in common garden-pots; some crept serpent-like along
the ground, or climbed on high, using whatever means of ascent
was offered them. One plant had wreathed itself round a statue of
Vertumnus, which was thus quite veiled and shrouded in a drapery
of hanging foliage, so happily arranged that it might have served a
sculptor for a study.

While Giovanni stood at the window, he heard a rustling behind
a screen of leaves, and became aware that a person was at work in
the garden. His figure soon emerged into view, and showed itself to
be that of no common labourer, but a tall, emaciated, sallow, and
sickly-looking man, dressed in a scholar's garb of black. He was
beyond the middle term of life, with grey hair, a thin grey beard,
and a face singularly marked with intellect and cultivation, but which
could never, even in his more youthful days, have expressed much
warmth of heart.

Nothing could exceed the intentness with which this scientific
gardener examined every shrub which grew in his path; it seemed as
if he was looking into their inmost nature, making observations in
regard to their creative essence, and discovering why one leaf grew
in this shape, and another in that, and wherefore such and such flowers differed among themselves in hue and perfume. Nevertheless, in
spite of the deep intelligence on his part, there was no approach to
intimacy between himself and these vegetable existences. On the
contrary, he avoided their actual touch, or the direct inhaling of their
odours, with a caution that impressed Giovanni most disagreeably;

for the man's demeanour was that of one walking among malignant influences, such as savage beasts, or deadly snakes, or evil spirits, which, should he allow them one moment of licence, would wreak upon him some terrible fatality. It was strangely frightful to the young man's imagination, to see this air of insecurity in a person cultivating a garden, that most simple and innocent of human toils, and which had been alike the joy and labour of the unfallen parents of the race. Was this garden, then, the Eden of the present world?—and this man, with such a perception of harm in what his own hands caused to grow, was he the Adam?

The distrustful gardener, while plucking away the dead leaves, or pruning the too luxuriant growth of the shrubs, defended his hands with a pair of thick gloves. Nor were these his only armour. When, in his walk through the garden, he came to the magnificent plant that hung its purple gems beside the marble fountain, he placed a kind of mask over his mouth and nostrils, as if all this beauty did but conceal a deadlier malice. But finding his task still too dangerous, he drew back, removed the mask, and called loudly, but in the infirm voice of a person affected with inward disease:

"Beatrice!—Beatrice!"

"Here am I, my father! What would you?" cried a rich and youthful voice from the window of the opposite house; a voice as rich as a tropical sunset, and which made Giovanni, though he knew not why, think of deep hues of purple or crimson, and of perfumes heavily delectable—"Are you in the garden?"

"Yes, Beatrice," answered the gardener, "and I need your help."

Soon there emerged from under a sculptured portal the figure of a young girl, arrayed with as much richness of taste as the most splendid of the flowers, beautiful as the day, and with a bloom so deep and vivid, that one shade more would have been too much. She looked redundant with life, health, and energy; all of which attributes were bound down and compressed, as it were, and girdled tensely, in their luxuriance, by her virgin zone. Yet Giovanni's fancy must have grown morbid, while he looked down into the garden; for the impression which the fair stranger made upon him was as if here were another flower, the human sister of those vegetable ones, as beautiful as they—more beautiful than the richest of them, but still to be touched only with a glove, nor to be approached without a mask. As Beatrice came down the garden-path, it was observable that she handled and inhaled the odour of several of the plants, which her father had most sedulously avoided.

"Here, Beatrice!" said the latter,—"see how many needful offices require to be done to our chief treasure. Yet, shattered as I am, my life might pay the penalty of approaching it so closely as circumstances demand. Henceforth, I fear, this plant must be consigned to your sole charge."

"And gladly will I undertake it," cried again the rich tones of the young lady, as she bent towards the magnificent plant, and opened her arms as if to embrace it. "Yes, my sister, my splendour, it shall be Beatrice's task to nurse and serve thee; and thou shalt reward her with thy kisses and perfume-breath, which to her is as the breath of life!"

Then, with all the tenderness in her manner that was so strikingly expressed in her words, she busied herself with such attentions as the plant seemed to require; and Giovanni, at his lofty window, rubbed his eyes, and almost doubted whether it were a girl tending her favourite flower, or one sister performing the duties of affection to another. The scene soon terminated. Whether Doctor Rappaccini had finished his labours in the garden, or that his watchful eye had caught the stranger's face, he now took his daughter's arm and retired. Night was already closing in; oppressive exhalations seemed to proceed from the plants, and steal upward past the open window; and Giovanni, closing the lattice, went to his couch, and dreamed of

a rich flower and beautiful girl. Flower and maiden were different and
yet the same, and fraught with some strange peril in either shape.

But there is an influence in the light of morning that tends to
rectify whatever errors of fancy, or even of judgment, we may have
incurred during the sun's decline, or among the shadows of the night,
or in the less wholesome glow of moonshine. Giovanni's first movement on starting from sleep, was to throw open the window, and
gaze down into the garden which his dreams had made so fertile of
mysteries. He was surprised, and a little ashamed to find how real
and matter-of-fact an affair it proved to be, in the first rays of the sun,
which gilded the dew-drops that hung upon leaf and blossom, and
while giving a brighter beauty to each rare flower, brought everything
within the limits of ordinary experience. The young man rejoiced,
that, in the heart of the barren city, he had the privilege of overlook-
ing this spot of lovely and luxuriant vegetation. It would serve, he
said to himself, as a symbolic language, to keep him in communion
with nature. Neither the sickly and thought-worn Doctor Giacomo
Rappaccini, it is true, nor his brilliant daughter, were now visible;
so that Giovanni could not determine how much of the singularity
which he attributed to both, was due to their own qualities, and how
much to his wonder-working fancy. But he was inclined to take a
most rational view of the whole matter.

In the course of the day, he paid his respects to Signor Pietro
Baglioni, professor of medicine in the University, a physician of
eminent repute, to whom Giovanni had brought a letter of introduction. The Professor was an elderly personage, apparently of
genial nature, and habits that might almost be called jovial; he kept
the young man to dinner, and made himself very agreeable by the
freedom and liveliness of his conversation, especially when warmed
by a flask or two of Tuscan wine. Giovanni, conceiving that men
of science, inhabitants of the same city, must needs be on familiar

terms with one another, took an opportunity to mention the name of Dr. Rappaccini. But the Professor did not respond with so much cordiality as he had anticipated.

"Ill would it become a teacher of the divine art of medicine," said Professor Pietro Baglioni, in answer to a question of Giovanni, "to withhold due and well-considered praise of a physician so eminently skilled as Rappaccini. But, on the other hand, I should answer it but scantily to my conscience, were I to permit a worthy youth like yourself, Signor Giovanni, the son of an ancient friend, to imbibe erroneous ideas respecting a man who might hereafter chance to hold your life and death in his hands. The truth is, our worshipful Doctor Rappaccini has as much science as any member of the faculty—with perhaps one single exception—in Padua, or all Italy. But there are certain grave objections to his professional character."

"And what are they?" asked the young man.

"Has my friend Giovanni any disease of body or heart, that he is so inquisitive about physicians?" said the Professor, with a smile. "But as for Rappaccini, it is said of him—and I, who know the man well, can answer for its truth—that he cares infinitely more for science than for mankind. His patients are interesting to him only as subjects for some new experiment. He would sacrifice human life, his own among the rest, or whatever else was dearest to him, for the sake of adding so much as a grain of mustard-seed to the great heap of his accumulated knowledge."

"Methinks he is an awful man, indeed," remarked Guasconti, mentally recalling the cold and purely intellectual aspect of Rappaccini. "And yet, worshipful Professor, is it not a noble spirit? Are there many men capable of so spiritual a love of science?"

"God forbid," answered the Professor, somewhat testily—"at least, unless they take sounder views of the healing art than those adopted by Rappaccini. It is his theory, that all medicinal virtues are comprised within those substances which we term vegetable poisons. These he cultivates with his own hands, and is said even to have produced new varieties of poison, more horribly deleterious than Nature, without the assistance of this learned person, would ever have plagued the world with. That the Signor Doctor does less mischief than might be expected, with such dangerous substances, is undeniable. Now and then, it must be owned, he has effected—or seemed to effect—a marvellous cure. But, to tell you my private mind, Signor Giovanni, he should receive little credit for such instances of success—they being probably the work of chance—but should be held strictly accountable for his failures, which may justly be considered his own work."

The youth might have taken Baglioni's opinions with many grains of allowance, had he known that there was a professional warfare of long continuance between him and Doctor Rappaccini, in which the latter was generally thought to have gained the advantage. If the reader be inclined to judge for himself, we refer him to certain black-letter tracts on both sides, preserved in the medical department of the University of Padua.

"I know not, most learned Professor," returned Giovanni, after musing on what had been said of Rappaccini's exclusive zeal for science—"I know not how dearly this physician may love his art; but surely there is one object more dear to him. He has a daughter."

"Aha!" cried the Professor, with a laugh. "So, now our friend Giovanni's secret is out. You have heard of this daughter, whom all the young men in Padua are wild about, though not half a dozen have ever had the good hap to see her face. I know little of the Signora Beatrice, save that Rappaccini is said to have instructed her deeply in his science, and that, young and beautiful as fame reports her, she is already qualified to fill a professor's chair. Perchance her father destines her for mine! Other absurd rumours there be, not worth talking about, or listening to. So now, Signor Giovanni, drink off your glass of Lacryma."

Guasconti returned to his lodgings somewhat heated with the wine he had quaffed, and which caused his brain to swim with strange fantasies in reference to Doctor Rappaccini and the beautiful Beatrice. On his way, happening to pass by a florist's, he bought a fresh bouquet of flowers.

Ascending to his chamber, he seated himself near the window, but within the shadow thrown by the depth of the wall, so that he could look down into the garden with little risk of being discovered. All beneath his eye was a solitude. The strange plants were basking in the sunshine, and now and then nodding gently to one another, as if in acknowledgment of sympathy and kindred. In the midst, by the shattered fountain, grew the magnificent shrub, with its purple gems clustering all over it; they glowed in the air, and gleamed back again out of the depths of the pool, which thus seemed to overflow with coloured radiance from the rich reflection that was steeped in it. At first, as we have said, the garden was a solitude. Soon, however,—as Giovanni had half-hoped, half-feared, would be the case,—a figure appeared beneath the antique sculptured portal, and came down between the rows of plants, inhaling their various perfumes, as if she were one of those beings of old classic fable, that lived upon sweet odours. On again beholding Beatrice, the young man was even startled to perceive how much her beauty exceeded his recollection of it; so brilliant, so vivid in its character, that she glowed amid the sunlight, and, as Giovanni whispered to himself, positively illuminated the more shadowy intervals of the garden path. Her face being now more revealed than on the former occasion, he was struck by its expression of simplicity and sweetness; qualities that had not entered into his idea of her character, and which made him ask anew, what manner of mortal she might be. Nor did he fail again to observe, or imagine, an analogy between the beautiful girl and the gorgeous shrub that hung its gem-like flowers over the fountain; a resemblance which Beatrice seemed to have indulged a fantastic humour in heightening, both by the arrangement of her dress and the selection of its hues.

Approaching the shrub, she threw open her arms, as with a passionate ardour, and drew its branches into an intimate embrace; so intimate, that her features were hidden in its leafy bosom, and her glistening ringlets all intermingled with the flowers.

"Give me thy breath, my sister," exclaimed Beatrice; "for I am faint with common air! And give me this flower of thine, which I separate with gentlest fingers from the stem, and place it close beside my heart."

With these words, the beautiful daughter of Rappaccini plucked one of the richest blossoms of the shrub, and was about to fasten it in her bosom. But now, unless Giovanni's draughts of wine had bewildered his senses, a singular incident occurred. A small orange-coloured reptile, of the lizard or chameleon species, chanced to be creeping along the path, just at the feet of Beatrice. It appeared to Giovanni—but, at the distance from which he gazed, he could scarcely have seen anything so minute—it appeared to him, however, that a drop or two of moisture from the broken stem of the flower descended upon the lizard's head. For an instant, the reptile contorted itself violently, and then lay motionless in the sunshine. Beatrice observed this remarkable phenomenon, and crossed herself, sadly, but without surprise; nor did she therefore hesitate to arrange the fatal flower in her bosom. There it blushed, and almost glimmered with the dazzling effect of a precious stone, adding to her dress and aspect the one appropriate charm, which nothing else in the world could have supplied. But Giovanni, out of the shadow of his window, bent forward and shrank back, and murmured and trembled.

"Am I awake? Have I my senses?" said he to himself. "What is this being?—beautiful, shall I call her?—or inexpressibly terrible?"

Beatrice now strayed carelessly through the garden, approaching closer beneath Giovanni's window, so that he was compelled to thrust his head quite out of its concealment, in order to gratify the intense and painful curiosity which she excited. At this moment, there came a beautiful insect over the garden wall; it had perhaps wandered through the city and found no flowers nor verdure among those antique haunts of men, until the heavy perfumes of Doctor Rappaccini's shrubs had lured it from afar. Without alighting on the flowers, this winged brightness seemed to be attracted by Beatrice, and lingered in the air and fluttered about her head. Now here it could not be but that Giovanni Guasconti's eyes deceived him. Be that as it might, he fancied that while Beatrice was gazing at the insect with childish delight, it grew faint and fell at her feet!—its bright wings shivered! it was dead!—from no cause that he could discern, unless it were the atmosphere of her breath. Again Beatrice crossed herself and sighed heavily, as she bent over the dead insect.

An impulsive movement of Giovanni drew her eyes to the window. There she beheld the beautiful head of the young man—rather a Grecian than an Italian head, with fair, regular features, and a glistening of gold among his ringlets—gazing down upon her like a being that hovered in mid-air. Scarcely knowing what he did, Giovanni threw down the bouquet which he had hitherto held in his hand.

"Signora," said he, "there are pure and healthful flowers. Wear them for the sake of Giovanni Guasconti!"

"Thanks, Signor," replied Beatrice, with her rich voice, that came forth as if it were like a gush of music; and with a mirthful expression half childish and half woman-like. "I accept your gift, and would fain recompense it with this precious purple flower; but if I toss it into the air, it will not reach you. So Signor Guasconti must even content himself with my thanks."

She lifted the bouquet from the ground, and then as if inwardly ashamed at having stepped aside from her maidenly reserve to respond to a stranger's greeting, passed swiftly homeward through the garden. But, few as the moments were, it seemed to Giovanni when she was on the point of vanishing beneath the sculptured portal, that his beautiful bouquet was already beginning to wither in her grasp. It was an idle thought; there could be no possibility of distinguishing a faded flower from a fresh one, at so great a distance.

For many days after this incident, the young man avoided the window that looked into Doctor Rappaccini's garden, as if something ugly and monstrous would have blasted his eye-sight, had he been betrayed into a glance. He felt conscious of having put himself, to a certain extent, within the influence of an unintelligible power, by the communication which he had opened with Beatrice. The wisest course would have been, if his heart were in any real danger, to quit his lodgings and Padua itself, at once; the next wiser, to have accustomed himself, as far as possible, to the familiar and day-light view of Beatrice; thus bringing her rigidly and systematically within the limits of ordinary experience. Least of all, while avoiding her sight, should Giovanni have remained so near this extraordinary being, that the proximity and possibility even of intercourse, should give a kind of substance and reality to the wild vagaries which his imagination ran riot continually in producing. Guasconti had not a deep heart—or at all events, its depths were not sounded now—but he had a quick fancy, and an ardent southern temperament, which rose every instant to a higher fever-pitch. Whether or no Beatrice possessed those terrible attributes—that fatal breath—the affinity with those so beautiful and deadly flowers—which were indicated by what Giovanni had witnessed, she had at least instilled a fierce

and subtle poison into his system. It was not love, although her rich
beauty was a madness to him; nor horror, even while he fancied her
spirit to be imbued with the same baneful essence that seemed to
pervade her physical frame; but a wild offspring of both love and
horror that had each parent in it, and burned like one and shivered
like the other. Giovanni knew not what to dread; still less did he
know what to hope; yet hope and dread kept a continual warfare in
his breast, alternately vanquishing one another and starting up afresh
to renew the contest. Blessed are all simple emotions, be they dark
or bright! It is the lurid intermixture of the two that produces the
illuminating blaze of the infernal regions.

Sometimes he endeavoured to assuage the fever of his spirit by
a rapid walk through the streets of Padua, or beyond its gates; his
footsteps kept time with the throbbings of his brain, so that the
walk was apt to accelerate itself to a race. One day, he found himself
arrested; his arm was seized by a portly personage who had turned
back on recognizing the young man, and expended much breath in
overtaking him.

"Signor Giovanni!—stay, my young friend!" cried he. "Have you
forgotten me? That might well be the case, if I were as much altered
as yourself."

It was Baglioni, whom Giovanni had avoided, ever since their first
meeting, from a doubt that the Professor's sagacity would look too
deeply into his secrets. Endeavouring to recover himself, he stared
forth wildly from his inner world into the outer one, and spoke like
a man in a dream.

"Yes; I am Giovanni Guasconti. You are Professor Pietro Baglioni.
Now let me pass!"

"Not yet—not yet, Signor Giovanni Guasconti," said the Professor,
smiling, but at the same time scrutinizing the youth with an earnest
glance. "What, did I grow up side by side with your father, and shall

his son pass me like a stranger, in these old streets of Padua? Stand still, Signor Giovanni; for we must have a word or two before we part."

"Speedily, then, most worshipful Professor—speedily!" said Giovanni, with feverish impatience. "Does not your worship see that I am in haste?"

Now, while he was speaking, there came a man in black along the street, stooping and moving feebly, like a person in inferior health. His face was all overspread with a most sickly and sallow hue, but yet so pervaded with an expression of piercing and active intellect, that an observer might easily have overlooked the merely physical attributes, and have seen only this wonderful energy. As he passed, this person exchanged a cold and distant salutation with Baglioni, but fixed his eyes upon Giovanni with an intentness that seemed to bring out whatever was within him worthy of notice. Nevertheless, there was a peculiar quietness in the look, as if taking merely a speculative, not a human interest, in the young man.

"It is Doctor Rappaccini!" whispered the Professor, when the stranger had passed. "Has he ever seen your face before?"

"Not that I know," answered Giovanni, starting at the name.

"He *has* seen you!—he must have seen you!" said Baglioni, hastily. "For some purpose or other, this man of science is making a study of you. I know that look of his! It is the same that coldly illuminates his face, as he bends over a bird, a mouse, or a butterfly, which, in pursuance of some experiment, he has killed by the perfume of a flower;—a look as deep as nature itself, but without nature's warmth of love. Signor Giovanni, I will stake my life upon it, you are the subject of one of Rappaccini's experiments!"

"Will you make a fool of me?" cried Giovanni, passionately. "*That*, Signor Professor, were an untoward experiment."

"Patience, patience!" replied the imperturbable Professor. "I tell thee, my poor Giovanni, that Rappaccini has a scientific interest in thee. Thou hast fallen into fearful hands! And the Signora Beatrice? What part does she act in this mystery?"

But Guasconti, finding Baglioni's pertinacity intolerable, here broke away, and was gone before the Professor could again seize his arm. He looked after the young man intently, and shook his head.

"This must not be," said Baglioni to himself. "The youth is the son of my old friend, and shall not come to any harm from which the arcana of medical science can preserve him. Besides, it is too insufferable an impertinence in Rappaccini thus to snatch the lad out of my own hands, as I may say, and make use of him for his infernal experiments. This daughter of his! It shall be looked to. Perchance, most learned Rappaccini, I may foil you where you little dream of it!"

Meanwhile, Giovanni had pursued a circuitous route, and at length found himself at the door of his lodgings. As he crossed the threshold, he was met by old Lisabetta, who smirked and smiled, and was evidently desirous to attract his attention; vainly, however, as the ebullition of his feelings had momentarily subsided into a cold and dull vacuity. He turned his eyes full upon the withered face that was puckering itself into a smile, but seemed to behold it not. The old dame, therefore, laid her grasp upon his cloak.

"Signor!—Signor!" whispered she, still with a smile over the whole breadth of her visage, so that it looked not unlike a grotesque carving in wood, darkened by centuries—"Listen, Signor! There is a private entrance into the garden!"

"What do you say?" exclaimed Giovanni, turning quickly about, as if an inanimate thing should start into feverish life. "A private entrance into Doctor Rappaccini's garden!"

"Hush! hush!—not so loud!" whispered Lisabetta, putting her hand over his mouth. "Yes; into the worshipful Doctor's garden, where you may see all his fine shrubbery. Many a young man in Padua would give gold to be admitted among those flowers."

Giovanni put a piece of gold into her hand.

"Show me the way," said he.

A surmise, probably excited by his conversation with Baglioni, crossed his mind, that this interposition of old Lisabetta might perchance be connected with the intrigue, whatever were its nature, in which the Professor seemed to suppose that Doctor Rappaccini was involving him. But such a suspicion, though it disturbed Giovanni, was inadequate to restrain him. The instant he was aware of the possibility of approaching Beatrice, it seemed an absolute necessity of his existence to do so. It mattered not whether she were angel or demon; he was irrevocably within her sphere, and must obey the law that whirled him onward, in ever lessening circles, towards a result which he did not attempt to foreshadow. And yet, strange to say, there came across him a sudden doubt, whether this intense interest on his part were not delusory—whether it were really of so deep and positive a nature as to justify him in now thrusting himself into an incalculable position—whether it were not merely the fantasy of a young man's brain, only slightly, or not at all, connected with his heart!

He paused—hesitated—turned half about—but again went on. His withered guide led him along several obscure passages, and finally undid a door, through which, as it was opened, there came the sight and sound of rustling leaves, with the broken sunshine glimmering among them. Giovanni stepped forth, and forcing himself through the entanglement of a shrub that wreathed its tendrils over the hidden entrance, he stood beneath his own window, in the open area of Doctor Rappaccini's garden.

How often is it the case, that, when impossibilities have come to pass, and dreams have condensed their misty substance into tangible realities, we find ourselves calm, and even coldly self-possessed, amid circumstances which it would have been a delirium of joy or agony to anticipate! Fate delights to thwart us thus. Passion will choose his own time to rush upon the scene, and lingers sluggishly behind, when an appropriate adjustment of events would seem to summon his appearance. So was it now with Giovanni. Day after day, his pulses had throbbed with feverish blood, at the improbable idea of an interview with Beatrice, and of standing with her, face to face, in this very garden, basking in the oriental sunshine of her beauty, and snatching from her full gaze the mystery which he deemed the riddle of his own existence. But now there was a singular and untimely equanimity within his breast. He threw a glance around the garden to discover if Beatrice or her father were present, and perceiving that he was alone, began a critical observation of the plants.

The aspect of one and all of them dissatisfied him; their gorgeousness seemed fierce, passionate, and even unnatural. There was hardly an individual shrub which a wanderer, straying by himself through a forest, would not have been startled to find growing wild, as if an unearthly face had glared at him out of the thicket. Several, also, would have shocked a delicate instinct by an appearance of artificialness, indicating that there had been such commixture, and, as it were, adultery of various vegetable species, that the production was no longer of God's making, but the monstrous offspring of man's depraved fancy, glowing with only an evil mockery of beauty. They were probably the result of experiment, which, in one or two cases, had succeeded in mingling plants individually lovely into a compound possessing the questionable and ominous character that distinguished the whole growth of the garden. In fine, Giovanni recognized but two or three plants in the collection, and those of a kind that he well knew to be poisonous. While busy with these contemplations, he heard the rustling of a silken garment, and turning, beheld Beatrice emerging from beneath the sculptured portal.

Giovanni had not considered with himself what should be his deportment; whether he should apologize for his intrusion into the garden, or assume that he was there with the privity, at least, if not by the desire, of Doctor Rappaccini or his daughter. But Beatrice's manner placed him at his ease, though leaving him still in doubt by what agency he had gained admittance. She came lightly along the path, and met him near the broken fountain. There was surprise in her face, but brightened by a simple and kind expression of pleasure.

"You are a connoisseur in flowers, Signor," said Beatrice with a smile, alluding to the bouquet which he had flung her from the window. "It is no marvel, therefore, if the sight of my father's rare collection has tempted you to take a nearer view. If he were here, he could tell you many strange and interesting facts as to the nature and habits of these shrubs, for he has spent a life-time in such studies, and this garden is his world."

"And yourself, lady"—observed Giovanni—"if fame says true, you, likewise, are deeply skilled in the virtues indicated by these rich blossoms, and these spicy perfumes. Would you deign to be my instructress, I should prove an apter scholar than under Signor Rappaccini himself."

"Are there such idle rumours?" asked Beatrice, with the music of a pleasant laugh. "Do people say that I am skilled in my father's science of plants? What a jest is there! No; though I have grown up among these flowers, I know no more of them than their hues and perfume; and sometimes, methinks I would fain rid myself of even that small knowledge. There are many flowers here, and those not the least brilliant, that shock and offend me, when they meet my eye. But, pray, Signor, do not believe these stories about my science. Believe nothing of me save what you see with your own eyes."

"And must I believe all that I have seen with my own eyes?" asked Giovanni pointedly, while the recollection of former scenes made him shrink. "No, Signora, you demand too little of me. Bid me believe nothing, save what comes from your own lips."

It would appear that Beatrice understood him. There came a deep flush to her cheek; but she looked full into Giovanni's eyes, and responded to his gaze of uneasy suspicion with a queen-like haughtiness.

"I do so bid you, Signor!" she replied. "Forget whatever you may have fancied in regard to me. If true to the outward senses, still it may be false in its essence. But the words of Beatrice Rappaccini's lips are true from the heart outward. Those you may believe!"

A fervour glowed in her whole aspect, and beamed upon Giovanni's consciousness like the light of truth itself. But while she spoke, there was a fragrance in the atmosphere around her rich and delightful, though evanescent, yet which the young man, from an indefinable reluctance, scarcely dared to draw into his lungs. It might be the odour of the flowers. Could it be Beatrice's breath, which thus embalmed her words with a strange richness, as if by steeping them in her heart? A faintness passed like a shadow over Giovanni, and flitted away; he seemed to gaze through the beautiful girl's eyes into her transparent soul, and felt no more doubt or fear.

The tinge of passion that had coloured Beatrice's manner vanished; she became gay, and appeared to derive a pure delight from her communion with the youth, not unlike what the maiden of a lonely island might have felt, conversing with a voyager from the civilized world. Evidently her experience of life had been confined within the limits of that garden. She talked now about matters as simple as the daylight or summer clouds, and now asked questions in reference to the city, or Giovanni's distant home, his friends, his mother, and his sisters; questions indicating such seclusion, and such lack of familiarity with modes and forms, that Giovanni responded as if to an infant. Her spirit gushed out before him like a fresh rill, that was just catching its first glimpse of the sunlight, and wondering, at the reflections of earth and sky which were flung into its bosom. There came thoughts, too, from a deep source, and fantasies of a gem-like brilliancy, as if diamonds and rubies sparkled upward among the bubbles of the fountain. Ever and anon, there gleamed across the young man's mind a sense of wonder, that he should be walking side by side with the being who had so wrought upon his imagination—whom he had idealized in such hues of terror—in whom he had positively witnessed such manifestations of dreadful attributes—that he should be conversing with Beatrice like a brother, and should find her so human and so maiden-like. But such reflections were only momentary; the effect of her character was too real, not to make itself familiar at once.

In this free intercourse, they had strayed through the garden, and now, after many turns among its avenues, were come to the shattered fountain, beside which grew the magnificent shrub with its treasury of glowing blossoms. A fragrance was diffused from it, which Giovanni recognized as identical with that which he had attributed to Beatrice's breath, but incomparably more powerful. As her eyes fell upon it, Giovanni beheld her press her hand to her bosom, as if her heart were throbbing suddenly and painfully.

"For the first time in my life," murmured she, addressing the shrub, "I had forgotten thee!"

"I remember, signora," said Giovanni, "that you once promised to reward me with one of these living gems for the bouquet, which I had the happy boldness to fling to your feet. Permit me now to pluck it as a memorial of this interview."

He made a step towards the shrub, with extended hand. But Beatrice darted forward, uttering a shriek that went through his heart like a dagger. She caught his hand, and drew it back with the whole force of her slender figure. Giovanni felt her touch thrilling through his fibres.

"Touch it not!" exclaimed she, in a voice of agony. "Not for thy life! It is fatal!"

Then, hiding her face, she fled from him, and vanished beneath the sculptured portal. As Giovanni followed her with his eyes, he beheld the emaciated figure and pale intelligence of Doctor Rappaccini, who had been watching the scene, he knew not how long, within the shadow of the entrance.

No sooner was Guasconti alone in his chamber, than the image of Beatrice came back to his passionate musings, invested with all the witchery that had been gathering around it ever since his first glimpse of her, and now likewise imbued with a tender warmth of girlish womanhood. She was human: her nature was endowed with all gentle and feminine qualities; she was worthiest to be worshipped; she was capable, surely, on her part, of the height and heroism of love. Those tokens, which he had hitherto considered as proofs of a frightful peculiarity in her physical and moral system, were now either forgotten, or, by the subtle sophistry of passion, transmuted into a golden crown of enchantment, rendering Beatrice the more admirable, by so much as she was the more unique. Whatever had looked ugly, was now beautiful; or, if incapable of such a change, it stole away and hid itself among those shapeless half-ideas, which throng the dim region beyond the daylight of our perfect consciousness. Thus did Giovanni spend the night, nor fell asleep, until the dawn had begun to awake the slumbering flowers in Doctor Rappaccini's garden, whither his dreams doubtless led him. Up rose the sun in his due season, and flinging his beams upon the young man's eyelids, awoke him to a sense of pain. When thoroughly aroused, he became sensible of a burning and tingling agony in his hand—in his right hand—the very hand which Beatrice had grasped in her own, when he was on the point of plucking one of the gem-like flowers. On the back of that hand there was now a purple print,

like that of four small fingers, and the likeness of a slender thumb
upon his wrist.

Oh, how stubbornly does love—or even that cunning semblance
of love which flourishes in the imagination, but strikes no depth of
root into the heart—how stubbornly does it hold its faith, until the
moment come, when it is doomed to vanish into thin mist! Giovanni
wrapt a handkerchief about his hand, and wondered what evil thing
had stung him, and soon forgot his pain in a reverie of Beatrice.

After the first interview, a second was in the inevitable course of
what we call fate. A third; a fourth; and a meeting with Beatrice in
the garden was no longer an incident in Giovanni's daily life, but the
whole space in which he might be said to live; for the anticipation
and memory of that ecstatic hour made up the remainder. Nor was
it otherwise with the daughter of Rappaccini. She watched for the
youth's appearance, and flew to his side with confidence as unre-
served as if they had been playmates from early infancy—as if they
were such playmates still. If, by any unwonted chance, he failed to
come at the appointed moment, she stood beneath the window, and
sent up the rich sweetness of her tones to float around him in his
chamber, and echo and reverberate throughout his heart—"Giovanni!
Giovanni! Why tarriest thou? Come down!" And down he hastened
into that Eden of poisonous flowers.

But, with all this intimate familiarity, there was still a reserve in
Beatrice's demeanour, so rigidly and invariably sustained, that the idea
of infringing it scarcely occurred to his imagination. By all appreci-
able signs, they loved; they had looked love, with eyes that conveyed
the holy secret from the depths of one soul into the depths of the
other, as if it were too sacred to be whispered by the way; they had
even spoken love, in those gushes of passion when their spirits darted
forth in articulated breath, like tongues of long-hidden flame; and
yet there had been no seal of lips, no clasp of hands, nor any slightest

caress, such as love claims and hallows. He had never touched one of the gleaming ringlets of her hair; her garment—so marked was the physical barrier between them—had never been waved against him by a breeze. On the few occasions when Giovanni had seemed tempted to overstep the limit, Beatrice grew so sad, so stern, and withal wore such a look of desolate separation, shuddering at itself, that not a spoken word was requisite to repel him. At such times, he was startled at the horrible suspicions that rose, monster-like, out of the caverns of his heart, and stared him in the face; his love grew thin and faint as the morning-mist; his doubts alone had substance. But when Beatrice's face brightened again, after the momentary shadow, she was transformed at once from the mysterious, questionable being, whom he had watched with so much awe and horror; she was now the beautiful and unsophisticated girl, whom he felt that his spirit knew with a certainty beyond all other knowledge.

A considerable time had now passed since Giovanni's last meeting with Baglioni. One morning, however, he was disagreeably surprised by a visit from the Professor, whom he had scarcely thought of for whole weeks, and would willingly have forgotten still longer. Given up, as he had long been, to a pervading excitement, he could tolerate no companions, except upon condition of their perfect sympathy with his present state of feeling. Such sympathy was not to be expected from Professor Baglioni.

The visitor chatted carelessly, for a few moments, about the gossip of the city and the University, and then took up another topic.

"I have been reading an old classic author lately," said he, "and met with a story that strangely interested me. Possibly you may remember it. It is of an Indian prince, who sent a beautiful woman as a present to Alexander the Great. She was as lovely as the dawn, and gorgeous as the sunset; but what especially distinguished her was a certain rich perfume in her breath—richer than a garden of

Persian roses. Alexander, as was natural to a youthful conqueror, fell in love at first sight with this magnificent stranger. But a certain sage physician, happening to be present, discovered a terrible secret in regard to her."

"And what was that?" asked Giovanni, turning his eyes downward to avoid those of the Professor.

"That this lovely woman," continued Baglioni, with emphasis, "had been nourished with poisons from her birth upward, until her whole nature was so imbued with them, that she herself had become the deadliest poison in existence. Poison was her element of life. With that rich perfume of her breath, she blasted the very air. Her love would have been poison!—her embrace death! Is not this a marvellous tale?"

"A childish fable," answered Giovanni, nervously starting from his chair. "I marvel how your worship finds time to read such nonsense, among your graver studies."

"By the bye," said the Professor, looking uneasily about him, "what singular fragrance is this in your apartment? Is it the perfume of your gloves? It is faint, but delicious, and yet, after all, by no means agreeable. Were I to breathe it long, methinks it would make me ill. It is like the breath of a flower—but I see no flowers in the chamber."

"Nor are there any," replied Giovanni, who had turned pale as the Professor spoke; "nor, I think, is there any fragrance, except in your worship's imagination. Odours, being a sort of element combined of the sensual and the spiritual, are apt to deceive us in this manner. The recollection of a perfume—the bare idea of it—may easily be mistaken for a present reality."

"Ay; but my sober imagination does not often play such tricks," said Baglioni; "and were I to fancy any kind of odour, it would be that of some vile apothecary drug, wherewith my fingers are likely enough to be imbued. Our worshipful friend Rappaccini, as I have heard, tinctures his medicaments with odours richer than those of Araby. Doubtless, likewise, the fair and learned Signora Beatrice would minister to her patients with draughts as sweet as a maiden's breath. But woe to him that sips them!"

Giovanni's face evinced many contending emotions. The tone in which the Professor alluded to the pure and lovely daughter of Rappaccini was a torture to his soul; and yet, the intimation of a view of her character, opposite to his own, gave instantaneous distinctness to a thousand dim suspicions, which now grinned at him like so many demons. But he strove hard to quell them, and to respond to Baglioni with a true lover's perfect faith.

"Signor Professor," said he, "you were my father's friend—perchance, too, it is your purpose to act a friendly part towards his son. I would fain feel nothing towards you save respect and deference. But I pray you to observe, Signor, that there is one subject on which we must not speak. You know not the Signora Beatrice. You cannot, therefore, estimate the wrong—the blasphemy, I may even say—that is offered to her character by a light or injurious word."

"Giovanni!—my poor Giovanni!" answered the Professor, with a calm expression of pity, "I know this wretched girl far better than yourself. You shall hear the truth in respect to the poisoner Rappaccini, and his poisonous daughter. Yes; poisonous as she is beautiful! Listen! for even should you do violence to my grey hairs, it shall not silence me. That old fable of the Indian woman has become a truth, by the deep and deadly science of Rappaccini, and in the person of the lovely Beatrice!"

Giovanni groaned, and hid his face.

"Her father," continued Baglioni, "was not restrained by natural affection from offering up his child, in this horrible manner, as the victim of his insane zeal for science. For—let us do him justice—he is as true a man of science as ever distilled his own heart in an alembic.

What, then, will be your fate? Beyond a doubt, you are selected as the material of some new experiment. Perhaps the result is to be death—perhaps a fate more awful still! Rappaccini, with what he calls the interest of science before his eyes, will hesitate at nothing."

"It is a dream!" muttered Giovanni to himself; "surely, it is a dream!"

"But," resumed the Professor, "be of good cheer, son of my friend! It is not yet too late for the rescue. Possibly, we may even succeed in bringing back this miserable child within the limits of ordinary nature, from which her father's madness has estranged her. Behold this little silver vase! It was wrought by the hands of the renowned Benvenuto Cellini, and is well worthy to be a love-gift to the fairest dame in Italy. But its contents are invaluable. One little sip of this antidote would have rendered the most virulent poisons of the Borgias innocuous. Doubt not that it will be as efficacious against those of Rappaccini. Bestow the vase, and the precious liquid within it, on your Beatrice, and hopefully await the result."

Baglioni laid a small, exquisitely-wrought silver phial on the table, and withdrew, leaving what he had said to produce its effect upon the young man's mind.

"We will thwart Rappaccini yet!" thought he, chuckling to himself, as he descended the stairs. "But, let us confess the truth of him, he is a wonderful man!—a wonderful man, indeed! A vile empiric, however, in his practice, and therefore not to be tolerated by those who respect the good old rules of the medical profession!"

Throughout Giovanni's whole acquaintance with Beatrice, he had occasionally, as we have said, been haunted by dark surmises as to her character. Yet, so thoroughly had she made herself felt by him as a simple, natural, most affectionate and guileless creature, that the image now held up by Professor Baglioni, looked as strange and incredible, as if it were not in accordance with his own original conception. True, there were ugly recollections connected with his first glimpses of the beautiful girl; he could not quite forget the bouquet that withered in her grasp, and the insect that perished amid the sunny air, by no ostensible agency save the fragrance of her breath. These incidents, however, dissolving in the pure light of her character, had no longer the efficacy of facts, but were acknowledged as mistaken fantasies, by whatever testimony of the senses they might appear to be substantiated. There is something truer and more real, than what we can see with the eyes, and touch with the finger. On such better evidence, had Giovanni founded his confidence in Beatrice, though rather by the necessary force of her high attributes, than by any deep and generous faith on his part. But, now, his spirit was incapable of sustaining itself at the height to which the early enthusiasm of passion had exalted it; he fell down, grovelling among earthly doubts, and defiled therewith the pure whiteness of Beatrice's image. Not that he gave her up; he did but distrust. He resolved to institute some decisive test that should satisfy him, once for all, whether there were those dreadful peculiarities in her physical nature, which could not be supposed to exist without some corresponding monstrosity of soul. His eyes, gazing down afar, might have deceived him as to the lizard, the insect, and the flowers. But if he could witness, at the distance of a few paces, the sudden blight of one fresh and healthful flower in Beatrice's hand, there would be room for no further question. With this idea, he hastened to the florist's, and purchased a bouquet that was still gemmed with the morning dew-drops.

It was now the customary hour of his daily interview with Beatrice. Before descending into the garden, Giovanni failed not to look at his figure in the mirror; a vanity to be expected in a beautiful young man, yet, as displaying itself at that troubled and feverish moment, the token of a certain shallowness of feeling and insincerity of character. He did gaze, however, and said to himself, that his features had never before possessed so rich a grace, nor his eyes such vivacity, nor his cheeks so warm a hue of superabundant life.

"At least," thought he, "her poison has not yet insinuated itself into my system. I am no flower to perish in her grasp!"

With that thought, he turned his eyes on the bouquet, which he had never once laid aside from his hand. A thrill of indefinable horror shot through his frame, on perceiving that those dewy flowers were already beginning to droop; they wore the aspect of things that had been fresh and lovely, yesterday. Giovanni grew white as marble, and stood motionless before the mirror, staring at his own reflection there, as at the likeness of something frightful. He remembered Baglioni's remark about the fragrance that seemed to pervade the chamber. It must have been the poison in his breath! Then he shuddered—shuddered at himself! Recovering from his stupor, he began to watch, with curious eye, a spider that was busily at work, hanging its web from the antique cornice of the apartment, crossing and re-crossing the artful system of interwoven lines, as vigorous and active a spider as ever dangled from an old ceiling. Giovanni bent towards the insect, and emitted a deep, long breath. The spider suddenly ceased its toil; the web vibrated with a tremor originating in the body of the small artisan. Again Giovanni sent forth a breath, deeper, longer, and imbued with a venomous feeling out of his heart; he knew not whether he were wicked, or only desperate. The spider made a convulsive gripe with his limbs, and hung dead across the window.

"Accursed! accursed!" muttered Giovanni, addressing himself. "Hast thou grown so poisonous, that this deadly insect perishes by thy breath?"

At that moment, a rich, sweet voice came floating up from the garden:—

"Giovanni! Giovanni! It is past the hour! Why tarriest thou? Come down!"

"Yes," muttered Giovanni again—"she is the only being whom my breath may not slay! Would that it might!"

He rushed down, and, in an instant, was standing before the bright and loving eyes of Beatrice. A moment ago, his wrath and despair had been so fierce that he could have desired nothing so much as to wither her by a glance. But, with her actual presence, there came influences which had too real an existence to be at once shaken off; recollections of the delicate and benign power of her feminine nature, which had so often enveloped him in a religious calm; recollections of many a holy and passionate out-gush of her heart, when the pure fountain had been unsealed from its depths, and made visible in its transparency to his mental eye; recollections which, had Giovanni known how to estimate them, would have assured him that all this ugly mystery was but an earthly illusion, and that, whatever mist of evil might seem to have gathered over her, the real Beatrice was a heavenly angel. Incapable as he was of such high faith, still her presence had not utterly lost its magic. Giovanni's rage was quelled into an aspect of sullen insensibility. Beatrice, with a quick spiritual sense, immediately felt that there was a gulf of blackness between them, which neither he nor she could pass. They walked on together, sad and silent, and came thus to the marble fountain, and to its pool of water on the ground, in the midst of which grew the shrub that bore gem-like blossoms. Giovanni was affrighted at the eager enjoyment—the appetite, as it were—with which he found himself inhaling the fragrance of the flowers.

"Beatrice," asked he, abruptly, "whence came this shrub?"

"My father created it," answered she, with simplicity.

"Created it! created it!" repeated Giovanni. "What mean you, Beatrice?"

"He is a man fearfully acquainted with the secrets of nature," replied Beatrice; "and, at the hour when I first drew breath, this plant sprang from the soil, the offspring of his science, of his intellect, while I was but his earthly child. Approach it not!" continued she, observing with terror that Giovanni was drawing nearer to the shrub. "It has qualities that you little dream of. But I, dearest Giovanni,—I grew up and blossomed with the plant, and was nourished with its breath. It was my sister, and I loved it with a human affection: for—alas! hast thou not suspected it?—there was an awful doom."

Here Giovanni frowned so darkly upon her that Beatrice paused and trembled. But her faith in his tenderness re-assured her, and made her blush that she had doubted for an instant.

"There was an awful doom," she continued,—"the effect of my father's fatal love of science—which estranged me from all society of my kind. Until Heaven sent thee, dearest Giovanni, oh! how lonely was thy poor Beatrice!"

"Was it a hard doom?" asked Giovanni, fixing his eyes upon her.

"Only of late have I known how hard it was," answered she, tenderly. "Oh, yes; but my heart was torpid, and therefore quiet."

Giovanni's rage broke forth from his sullen gloom like a lightning-flash out of a dark cloud.

"Accursed one!" cried he, with venomous scorn and anger—"and finding thy solitude wearisome, thou hast severed me, likewise, from all the warmth of life, and enticed me into thy region of unspeakable horror!"

"Giovanni!" exclaimed Beatrice, turning her large bright eyes upon his face. The force of his words had not found its way into her mind; she was merely thunderstruck.

"Yes, poisonous thing!" repeated Giovanni, beside himself with passion—"thou hast done it! Thou hast blasted me! Thou hast filled my veins with poison! Thou hast made me as hateful, as ugly, as loathsome and deadly a creature as thyself,—a world's wonder of hideous monstrosity! Now—if our breath be happily as fatal to ourselves as to all others—let us join our lips in one kiss of unutterable hatred, and so die!"

"What has befallen me?" murmured Beatrice, with a low moan out of her heart. "Holy Virgin, pity me, a poor heart-broken child!"

"Thou! dost thou pray?" cried Giovanni, still with the same fiendish scorn. "Thy very prayers, as they come from thy lips, taint the atmosphere with death. Yes, yes; let us pray! Let us to church, and dip our fingers in the holy water at the portal! They that come after us will perish as by a pestilence. Let us sign crosses in the air! It will be scattering curses abroad in the likeness of holy symbols!"

"Giovanni," said Beatrice calmly, for her grief was beyond passion, "Why dost thou join thyself with me thus in those terrible words? I, it is true, am the horrible thing thou namest me. But thou!— what hast thou to do, save with one other shudder at my hideous misery, to go forth out of the garden, and mingle with thy race, and forget that there ever crawled on earth such a monster as poor Beatrice?"

"Dost thou pretend ignorance?" asked Giovanni, scowling upon her. "Behold! This power have I gained from the pure daughter of Rappaccini!"

There was a swarm of summer-insects flitting through the air, in search of the food promised by the flower-odours of the fatal garden. They circled round Giovanni's head, and were evidently attracted towards him by the same influence which had drawn them, for an instant, within the sphere of several of the shrubs. He sent forth a breath among them, and smiled bitterly at Beatrice, as at least a score of the insects fell dead upon the ground.

"I see it! I see it!" shrieked Beatrice. "It is my father's fatal science? No, no, Giovanni; it was not I! Never, never! I dreamed only to love thee, and be with thee a little time, and so to let thee pass away, leaving but thine image in mine heart. For, Giovanni—believe it—though my body be nourished with poison, my spirit is God's creature, and craves love as its daily food. But my father!—he has united us in this fearful sympathy. Yes; spurn me!—tread upon me!—kill me! Oh, what is death, after such words as thine? But it was not I! Not for a world of bliss would I have done it!"

Giovanni's passion had exhausted itself in its outburst from his lips. There now came across him a sense, mournful, and not without tenderness, of the intimate and peculiar relationship between Beatrice and himself. They stood, as it were, in an utter solitude, which would be made none the less solitary by the densest throng of human life. Ought not, then, the desert of humanity around them to press this insulated pair closer together? If they should be cruel to one another, who was there to be kind to them? Besides, thought Giovanni, might there not still be a hope of his returning within the limits of ordinary nature, and leading Beatrice—the redeemed Beatrice—by the hand? Oh, weak, and selfish, and unworthy spirit, that could dream of an earthly union and earthly happiness as possible, after such deep love had been so bitterly wronged as was Beatrice's love by Giovanni's blighting words! No, no; there could be no such hope. She must pass heavily, with that broken heart, across the borders—she must bathe her hurts in some fount of Paradise, and forget her grief in the light of immortality—and *there* be well!

But Giovanni did not know it.

"Dear Beatrice," said he, approaching her, while she shrank away, as always, at his approach, but now with a different impulse,— "dearest Beatrice, our fate is not yet so desperate. Behold! There is a medicine, potent, as a wise physician has assured me, and almost divine in its efficacy. It is composed of ingredients the most opposite to those by which thy awful father has brought this calamity upon thee and me. It is distilled of blessed herbs. Shall we not quaff it together, and thus be purified from evil?"

"Give it me!" said Beatrice, extending her hand to receive the little silver phial which Giovanni took from his bosom. She added, with a peculiar emphasis: "I will drink—but do thou await the result."

She put Baglioni's antidote to her lips; and, at the same moment, the figure of Rappaccini emerged from the portal, and came slowly towards the marble fountain. As he drew near, the pale man of science seemed to gaze with a triumphant expression at the beautiful youth and maiden, as might an artist who should spend his life in achieving a picture or a group of statuary, and finally be satisfied with his success. He paused—his bent form grew erect with conscious power, he spread out his hand over them, in the attitude of a father imploring a blessing upon his children. But those were the same hands that had thrown poison into the stream of their lives! Giovanni trembled. Beatrice shuddered very nervously, and pressed her hand upon her heart.

"My daughter," said Rappaccini, "thou art no longer lonely in the world! Pluck one of those precious gems from thy sister shrub, and bid thy bridegroom wear it in his bosom. It will not harm him now! My science, and the sympathy between thee and him, have so wrought within his system, that he now stands apart from common men, as thou dost, daughter of my pride and triumph, from ordinary women. Pass on, then, through the world, most dear to one another, and dreadful to all besides!"

"My father," said Beatrice, feebly—and still, as she spoke, she kept her hand upon her heart—"wherefore didst thou inflict this miserable doom upon thy child?"

"Miserable!" exclaimed Rappaccini. "What mean you, foolish girl? Dost thou deem it misery to be endowed with marvellous gifts, against which no power nor strength could avail an enemy? Misery, to be able to quell the mightiest with a breath? Misery, to be as terrible as thou art beautiful? Wouldst thou, then, have preferred the condition of a weak woman, exposed to all evil, and capable of none?"

"I would fain have been loved, not feared," murmured Beatrice, sinking down upon the ground. "But now it matters not; I am going, father, where the evil, which thou hast striven to mingle with my being, will pass away like a dream—like the fragrance of these poisonous flowers, which will no longer taint my breath among the flowers of Eden. Farewell, Giovanni! Thy words of hatred are like lead within my heart—but they, too, will fall away as I ascend. Oh, was there not, from the first, more poison in thy nature than in mine?"

To Beatrice—so radically had her earthly part been wrought upon by Rappaccini's skill—as poison had been life, so the powerful antidote was death. And thus the poor victim of man's ingenuity and of thwarted nature, and of the fatality that attends all such efforts of perverted wisdom, perished there, at the feet of her father and Giovanni. Just at that moment, Professor Pietro Baglioni looked forth from the window, and called loudly, in a tone of triumph, mixed with horror, to the thunder-stricken man of science:

"Rappaccini! Rappaccini! And is *this* the upshot of your experiment?"

THE SIGNAL-MAN (1866)

Charles Dickens

Few authors either before or since have achieved quite the fame of Charles Dickens (1812–70). Born in Portsmouth Dickens endured a difficult childhood, being denied much in the way of a formal education. He was also forced into working in a factory when his father was incarcerated in a debtors' prison. His literary success began with the publication of his first book, *The Pickwick Papers* (1836), and within a very few years he was an international literary celebrity. Several successful novels followed including *The Old Curiosity Shop* (1840–41), *Bleak House* (1852–53), *Great Expectations* (1860–61) and *Our Mutual Friend* (1864–65).

Dickens wrote many short stories of which 'The Signal-Man', first published in the 1866 Christmas edition of *All the Year Round*, is arguably the finest. Dickens had been involved in the Staplehurst rail crash on 9th June 1865. The crash left ten people dead and forty injured. Dickens helped tend to the wounded and the traumatic experience left a deep and lasting impression. 'The Signal-Man' tells of a lonely individual, ill at ease with the world, who begins to receive eerie warnings of impending disaster. Dickens himself died on the 9th June 1870, five years to the day after the Staplehurst rail crash.

"HALLOA! BELOW THERE!"

When he heard a voice thus calling to him, he was standing at the door of his box, with a flag in his hand, furled round its short pole. One would have thought, considering the nature of the ground, that he could not have doubted from what quarter the voice came; but, instead of looking up to where I stood on the top of the steep cutting nearly over his head, he turned himself about and looked down the Line. There was something remarkable in his manner of doing so, though I could not have said, for my life, what. But, I know it was remarkable enough to attract my notice, even though his figure was foreshortened and shadowed, down in the deep trench, and mine was high above him, so steeped in the glow of an angry sunset that I had shaded my eyes with my hand before I saw him at all.

"Halloa! Below!"

From looking down the Line, he turned himself about again, and, raising his eyes, saw my figure high above him.

"Is there any path by which I can come down and speak to you?"

He looked up at me without replying, and I looked down at him without pressing him too soon with a repetition of my idle question. Just then, there came a vague vibration in the earth and air, quickly changing into a violent pulsation, and an oncoming rush that caused me to start back, as though it had force to draw me down. When such vapour as rose to my height from this rapid train, had passed me and was skimming away over the landscape, I looked down again, and saw him re-furling the flag he had shown while the train went by.

I repeated my inquiry. After a pause, during which he seemed to regard me with fixed attention, he motioned with his rolled-up flag towards a point on my level, some two or three hundred yards distant. I called down to him, "All right!" and made for that point. There, by dint of looking closely about me, I found a rough zig-zag descending path notched out: which I followed.

The cutting was extremely deep, and unusually precipitate. It was made through a clammy stone that became oozier and wetter as I went down. For these reasons, I found the way long enough to give me time to recall a singular air of reluctance or compulsion with which he had pointed out the path.

When I came down low enough upon the zig-zag descent, to see him again, I saw that he was standing between the rails on the way by which the train had lately passed, in an attitude as if he were waiting for me to appear. He had his left hand at his chin, and that left elbow rested on his right hand crossed over his breast. His attitude was one of such expectation and watchfulness, that I stopped a moment, wondering at it.

I resumed my downward way, and, stepping out upon the level of the railroad and drawing nearer to him, saw that he was a dark sallow man, with a dark beard and rather heavy eyebrows. His post was in as solitary and dismal a place as ever I saw. On either side, a dripping-wet wall of jagged stone, excluding all view but a strip of sky; the perspective one way, only a crooked prolongation of this great dungeon; the shorter perspective in the other direction, terminating in a gloomy red light, and the gloomier entrance to a black tunnel, in whose massive architecture there was a barbarous, depressing, and forbidding air. So little sunlight ever found its way to this spot, that it had an earthy deadly smell; and so much cold wind rushed through it, that it struck chill to me, as if I had left the natural world.

Before he stirred, I was near enough to him to have touched him. Not even then removing his eyes from mine, he stepped back one step, and lifted his hand.

This was a lonesome post to occupy (I said), and it had riveted my attention when I looked down from up yonder. A visitor was a rarity, I should suppose; not an unwelcome rarity, I hoped? In me, he merely saw a man who had been shut up within narrow limits all his life, and who, being at last set free, had a newly-awakened interest in these great works. To such purpose I spoke to him; but I am far from sure of the terms I used, for, besides that I am not happy in opening any conversation, there was something in the man that daunted me.

He directed a most curious look towards the red light near the tunnel's mouth, and looked all about it, as if something were missing from it, and then looked at me.

That light was part of his charge? Was it not?

He answered in a low voice: "Don't you know it is?"

The monstrous thought came into my mind as I perused the fixed eyes and the saturnine face, that this was a spirit, not a man. I have speculated since, whether there may have been infection in his mind.

In my turn, I stepped back. But in making the action, I detected in his eyes some latent fear of me. This put the monstrous thought to flight.

"You look at me," I said, forcing a smile, "as if you had a dread of me."

"I was doubtful," he returned, "whether I had seen you before."

"Where?"

He pointed to the red light he had looked at.

"There?" I said.

Intently watchful of me, he replied (but without sound), Yes.

"My good fellow, what should I do there? However, be that as it may, I never was there, you may swear."

"I think I may," he rejoined. "Yes. I am sure I may."

His manner cleared, like my own. He replied to my remarks with readiness, and in well-chosen words. Had he much to do there? Yes; that was to say, he had enough responsibility to bear; but exactness and watchfulness were what was required of him, and of actual work—manual labour—he had next to none. To change that signal, to trim those lights, and to turn this iron handle now and then, was all he had to do under that head. Regarding those many long and lonely hours of which I seemed to make so much, he could only say that the routine of his life had shaped itself into that form, and he had grown used to it. He had taught himself a language down here—if only to know it by sight, and to have formed his own crude ideas of its pronunciation, could be called learning it. He had also worked at fractions and decimals, and tried a little algebra; but he was, and had been as a boy, a poor hand at figures. Was it necessary for him when on duty, always to remain in that channel of damp air, and could he never rise into the sunshine from between those high stone walls? Why, that depended upon times and circumstances. Under some conditions there would be less upon the Line than under others, and the same held good as to certain hours of the day and night. In bright weather, he did choose occasions for getting a little above these lower shadows; but, being at all times liable to be called by his electric bell, and at such times listening for it with redoubled anxiety, the relief was less than I would suppose.

He took me into his box, where there was a fire, a desk for an official book in which he had to make certain entries, a telegraphic instrument with its dial face and needles, and the little bell of which he had spoken. On my trusting that he would excuse the remark that he had been well educated, and (I hoped I might say without offence), perhaps educated above that station, he observed that instances of slight incongruity in such-wise would rarely be found wanting among large bodies of men; that he had heard it was so in workhouses, in the police force, even in that last desperate resource, the army; and that he knew it was so, more or less, in any great railway staff. He had been, when young (if I could believe it, sitting in that, hut; he scarcely could), a student of natural philosophy, and had attended lectures; but he had run wild, misused his opportunities, gone down, and never risen again. He had no complaint to offer about that. He had made his bed, and he lay upon it. It was far too late to make another.

All that I have here condensed, he said in a quiet manner, with his grave dark regards divided between me and the fire. He threw in the word "Sir," from time to time, and especially when he referred to his youth: as though to request me to understand that he claimed to be nothing but what I found him. He was several times interrupted by the little bell, and had to read off messages, and send replies. Once, he had to stand without the door, and display a flag as a train passed, and make some verbal communication to the driver. In the discharge of his duties I observed him to be remarkably exact and vigilant, breaking off his discourse at a syllable, and remaining silent until what he had to do was done.

In a word, I should have set this man down as one of the safest of men to be employed in that capacity, but for the circumstance that while he was speaking to me he twice broke off with a fallen colour, turned his face towards the little bell when it did NOT ring, opened the door of the hut (which was kept shut to exclude the unhealthy damp), and looked out towards the red light near the mouth of the tunnel. On both of those occasions, he came back to the fire with the inexplicable air upon him which I had remarked, without being able to define, when we were so far asunder.

Said I when I rose to leave him: "You almost make me think that I have met with a contented man."

(I am afraid I must acknowledge that I said it to lead him on.)

"I believe I used to be so," he rejoined, in the low voice in which he had first spoken; "but I am troubled, sir, I am troubled."

He would have recalled the words if he could. He had said them, however, and I took them up quickly.

"With what? What is your trouble?"

"It is very difficult to impart, sir. It is very, very, difficult to speak of. If ever you make me another visit, I will try to tell you."

"But I expressly intend to make you another visit. Say, when shall it be?"

"I go off early in the morning, and I shall be on again at ten tomorrow night, sir."

"I will come at eleven."

He thanked me, and went out at the door with me. "I'll show my white light, sir," he said, in his peculiar low voice, "till you have found the way up. When you have found it, don't call out! And when you are at the top, don't call out!"

His manner seemed to make the place strike colder to me, but I said no more than "Very well."

"And when you come down tomorrow night, don't call out! Let me ask you a parting question. What made you cry 'Halloa! Below there!' tonight?"

"Heaven knows," said I. "I cried something to that effect—"

"Not to that effect, sir. Those were the very words. I know them well."

"Admit those were the very words. I said them, no doubt, because I saw you below."

"For no other reason?"

"What other reason could I possibly have!"

"You had no feeling that they were conveyed to you in any supernatural way?"

"No."

He wished me good night, and held up his light. I walked by the side of the down Line of rails (with a very disagreeable sensation of a train coming behind me), until I found the path. It was easier to mount than to descend, and I got back to my inn without any adventure.

Punctual to my appointment, I placed my foot on the first notch of the zig-zag next night, as the distant clocks were striking eleven. He was waiting for me at the bottom, with his white light on. "I have not called out," I said, when we came close together; "may I speak now?" "By all means, sir." "Good night then, and here's my hand." "Good night, sir, and here's mine." With that, we walked side by side to his box, entered it, closed the door, and sat down by the fire.

"I have made up my mind, sir," he began, bending forward as soon as we were seated, and speaking in a tone but a little above a whisper, "that you shall not have to ask me twice what troubles me. I took you for someone else yesterday evening. That troubles me."

"That mistake?"

"No. That someone else."

"Who is it?"

"I don't know."

"Like me?"

"I don't know. I never saw the face. The left arm is across the face, and the right arm is waved. Violently waved. This way."

I followed his action with my eyes, and it was the action of an arm gesticulating with the utmost passion and vehemence: "For God's sake clear the way!"

"One moonlight night," said the man, "I was sitting here, when I heard a voice cry 'Halloa! Below there!' I started up, looked from that door, and saw this Someone else standing by the red light near the tunnel, waving as I just now showed you. The voice seemed hoarse with shouting, and it cried, 'Look out! Look out!' And then again

'Halloa! Below there! Look out!' I caught up my lamp, turned it on red, and ran towards the figure, calling, 'What's wrong? What has happened? Where?' It stood just outside the blackness of the tunnel. I advanced so close upon it that I wondered at its keeping the sleeve across its eyes. I ran right up at it, and had my hand stretched out to pull the sleeve away, when it was gone."

"Into the tunnel," said I.

"No, I ran on into the tunnel, five hundred yards. I stopped and held my lamp above my head, and saw the figures of the measured distance, and saw the wet stains stealing down the walls and trickling through the arch. I ran out again, faster than I had run in (for I had a mortal abhorrence of the place upon me), and I looked all round the red light with my own red light, and I went up the iron ladder to the gallery atop of it, and I came down again, and ran back here. I telegraphed both ways: 'An alarm has been given. Is anything wrong?' The answer came back, both ways: 'All well.'"

Resisting the slow touch of a frozen finger tracing out my spine, I showed him how that this figure must be a deception of his sense of sight, and how that figures, originating in disease of the delicate nerves that minister to the functions of the eye, were known to have often troubled patients, some of whom had become conscious of the nature of their affliction, and had even proved it by experiments upon themselves. "As to an imaginary cry," said I, "do but listen for a moment to the wind in this unnatural valley while we speak so low, and to the wild harp it makes of the telegraph wires!"

That was all very well, he returned, after we had sat listening for a while, and he ought to know something of the wind and the wires, he who so often passed long winter nights there, alone and watching. But he would beg to remark that he had not finished.

I asked his pardon, and he slowly added these words, touching my arm:

"Within six hours after the Appearance, the memorable accident on this Line happened, and within ten hours the dead and wounded were brought along through the tunnel over the spot where the figure had stood."

A disagreeable shudder crept over me, but I did my best against it. It was not to be denied, I rejoined, that this was a remarkable coincidence, calculated deeply to impress his mind. But, it was unquestionable that remarkable coincidences did continually occur, and they must be taken into account in dealing with such a subject. Though to be sure I must admit, I added (for I thought I saw that he was going to bring the objection to bear upon me), men of common sense did not allow much for coincidences in making the ordinary calculations of life.

He again begged to remark that he had not finished.

I again begged his pardon for being betrayed into interruptions.

"This," he said, again laying his hand upon my arm, and glancing over his shoulder with hollow eyes, "was just a year ago. Six or seven months passed, and I had recovered from the surprise and shock, when one morning, as the day was breaking, I, standing at that door, looked towards the red light, and saw the spectre again." He stopped, with a fixed look at me.

"Did it cry out?"

"No. It was silent."

"Did it wave its arm?"

"No. It leaned against the shaft of the light, with both hands before the face. Like this."

Once more, I followed his action with my eyes. It was an action of mourning. I have seen such an attitude in stone figures on tombs.

"Did you go up to it?"

"I came in and sat down, partly to collect my thoughts, partly because it had turned me faint. When I went to the door again, daylight was above me, and the ghost was gone."

"But nothing followed? Nothing came of this?"

He touched me on the arm with his forefinger twice or thrice, giving a ghastly nod each time:

"That very day, as a train came out of the tunnel, I noticed, at a carriage window on my side, what looked like a confusion of hands and heads, and something waved. I saw it, just in time to signal the driver, Stop! He shut off, and put his brake on, but the train drifted past here a hundred and fifty yards or more. I ran after it, and, as I went along, heard terrible screams and cries. A beautiful young lady had died instantaneously in one of the compartments, and was brought in here, and laid down on this floor between us."

Involuntarily, I pushed my chair back, as I looked from the boards at which he pointed, to himself.

"True, sir. True. Precisely as it happened, so I tell it you."

I could think of nothing to say, to any purpose, and my mouth was very dry. The wind and the wires took up the story with a long lamenting wail.

He resumed. "Now, sir, mark this, and judge how my mind is troubled. The spectre came back, a week ago. Ever since, it has been there, now and again, by fits and starts."

"At the light?"

"At the Danger-light."

"What does it seem to do?"

He repeated, if possible with increased passion and vehemence, that former gesticulation of "For God's sake clear the way!"

Then, he went on. "I have no peace or rest for it. It calls to me, for many minutes together, in an agonized manner, 'Below there! Look out! Look out!' It stands waving to me. It rings my little bell—"

I caught at that. "Did it ring your bell yesterday evening when I was here, and you went to the door?"

"Twice."

"Why, see," said I, "how your imagination misleads you. My eyes were on the bell, and my ears were open to the bell, and if I am a living man, it did NOT ring at those times. No, nor at any other time, except when it was rung in the natural course of physical things by the station communicating with you."

He shook his head. "I have never made a mistake as to that, yet, sir. I have never confused the spectre's ring with the man's. The ghost's ring is a strange vibration in the bell that it derives from nothing else, and I have not asserted that the bell stirs to the eye. I don't wonder that you failed to hear it. But I heard it."

"And did the spectre seem to be there, when you looked out?"

"It WAS there."

"Both times?"

He repeated firmly: "Both times."

"Will you come to the door with me, and look for it now?"

He bit his under-lip as though he were somewhat unwilling, but arose. I opened the door, and stood on the step, while he stood in the doorway. There, was the Danger-light. There, was the dismal mouth of the tunnel. There, were the high wet stone walls of the cutting. There, were the stars above them.

"Do you see it?" I asked him, taking particular note of his face. His eyes were prominent and strained; but not very much more so, perhaps, than my own had been when I had directed them earnestly towards the same spot.

"No," he answered. "It is not there."

"Agreed," said I.

We went in again, shut the door, and resumed our seats. I was thinking how best to improve this advantage, if it might be called one, when he took up the conversation in such a matter of course way, so assuming that there could be no serious question of fact between us, that I felt myself placed in the weakest of positions.

"By this time you will fully understand, sir," he said, "that what troubles me so dreadfully, is the question, What does the spectre mean?"

I was not sure, I told him, that I did fully understand.

"What is its warning against?" he said, ruminating, with his eyes on the fire, and only by times turning them on me. "What is the danger? Where is the danger? There is danger overhanging, somewhere on the Line. Some dreadful calamity will happen. It is not to be doubted this third time, after what has gone before. But surely this is a cruel haunting of *me*. What can *I* do!"

He pulled out his handkerchief, and wiped the drops from his heated forehead.

"If I telegraph Danger, on either side of me, or on both, I can give no reason for it," he went on, wiping the palms of his hands. "I should get into trouble, and do no good. They would think I was mad. This is the way it would work:—Message: 'Danger! Take care!' Answer: 'What Danger? Where?' Message: 'Don't know. But for God's sake take care!' They would displace me. What else could they do?"

His pain of mind was most pitiable to see. It was the mental torture of a conscientious man, oppressed beyond endurance by an unintelligible responsibility involving life.

"When it first stood under the Danger-light," he went on, putting his dark hair back from his head, and drawing his hands outward across and across his temples in an extremity of feverish distress, "why not tell me where that accident was to happen—if it must happen? Why not tell me how it could be averted—if it could have been averted? When on its second coming it hid its face, why not tell me instead: 'She is going to die. Let them keep her at home'? If it came, on those two occasions, only to show me that its warnings were true, and so to prepare me for the third, why not warn me plainly now? And I, Lord help me! A mere poor signalman on this solitary station! Why not go to somebody with credit to be believed, and power to act!"

When I saw him in this state, I saw that for the poor man's sake, as well as for the public safety, what I had to do for the time was, to compose his mind. Therefore, setting aside all question of reality or unreality between us, I represented to him that whoever thoroughly discharged his duty, must do well, and that at least it was his comfort that he understood his duty, though he did not understand these confounding Appearances. In this effort I succeeded far better than in the attempt to reason him out of his conviction. He became calm; the occupations incidental to his post as the night advanced, began to make larger demands on his attention; and I left him at two in the morning. I had offered to stay through the night, but he would not hear of it.

That I more than once looked back at the red light as I ascended the pathway, that I did not like the red light, and that I should have slept but poorly if my bed had been under it, I see no reason to conceal. Nor, did I like the two sequences of the accident and the dead girl. I see no reason to conceal that, either.

But, what ran most in my thoughts was the consideration how ought I to act, having become the recipient of this disclosure? I had proved the man to be intelligent, vigilant, painstaking, and exact; but how long might he remain so, in his state of mind? Though in a subordinate position, still he held a most important trust, and would I (for instance) like to stake my own life on the chances of his continuing to execute it with precision?

Unable to overcome a feeling that there would be something treacherous in my communicating what he had told me, to his superiors in the Company, without first being plain with himself and proposing a middle course to him, I ultimately resolved to offer to accompany him (otherwise keeping his secret for the present) to the wisest medical practitioner we could hear of in those parts, and to take his opinion. A change in his time of duty would come round next night, he had apprised me, and he would be off an hour or two after sunrise, and on again soon after sunset. I had appointed to return accordingly.

Next evening was a lovely evening, and I walked out early to enjoy it. The sun was not yet quite down when I traversed the field-path near the top of the deep cutting. I would extend my walk for an hour, I said to myself, half an hour on and half an hour back, and it would then be time to go to my signalman's box.

Before pursuing my stroll, I stepped to the brink, and mechanically looked down, from the point from which I had first seen him. I cannot describe the thrill that seized upon me, when, close at the mouth of the tunnel, I saw the appearance of a man, with his left sleeve across his eyes, passionately waving his right arm.

The nameless horror that oppressed me, passed in a moment, for in a moment I saw that this appearance of a man was a man indeed, and that there was a little group of other men standing at a short distance, to whom he seemed to be rehearsing the gesture he made. The Danger-light was not yet lighted. Against its shaft, a little low hut, entirely new to me, had been made of some wooden supports and tarpaulin. It looked no bigger than a bed.

With an irresistible sense that something was wrong—with a flashing self-reproachful fear that fatal mischief had come of my leaving the man there, and causing no one to be sent to overlook or correct what he did—I descended the notched path with all the speed I could make.

"What is the matter?" I asked the men.

"Signalman killed this morning, sir."

"Not the man belonging to that box?"

"Yes, sir."

"Not the man I know?"

"You will recognize him, sir, if you knew him," said the man who spoke for the others, solemnly uncovering his own head and raising an end of the tarpaulin, "for his face is quite composed."

"O! how did this happen, how did this happen?" I asked, turning from one to another as the hut closed in again.

"He was cut down by an engine, sir. No man in England knew his work better. But somehow he was not clear of the outer rail. It was just at broad day. He had struck the light, and had the lamp in his hand. As the engine came out of the tunnel, his back was towards her, and she cut him down. That man drove her, and was showing how it happened. Show the gentleman, Tom."

The man, who wore a rough dark dress, stepped back to his former place at the mouth of the tunnel:

"Coming round the curve in the tunnel, sir," he said, "I saw him at the end, like as if I saw him down a perspective-glass. There was no time to check speed, and I knew him to be very careful. As he didn't seem to take heed of the whistle, I shut it off when we were running down upon him, and called to him as loud as I could call."

"What did you say?"

"I said, Below there! Look out! Look out! For God's sake clear the way!"

I started.

"Ah! it was a dreadful time, sir. I never left off calling to him. I put this arm before my eyes, not to see, and I waved this arm to the last; but it was no use."

Without prolonging the narrative to dwell on any one of its curious circumstances more than on any other, I may, in closing it, point out the coincidence that the warning of the Engine-Driver included, not only the words which the unfortunate Signalman had repeated to me as haunting him, but also the words which I myself—not he—had attached, and that only in my own mind, to the gesticulation he had imitated.

AN OCCURRENCE AT
OWL CREEK BRIDGE (1890)

Ambrose Bierce

The American short story writer, journalist, poet and Civil War veteran, Ambrose Bierce (1842–c.1914), lived a life and career every bit as adventurous as a character in one of his horror stories. His experiences as a Unionist soldier, particularly those dating from the Battle of Shiloh (April 1862), became the source material for many of his stories. His death, or more accurately his enigmatic disappearance, is also like something from one of his tales. In December 1913 he travelled to Chihuahua in Mexico to gain first-hand experience of the Mexican Revolution. He disappeared soon afterwards and, in spite of an official investigation, his fate was never established.

Bierce's literary work has been hugely influential and has provided inspiration for writers such as Stephen Crane, Ernest Hemingway and Ray Bradbury. His work, like that of Edgar Allan Poe, is also frequently credited with giving the horror story a psychological realism and depth previously absent from the genre. 'An Occurrence at Owl Creek Bridge' is one of his finest tales and the ending, once read, can never be forgotten.

A MAN STOOD UPON A RAILROAD BRIDGE IN NORTHERN Alabama, looking down into the swift waters twenty feet below. The man's hands were behind his back, the wrists bound with a cord. A rope loosely encircled his neck. It was attached to a stout cross-timber above his head, and the slack fell to the level of his knees. Some loose boards laid upon the sleepers supporting the metals of the railway supplied a footing for him, and his executioners—two private soldiers of the Federal army, directed by a sergeant, who in civil life may have been a deputy sheriff. At a short remove upon the same temporary platform was an officer in the uniform of his rank, armed. He was a captain. A sentinel at each end of the bridge stood with his rifle in the position known as "support," that is to say, vertical in front of the left shoulder, the hammer resting on the forearm thrown straight across the chest—a formal and unnatural position, enforcing an erect carriage of the body. It did not appear to be the duty of these two men to know what was occurring at the centre of the bridge; they merely blockaded the two ends of the foot plank which traversed it.

Beyond one of the sentinels nobody was in sight; the railroad ran straight away into a forest for a hundred yards, then, curving, was lost to view. Doubtless there was an outpost further along. The other bank of the stream was open ground—a gentle acclivity crowned with a stockade of vertical tree trunks, loop-holed for rifles, with a single embrasure through which protruded the muzzle of a brass cannon commanding the bridge. Midway of the slope between bridge and fort were the spectators—a single company of infantry in line, at "parade rest," the butts of the rifles on the ground, the barrels inclining slightly backward against the right shoulder, the hands crossed upon the stock. A lieutenant stood at the right of the line, the point of his sword upon the ground, his left hand resting upon his right. Excepting the group of four at the centre of the bridge not a man moved. The company faced the bridge, staring stonily, motionless. The sentinels, facing the banks of the stream, might have been statues to adorn the bridge. The captain stood with folded arms, silent, observing the work of his subordinates but making no sign. Death is a dignitary who, when he comes announced, is to be received with formal manifestations of respect, even by those most familiar with him. In the code of military etiquette silence and fixity are forms of deference.

The man who was engaged in being hanged was apparently about thirty-five years of age. He was a civilian, if one might judge from his dress, which was that of a planter. His features were good—a straight nose, firm mouth, broad forehead, from which his long, dark hair was combed straight back, falling behind his ears to the collar of his well-fitting frock coat. He wore a moustache and pointed beard but no whiskers; his eyes were large and dark grey and had a kindly expression which one would hardly have expected in one whose neck was in the hemp. Evidently this was no vulgar assassin. The liberal military code makes provision for hanging many kinds of people, and gentlemen are not excluded.

The preparations being complete, the two private soldiers stepped aside and each drew away the plank upon which he had been standing. The sergeant turned to the captain, saluted and placed himself immediately behind that officer, who in turn moved apart one pace. These movements left the condemned man and the sergeant standing on the two ends of the same plank, which spanned three of the cross-ties of the bridge. The end upon which the civilian stood almost, but not quite, reached a fourth. This plank had been held in place by the weight of the captain; it was now held by that of the sergeant. At a signal from the former, the latter would step aside, the plank would tilt and the condemned man go down between two ties. The arrangement commended itself to his judgment as simple and effective. His face had not been covered nor his eyes bandaged. He looked a moment at his "unsteadfast footing," then let his gaze wander to the swirling water of the stream racing madly beneath his feet. A piece of dancing driftwood caught his attention and his eyes followed it down the current. How slowly it appeared to move! What a sluggish stream!

He closed his eyes in order to fix his last thoughts upon his wife and children. The water, touched to gold by the early sun, the brooding mists under the banks at some distance down the stream, the fort, the soldiers, the piece of drift—all had distracted him. And now he became conscious of a new disturbance. Striking through the thought of his dear ones was a sound which he could neither ignore nor understand, a sharp, distinct, metallic percussion like the stroke of a blacksmith's hammer upon the anvil; it had the same ringing quality. He wondered what it was, and whether immeasurably distant or near by—it seemed both. Its recurrence was regular, but as slow as the tolling of a death knell. He awaited each stroke with impatience and—he knew not why—apprehension. The intervals of silence grew progressively longer; the delays became maddening. With their greater infrequency the sounds increased in strength and sharpness. They hurt his ear like the thrust of a knife; he feared he would shriek. What he heard was the ticking of his watch.

He unclosed his eyes and saw again the water below him. "If I could free my hands," he thought, "I might throw off the noose and spring into the stream. By diving I could evade the bullets, and, swimming vigorously, reach the bank, take to the woods, and get away home. My home, thank God, is as yet outside their lines; my wife and little ones are still beyond the invader's farthest advance."

As these thoughts, which have here to be set down in words, were flashed into the doomed man's brain rather than evolved from it, the captain nodded to the sergeant. The sergeant stepped aside.

II

Peyton Farquhar was a well-to-do planter, of an old and highly-respected Alabama family. Being a slave owner, and, like other slave owners, a politician, he was naturally an original secessionist and ardently devoted to the Southern cause. Circumstances of an imperious nature which it is unnecessary to relate here, had prevented him from taking service with the gallant army which had fought the disastrous campaigns ending with the fall of Corinth, and he chafed under the inglorious restraint, longing for the release of his energies, the larger life of the soldier, the opportunity for distinction. That opportunity, he felt, would come, as it comes to all in war time. Meanwhile he did what he could. No service was too humble for him to perform in aid of the South, no adventure too perilous for him to undertake if consistent with the character of a civilian who was at heart a soldier, and who in good faith and without too much qualification assented to at least a part of the frankly villainous dictum that all is fair in love and war.

One evening while Farquhar and his wife were sitting on a rustic bench near the entrance to his grounds, a grey-clad soldier rode up to the gate and asked for a drink of water. Mrs. Farquhar was only too happy to serve him with her own white hands. While she was gone to fetch the water, her husband approached the dusty horseman and inquired eagerly for news from the front.

"The Yanks are repairing the railroads," said the man, "and are getting ready for another advance. They have reached the Owl Creek bridge, put it in order, and built a stockade on the other bank. The commandant has issued an order, which is posted everywhere, declaring that any civilian caught interfering with the railroad, its bridges, tunnels, or trains, will be summarily hanged. I saw the order."

"How far is it to the Owl Creek bridge?" Farquhar asked.

"About thirty miles?"

"Is there no force on this side the creek?"

"Only a picket post half a mile out, on the railroad, and a single sentinel at this end of the bridge."

"Suppose a man—a civilian and student of hanging—should elude the picket post and perhaps get the better of the sentinel," said Farquhar, smiling, "what could he accomplish?"

The soldier reflected. "I was there a month ago," he replied. "I observed that the flood of last winter had lodged a great quantity of driftwood against the wooden pier at this end of the bridge. It is now dry and would burn like tow."

The lady had now brought the water, which the soldier drank. He thanked her ceremoniously, bowed to her husband, and rode away. An hour later, after nightfall, he repassed the plantation, going northward in the direction from which he had come. He was a Federal scout.

III

As Peyton Farquhar fell straight downward through the bridge, he lost consciousness and was as one already dead. From this state he was awakened—ages later, it seemed to him—by the pain of a sharp pressure upon his throat, followed by a sense of suffocation. Keen, poignant agonies seemed to shoot from his neck downward through every fibre of his body and limbs. These pains appeared to flash along well-defined lines of ramification and to beat with an inconceivably rapid periodicity. They seemed like streams of pulsating fire heating him to an intolerable temperature. As to his head, he was conscious of nothing but a feeling of fullness—of congestion. These sensations were unaccompanied by thought. The intellectual part of his nature was already effaced; he had power only to feel, and feeling was torment. He was conscious of motion. Encompassed in a luminous cloud, of which he was now merely the fiery heart, without material substance, he swung through unthinkable arcs of oscillation, like a vast pendulum. Then all at once, with terrible suddenness, the light about him shot upward with the noise of a loud plash; a frightful roaring was in his ears, and all was cold and dark. The power of thought was restored; he knew that the rope had broken and he had fallen into the stream. There was no additional strangulation; the noose about his neck was already suffocating him and kept the water from his lungs. To die of hanging at the bottom of a river!—the idea seemed to him ludicrous. He opened his eyes in the blackness and saw above him a gleam of light, but how distant, how inaccessible! He was still sinking, for the light became fainter and fainter until it was a mere glimmer. Then it began to grow and brighten, and he knew that he was rising toward the surface—knew it with reluctance, for he was now very comfortable. "To be hanged and drowned," he thought, "that is not so bad; but I do not wish to be shot. No; I will not be shot; that is not fair."

He was not conscious of an effort, but a sharp pain in his wrists apprised him that he was trying to free his hands. He gave the struggle his attention, as an idler might observe the feat of a juggler, without interest in the outcome. What splendid effort!—what magnificent, what superhuman strength! Ah, that was a fine endeavour! Bravo! The cord fell away; his arms parted and floated upward, the hands dimly seen on each side in the growing light. He watched them with a new interest as first one and then the other pounced upon the noose at his neck. They tore it away and thrust it fiercely aside, its undulations resembling those of a water snake. "Put it back, put it back!" He thought he shouted these words to his hands, for the undoing of the noose had been succeeded by the direst pang which he had yet experienced. His neck ached horribly; his brain was on fire; his heart, which had been fluttering faintly, gave a great leap, trying to force itself out at his mouth. His whole body was racked and wrenched with an insupportable anguish! But his disobedient hands gave no heed to the command. They beat the water vigorously with quick, downward strokes, forcing him to the surface. He felt his head emerge; his eyes were blinded by the sunlight; his chest expanded convulsively, and with a supreme and crowning agony his lungs engulfed a great draught of air, which instantly he expelled in a shriek!

He was now in full possession of his physical senses. They were, indeed, preternaturally keen and alert. Something in the awful disturbance of his organic system had so exalted and refined them that they made record of things never before perceived. He felt the ripples upon his face and heard their separate sounds as they struck. He looked at the forest on the bank of the stream, saw the individual trees, the leaves and the veining of each leaf—saw the very insects upon them, the locusts, the brilliant-bodied flies, the grey spiders stretching their webs from twig to twig. He noted the prismatic colours in all the dew-drops upon a million blades of grass. The humming of the gnats that danced above the eddies of the stream, the beating of the dragon flies' wings, the strokes of the water spiders' legs, like oars which had lifted their boat—all these made audible music. A fish slid along beneath his eyes and he heard the rush of its body parting the water.

He had come to the surface facing down the stream; in a moment the visible world seemed to wheel slowly round, himself the pivotal point, and he saw the bridge, the fort, the soldiers upon the bridge, the captain, the sergeant, the two privates, his executioners. They were in silhouette against the blue sky. They shouted and gesticulated, pointing at him; the captain had drawn his pistol, but did not fire; the others were unarmed. Their movements were grotesque and horrible, their forms gigantic.

Suddenly he heard a sharp report and something struck the water smartly within a few inches of his head, spattering his face with spray. He heard a second report, and saw one of the sentinels with his rifle at his shoulder, a light cloud of blue smoke rising from the muzzle. The man in the water saw the eye of the man on the bridge gazing into his own through the sights of the rifle. He observed that it was a grey eye, and remembered having read that grey eyes were keenest and that all famous marksmen had them. Nevertheless, this one had missed.

A counter swirl had caught Farquhar and turned him half round; he was again looking into the forest on the bank opposite the fort. The sound of a clear, high voice in a monotonous singsong now rang out behind him and came across the water with a distinctness that pierced and subdued all other sounds, even the beating of the ripples in his ears. Although no soldier, he had frequented camps enough to know the dread significance of that deliberate, drawling, aspirated chant; the lieutenant on shore was taking a part in the morning's work. How coldly and pitilessly—with what an even, calm intonation, presaging and enforcing tranquillity in the men—with what accurately-measured intervals fell those cruel words:

"Attention, company... Shoulder arms... Ready... Aim... Fire."

Farquhar dived—dived as deeply as he could. The water roared in his ears like the voice of Niagara, yet he heard the dulled thunder of the volley, and, rising again toward the surface, met shining bits of metal, singularly flattened, oscillating slowly downward. Some of them touched him on the face and hands, then fell away, continuing their descent. One lodged between his collar and neck; it was uncomfortably warm, and he snatched it out.

As he rose to the surface, gasping for breath, he saw that he had been a long time under water; he was perceptibly farther down stream—nearer to safety. The soldiers had almost finished reloading; the metal ramrods flashed all at once in the sunshine as they were drawn from the barrels, turned in the air, and thrust into their sockets. The two sentinels fired again, independently and ineffectually.

The hunted man saw all this over his shoulder; he was now swimming vigorously with the current. His brain was as energetic as his arms and legs; he thought with the rapidity of lightning.

"The officer," he reasoned, "will not make that martinet's error a second time. It is as easy to dodge a volley as a single shot. He has probably already given the command to fire at will. God help me, I cannot dodge them all!"

An appalling plash within two yards of him, followed by a loud rushing sound, *diminuendo*, which seemed to travel back through the air to the fort and died in an explosion which stirred the very river to its deeps! A rising sheet of water, which curved over him, fell down upon him, blinded him, strangled him! The cannon had taken a hand in the game. As he shook his head free from the commotion of the smitten water, he heard the deflected shot humming through the air ahead, and in an instant it was cracking and smashing the branches in the forest beyond.

"They will not do that again," he thought; "the next time they will use a charge of grape. I must keep my eye upon the gun; the smoke will apprise me—the report arrives too late; it lags behind the missile. It is a good gun."

Suddenly he felt himself whirled round and round—spinning like a top. The water, the banks, the forest, the now distant bridge, fort and men—all were commingled and blurred. Objects were represented by their colours only; circular horizontal streaks of colour—that was all he saw. He had been caught in a vortex and was being whirled on with a velocity of advance and gyration which made him giddy and sick. In a few moments he was flung upon the gravel at the foot of the left bank of the stream—the southern bank—and behind a projecting point which concealed him from his enemies. The sudden arrest of his motion, the abrasion of one of his hands on the gravel, restored him and he wept with delight. He dug his fingers into the sand, threw it over himself in handfuls and audibly blessed it. It looked like gold, like diamonds, rubies, emeralds; he could think of nothing beautiful which it did not resemble. The trees upon the bank were giant garden plants; he noted a definite order in their arrangement, inhaled the fragrance of their blooms. A strange, roseate light shone through the spaces among their trunks, and the wind made in their branches the music of æolian harps. He had no wish to perfect his escape, was content to remain in that enchanting spot until retaken.

A whizz and rattle of grapeshot among the branches high above his head roused him from his dream. The baffled cannoneer had fired him a random farewell. He sprang to his feet, rushed up the sloping bank, and plunged into the forest.

All that day he travelled, laying his course by the rounding sun. The forest seemed interminable; nowhere did he discover a break in it, not even a woodman's road. He had not known that he lived in so wild a region. There was something uncanny in the revelation.

By nightfall he was fatigued, footsore, famishing. The thought of his wife and children urged him on. At last he found a road which led him in what he knew to be the right direction. It was as wide and straight as a city street, yet it seemed untravelled. No fields bordered it, no dwelling anywhere. Not so much as the barking of a dog suggested human habitation. The black bodies of the great trees formed a straight wall on both sides, terminating on the horizon in a point, like a diagram in a lesson in perspective. Overhead, as he looked up through this rift in the wood, shone great golden stars looking unfamiliar and grouped in strange constellations. He was sure they were arranged in some order which had a secret and malign significance. The wood on either side was full of singular noises, among which—once, twice, and again—he distinctly heard whispers in an unknown tongue.

His neck was in pain, and, lifting his hand to it, he found it horribly swollen. He knew that it had a circle of black where the rope had bruised it. His eyes felt congested; he could no longer close them. His tongue was swollen with thirst; he relieved its fever by thrusting it forward from between his teeth into the cool air. How softly the turf had carpeted the untravelled avenue! He could no longer feel the roadway beneath his feet!

Doubtless, despite his suffering, he fell asleep while walking, for now he sees another scene—perhaps he has merely recovered from a delirium. He stands at the gate of his own home. All is as he left it, and all bright and beautiful in the morning sunshine. He must have travelled the entire night. As he pushes open the gate and passes up the wide white walk, he sees a flutter of female garments; his wife, looking fresh and cool and sweet, steps down from the veranda to meet him. At the bottom of the steps she stands waiting, with a smile of ineffable joy, an attitude of matchless grace and dignity. Ah, how beautiful she is! He springs forward with extended arms. As he is about to clasp her, he feels a stunning blow upon the back of the neck; a blinding white light blazes all about him, with a sound like the shock of a cannon—then all is darkness and silence!

Peyton Farquhar was dead; his body, with a broken neck, swung gently from side to side beneath the timbers of the Owl Creek bridge.

THE KING IS DEAD,
LONG LIVE THE KING (1890)

Mary Elizabeth Coleridge

Mary Elizabeth Coleridge (1861–1907), the great grandniece of the poet Samuel Taylor Coleridge, was a noted poet, novelist, short-story writer and essayist. Her father was Arthur Duke Coleridge, a lawyer and amateur musician who, along with the singer Jenny Lind, founded the London Bach Choir in 1875. Mary grew up in a very artistic atmosphere—guests to her father's house included the poets Robert Browning and Alfred, Lord Tennyson. She travelled widely throughout her life and was a great linguist, being fluent in Hebrew as well as French, German and Italian.

Her short story 'The King is Dead, Long Live the King' explores the attitudes of those still living to the recently deceased. The beautiful idea at the heart of the tale being that the dead, in this case a man who was once king, can listen in on those thoughts but is powerless to intervene. Coleridge had a great interest in the supernatural, once taking part in a séance with Alfred, Lord Tennyson, and the uncanny features prominently in much of her work.

I T WAS NOT VERY QUIET IN THE ROOM WHERE THE KING LAY dying. People were coming and going, rustling in and out with hushed footsteps, whispering eagerly to each other; and where a great many people are all busy making as little noise as possible, the result is apt to be a kind of bustle, that weakened nerves can scarcely endure.

But what did that matter? The doctors said he could hear nothing now. He gave no sign that he could. Surely the sobs of his beautiful young wife, as she knelt by the bedside, must else have moved him.

For days the light had been carefully shaded. Now, in the hurry, confusion, and distress, no one remembered to draw the curtains close, so that the dim eyes might not be dazzled. But what did that matter? The doctors said he could see nothing now.

For days no one but his attendants had been allowed to come near him. Now the room was free for all who chose to enter. What did it matter? The doctors said he knew no one.

So he lay for a long time, one hand flung out upon the counter-pane, as if in search of something. The queen took it softly in hers, but there was no answering pressure. At length the eyes and mouth closed, and the heart ceased to beat.

"How beautiful he looks," they whispered one to another.

When the king came to himself it was all very still—wonderfully and delightfully still, as he thought, wonderfully and delightfully dark. It was a strange, unspeakable relief to him—he lay as if in heaven. The room was full of the scent of flowers, and the cool night air came pleasantly through an open window. A row of wax tapers burned with soft radiance at the foot of the bed on which he was lying, covered with a velvet pall, only his head and face exposed. Four or five men were keeping guard around him, but they had fallen fast asleep.

So deep was the feeling of content which he experienced that he was loth to stir. Not till the great clock of the palace struck eleven, did he so much as move. Then he sat up with a light laugh.

He remembered how, when his mind was failing him, and he had rallied all his powers in one last passionate appeal against the injustice which was taking him away from the world just when the world most needed him, he had heard a voice saying, "I will give thee yet one hour after death. If, in that time, thou canst find three that desire thy life, live!"

This was his hour, his hour that he had snatched away from death. How much of it had he lost already? He had been a good king; he had worked night and day for his subjects; he had nothing to fear, and he knew that it was very pleasant to live, how pleasant he had never known before, for, to do him justice, he was not selfish; it was his unfinished work that he grieved about when the decree went forth against him. Yet, as he passed out of the room where the watchers sat heavily sleeping, things were changed to him somehow. The burning sense of injustice was gone. Now that he came to think of it, he had done very little. True that it was his utmost, but there were many better men in the world, and the world was large, very large it seemed to him now. Everything had grown larger. He loved his country and his home as well as ever, but in the night it had seemed as if they must perish with him, and now he knew that they were still unchanged.

Outside the door he paused a moment, hesitating whither to go first. Not to the queen. The very thought of her grief unnerved him. He would not see her till he could once more clasp her in his arms, and bid her weep tears of joy only because he was come again. After all, he had but an hour to wait. Before the castle clock struck twelve, he would be back again in life, remembering these things only as a dream. He sighed a little to think of it.

"All that to do over again some day," he said, as he recalled his last moments.

Almost he turned again to the couch he had so lately left.

"But I have never yet done anything through fear," said the king.

And he smiled as he thought of the terms of the compact. His city lay before him in the moonlight.

"I could find three thousand as easily as three," he said. "Are they not all my friends?"

As he passed out of the gate, he saw a child sitting on the steps, crying bitterly.

"What is the matter, little one?" said the sentinel on guard, stopping a moment.

"Father and mother have gone to the castle, because the king's dead," sobbed the child, "and they've never come back again; and I'm so tired and so hungry! And I've had no supper, and my doll's broken. Oh! I do wish the king were alive again!"

And she burst into a fresh storm of weeping. It amused the king not a little.

"So this is the first of my subjects that wants me back!" he said.

He had no child of his own. He would have liked to try and comfort the little maiden, but there were other calls upon him just then. He was on his way to the house of his great friend, the man whom he loved more than all others. A kind of malicious delight possessed him, as he pictured to himself the deep dejection he should find him in.

"Poor Amyas!" he said. "I know what I should be feeling in his place. I am glad he was not taken. I could not have borne his loss."

As he entered the courtyard of his friend's house, lights were being carried to and fro, horses were being saddled, an air of bustle and excitement pervaded the place. Look where he might, he could not see the face he knew so well. He entered at the open door. His friend was not in the hall. Room after room he vainly traversed— they were all empty. A sudden horror took him. Surely Amyas was not dead of grief?

He came at length to a small private apartment, in which they had spent many a happy, busy hour together; but his friend was not here either, though, to judge by appearances, he could only just have left it. Books and papers were tumbled all about in strange confusion, and bits of broken glass strewed the floor.

A little picture was lying on the ground. The king picked it up, and recognized a miniature of himself, the frame of which had been broken in the fall. He let it drop again, as if it had burnt him. The fire was blazing brightly, and the fragments of a half-destroyed letter lay, unconsumed as yet, in the fender. It was in his own writing. He snatched it up, and saw it was the last he had written, containing the details of an elaborate scheme which he had much at heart. He had only just thrown it back into the flames when two people entered the room, talking together, one a lady, the other a man, booted and spurred as though he came from a long distance.

"Where is Amyas?" he asked.

"Gone to proffer his services to the new king, of course," said the lady. "We are, as you may think, in great anxiety. He has none of the ridiculous notions of his predecessor, who, indeed, hated him cordially. The very favour Amyas has hitherto enjoyed will stand in his way at the new court. I only hope he may be in time to make his peace. He can, with truth, say that he utterly disapproved of the foolish reforms which his late master was bent on making. Of course, he was fond of him in a way; but we must think of ourselves, you know. People in our position have no time for sentiment. He started almost immediately after the king's death. I am sending his retinue after him."

"Quite right," said the gentleman, whom the king now knew as one of his ambassadors. "I shall follow him at once. Between you and me, it is no bad thing for the country. That poor boy had no notion of statesmanship. He forced me to conclude a peace which would have been disastrous to all our best interests. Happily, we shall have war directly now. Promotions in the army would have been at a standstill if he had had his way."

The king did not stay to hear more.

"I will go to my people," he said. "They at least have no interest to make peace with my successor. He will but take from them what I gave."

He heard the clock strike the first quarter as he went. He was, indeed, a very remarkable king, for he knew his way to the poorest part of his dominions. He had been there before, often and often, unknown to any one; and the misery which he had there beheld had stirred and steeled him to attempt what had never before been attempted.

No one about the palace knew where he had caught the malignant fever which carried him off. He had a shrewd suspicion himself, and he went straight to that quarter.

"Fevers won't hurt me now," he said laughing. The houses were as wretched, the people looked as sickly and squalid as ever. They were standing about in knots in the streets, late though it was, talking together about him. His name was in every mouth. The details of his illness, and the probable day of his funeral, seemed to interest them more than anything else.

Five or six men were sitting drinking round a table in a disreputable-looking public-house, and he stopped to overhear their conversation.

"And a good riddance, too!" said one of them, whom he knew well. "What's the use of a king as never spends a farthing more than he can help? It gives no impetus to trade, it don't. The new fellow's a very different sort. We shall have fine doings soon."

"Ay!" struck in another, "a meddlesome, priggish sort of chap, he was, always aworritting us about clean houses, and such like. What right's *he* got to interfere, I'd like to know?"

"Down with all kings! says I," put in a third; "but if we're to have 'em, let 'em behave as sich. I like a young fellow as isn't afraid of his missus, and knows port wine from sherry."

"Wanted to abolish capital punishment, he did!" cried a fourth. "Thought he'd get more work out of the poor fellows in prison, I suppose? Depend on it, there's some reason like that at the bottom of it. We ain't so very perticular about the lives of our subjects for nothing, we ain't"; an expression of opinion in which all the rest heartily concurred. The clock struck again as the king turned away; he felt as if a storm of abuse from some one he had always hated would be a precious balm just then. He entered the state prison, and made for the condemned cell. Capital punishment was not abolished yet, and in this particular instance he had certainly felt glad of it.

The cell was tenanted only by a little haggard-looking man, who was writing busily on his knee. The king had only seen him once before, and he looked at him curiously.

Presently the gaoler entered, and with him the first councillor, a man whom his late master had greatly loved and esteemed. The convict looked up quickly.

"It was not to be till tomorrow," he said. Then, as if afraid he had betrayed some cowardice, "but I am ready at any moment. May I ask you to give this paper to my wife?"

"The king is dead," said the first councillor gravely. "You are reprieved. His present majesty has other views. You will, in all probability, be set at large tomorrow."

"Dead?" said the man with a stunned look.

"Dead!" said the first councillor, with the impressiveness of a whole board.

The man stood up, passing his hand across his brow.

"Sir," he said earnestly, "I respected him. For all he was a king, he treated me like a gentleman. He, too, had a young wife. Poor fellow, I wish he were alive again!"

There were tears in the man's eyes as he spoke.

The third quarter struck as the king left the prison. He felt unutterably humiliated. The pity of his foe was harder to bear than the scorn of his friends. He would rather have died a thousand deaths than owe his life to such a man. And yet, because he was himself noble, he could not but rejoice to find nobility in another. He said to himself sternly that it was not worth what he had gone through. He reviewed his position in no very self-complacent mood. The affection he had so confidently relied upon was but a dream. The people he was fain to work for were not ripe for their own improvement. A foolish little child, a generous enemy, these were his only friends. After all, was it worth while to live? Had he not better go back quietly and submit, making no further effort? He had learnt his lesson; he could "lie down in peace, and sleep, and take his rest." The eternal powers had justified themselves. What matter though every man had proved a liar? The bitterness had passed away, and he seemed to see clearly.

Thick clouds had gathered over the moon, and the cold struck through him. All at once a sense of loneliness that cannot be described rushed over him, and his heart sank. Was there really no one who cared—no one? He would have given anything at that moment for a look, a single word of real sympathy. He longed with sick longing for the assurance of love.

There were yet a few moments left. How had he borne to wait so long? This, at least, he was sure of, and this was all the world to him. He began to find comfort and consolation in the thought; he forgave—indeed he almost forgot—the rest. Yet he had fallen very low, for, as he stood at the door of his wife's room, he hesitated whether to go in. What if this, too, were an illusion? Had he not best go back before he knew?

"But I have never yet done anything through fear," said the king.

His wife was sitting by the fire alone, her face hidden, her long hair falling round her like a veil. At the first sight of her, a pang of self-reproach shot through him. How could he ever have doubted?

She was wearing a ring that he had given her—a ring she wore always, and the light sparkled and flashed from the jewel. Except for this, there was nothing bright in the room.

He ardently desired to comfort her. He wondered why all her ladies had left her. Surely one might have stayed with her on this first night of her bereavement? She seemed to be lost in thought. If she would only speak, or call his name! But she was quite silent.

A slight noise made the king start. A secret door in the wall opened, the existence of which he had thought was known only to himself and his queen, and a man stood before her.

She put her finger to her lips, as though to counsel silence, and then threw herself into his arms.

"You have come," she said—"Oh, I am so glad! I had to hold his hand when he was dying. I was frightened sitting here by myself. I thought his ghost would come back, but he will never come back any more. We may be happy always now," and drawing the ring from her finger, she kissed it, weeping, and gave it to him.

When midnight struck, the watchers wakened with a start, to find the king lying stark and stiff, as before, but a great change had come over his countenance.

"We must not let the queen see him again," they said.

UNDER THE KNIFE (1896)

Herbert George Wells

Herbert George Wells (1866–1946), born in Bromley, Kent, was the son of Joseph Wells—a shopkeeper and professional cricketer—and Sarah Neal, a former domestic servant. A defining incident in Wells' early life occurred in 1874 when he broke his leg and was confined to bed. To pass the time he read library books brought to him by his father, a situation that resulted in a lifelong passion for literature and the desire to pursue a career as a writer. Today he probably remains most famous for his early science fiction novels such as *The Time Machine* (1895), *The Island of Dr Moreau* (1896), *The Invisible Man* (1897) and *The War of the Worlds* (1898).

First published in 1896, in *The New Review*, 'Under the Knife' tells of a man undergoing surgery. Life and death lie in the balance as the surgery proceeds with haunting implications for the patient's tenuous grip on the world he knows.

"WHAT IF I DIE UNDER IT?" THE THOUGHT RECURRED again and again, as I walked home from Haddon's. It was a purely personal question. I was spared the deep anxieties of a married man, and I knew there were few of my intimate friends but would find my death troublesome chiefly on account of their duty of regret. I was surprised indeed, and perhaps a little humiliated, as I turned the matter over, to think how few could possibly exceed the conventional requirement. Things came before me stripped of glamour, in a clear dry light, during that walk from Haddon's house over Primrose Hill. There were the friends of my youth: I perceived now that our affection was a tradition, which we foregathered rather laboriously to maintain. There were the rivals and helpers of my later career: I suppose I had been cold-blooded or undemonstrative—one perhaps implies the other. It may be that even the capacity for friendship is a question of physique. There had been a time in my own life when I had grieved bitterly enough at the loss of a friend; but as I walked home that afternoon the emotional side of my imagination was dormant. I could not pity myself, nor feel sorry for my friends, nor conceive of them as grieving for me.

I was interested in this deadness of my emotional nature—no doubt a concomitant of my stagnating physiology; and my thoughts wandered off along the line it suggested. Once before, in my hot youth, I had suffered a sudden loss of blood, and had been within an ace of death. I remembered now that my affections as well as my passions had drained out of me, leaving scarce anything but a tranquil resignation, a dreg of self-pity. It had been weeks before the old ambitions and tendernesses and all the complex moral interplay of a man had reasserted themselves. It occurred to me that the real meaning of this numbness might be a gradual slipping away from the pleasure-pain guidance of the animal man. It has been proven, I take it, as thoroughly as anything can be proven in this world, that the higher emotions, the moral feelings, even the subtle unselfishness of love, are evolved from the elemental desires and fears of the simple animal: they are the harness in which man's mental freedom goes. And it may be that as death overshadows us, as our possibility of acting diminishes, this complex growth of balanced impulse, propensity and aversion, whose interplay inspires our acts, goes with it. Leaving what?

I was suddenly brought back to reality by an imminent collision with the butcher-boy's tray. I found that I was crossing the bridge over the Regent's Park Canal, which runs parallel with that in the Zoological Gardens. The boy in blue had been looking over his shoulder at a black barge advancing slowly, towed by a gaunt white horse. In the Gardens a nurse was leading three happy little children over the bridge. The trees were bright green; the spring hopefulness was still unstained by the dusts of summer; the sky in the water was bright and clear, but broken by long waves, by quivering bands of black, as the barge drove through. The breeze was stirring; but it did not stir me as the spring breeze used to do.

Was this dulness of feeling in itself an anticipation? It was curious that I could reason and follow out a network of suggestion as clearly as ever: so, at least, it seemed to me. It was calmness rather than dulness that was coming upon me. Was there any ground for the belief in the presentiment of death? Did a man near to death begin instinctively to withdraw himself from the meshes of matter and sense, even before the cold hand was laid upon his? I felt strangely isolated—isolated without regret—from the life and existence about me. The children playing in the sun and gathering strength and experience for the business of life, the park-keeper gossiping with a nursemaid, the nursing mother, the young couple intent upon each other as they passed me, the trees by the wayside spreading new pleading leaves to the sunlight, the stir in their branches—I had been part of it all, but I had nearly done with it now.

Some way down the Broad Walk I perceived that I was tired, and that my feet were heavy. It was hot that afternoon, and I turned aside and sat down on one of the green chairs that line the way. In a minute I had dozed into a dream, and the tide of my thoughts washed up a vision of the resurrection. I was still sitting in the chair, but I thought myself actually dead, withered, tattered, dried, one eye (I saw) pecked out by birds. "Awake!" cried a voice; and incontinently the dust of the path and the mould under the grass became insurgent. I had never before thought of Regent's Park as a cemetery, but now, through the trees, stretching as far as eye could see, I beheld a flat plain of writhing graves and heeling tombstones. There seemed to be some trouble: the rising dead appeared to stifle as they struggled upward, they bled in their struggles, the red flesh was torn away from the white bones. "Awake!" cried a voice; but I determined I would not rise to such horrors. "Awake!" They would not let me alone. "Wike up!" said an angry voice. A cockney angel! The man who sells the tickets was shaking me, demanding my penny.

I paid my penny, pocketed my ticket, yawned, stretched my legs, and, feeling now rather less torpid, got up and walked on towards Langham Place. I speedily lost myself again in a shifting maze of thoughts about death. Going across Marylebone Road into that crescent at the end of Langham Place, I had the narrowest escape from the shaft of a cab, and went on my way with a palpitating heart and a bruised shoulder. It struck me that it would have been curious if my meditations on my death on the morrow had led to my death that day.

But I will not weary you with more of my experiences that day and the next. I knew more and more certainly that I should die under the operation; at times I think I was inclined to pose to myself. The doctors were coming at eleven, and I did not get up. It seemed scarce worth while to trouble about washing and dressing, and though I read my newspapers and the letters that came by the first post, I did not find them very interesting. There was a friendly note from Addison, my old school-friend, calling my attention to two discrepancies and a printer's error in my new book, with one from Langridge venting some vexation over Minton. The rest were business communications. I breakfasted in bed. The glow of pain at my side seemed more massive. I knew it was pain, and yet, if you can understand, I did not find it very painful. I had been awake and hot and thirsty in the night, but in the morning bed felt comfortable. In the night-time I had lain thinking of things that were past; in the morning I dozed over the question of immortality. Haddon came, punctual to the minute, with a neat black bag; and Mowbray soon followed. Their arrival stirred me up a little. I began to take a more personal interest in the proceedings. Haddon moved the little octagonal table close to the bedside, and, with his broad back to me, began taking things out of his bag. I heard the light click of steel upon steel. My imagination, I found, was not altogether stagnant. "Will you hurt me much?" I said in an off-hand tone.

"Not a bit," Haddon answered over his shoulder. "We shall chloroform you. Your heart's as sound as a bell." And as he spoke, I had a whiff of the pungent sweetness of the anæsthetic.

They stretched me out, with a convenient exposure of my side, and, almost before I realized what was happening, the chloroform was being administered. It stings the nostrils, and there is a suffocating sensation at first. I knew I should die—that this was the end of consciousness for me. And suddenly I felt that I was not prepared for death: I had a vague sense of a duty overlooked—I knew not what. What was it I had not done? I could think of nothing more to do, nothing desirable left in life; and yet I had the strangest disinclination to death. And the physical sensation was painfully oppressive. Of course the doctors did not know they were going to kill me. Possibly I struggled. Then I fell motionless, and a great silence, a monstrous silence, and an impenetrable blackness came upon me.

There must have been an interval of absolute unconsciousness, seconds or minutes. Then with a chilly, unemotional clearness, I perceived that I was not yet dead. I was still in my body; but all the multitudinous sensations that come sweeping from it to make up the background of consciousness had gone, leaving me free of it all. No, not free of it all; for as yet something still held me to the poor stark flesh upon the bed—held me, yet not so closely that I did not feel myself external to it, independent of it, straining away from it. I do not think I saw, I do not think I heard; but I perceived all that was going on, and it was as if I both heard and saw. Haddon was bending over me, Mowbray behind me; the scalpel—it was a large scalpel—was cutting my flesh at the side under the flying ribs. It was interesting to see myself cut like cheese, without a pang, without even a qualm. The interest was much of a quality with that one might feel in a game of chess between strangers. Haddon's face was firm and his hand steady; but I was surprised to perceive (*how* I know not) that he was feeling the gravest doubt as to his own wisdom in the conduct of the operation.

Mowbray's thoughts, too, I could see. He was thinking that Haddon's manner showed too much of the specialist. New suggestions came up like bubbles through a stream of frothing meditation, and burst one after another in the little bright spot of his consciousness. He could not help noticing and admiring Haddon's swift dexterity, in spite of his envious quality and his disposition to detract. I saw my liver exposed. I was puzzled at my own condition. I did not feel that I was dead, but I was different in some way from my living self. The grey depression, that had weighed on me for a year or more and coloured all my thoughts, was gone. I perceived and thought without any emotional tint at all. I wondered if everyone perceived things in this way under chloroform, and forgot it again when he came out of it. It would be inconvenient to look into some heads, and not forget.

Although I did not think that I was dead, I still perceived quite clearly that I was soon to die. This brought me back to the consideration of Haddon's proceedings. I looked into his mind, and saw that he was afraid of cutting a branch of the portal vein. My attention was distracted from details by the curious changes going on in his mind. His consciousness was like the quivering little spot of light which is thrown by the mirror of a galvanometer. His thoughts ran under it like a stream, some through the focus bright and distinct, some shadowy in the half-light of the edge. Just now the little glow was steady; but the least movement on Mowbray's part, the slightest sound from outside, even a faint difference in the slow movement of the living flesh he was cutting, set the light-spot shivering and spinning. A new sense-impression came rushing up through the flow of thoughts; and lo! the light-spot jerked away towards it, swifter than a frightened fish. It was wonderful to think that upon that unstable, fitful thing depended all the complex motions of the man; that for the next five minutes, therefore, my life hung upon its movements. And he was growing more and more nervous in his work. It was as if a little picture of a cut vein grew brighter, and struggled to oust from his brain another picture of a cut falling short of the mark. He was afraid: his dread of cutting too little was battling with his dread of cutting too far.

Then, suddenly, like an escape of water from under a lock-gate, a great uprush of horrible realization set all his thoughts swirling, and simultaneously I perceived that the vein was cut. He started back with a hoarse exclamation, and I saw the brown-purple blood gather in a swift bead, and run trickling. He was horrified. He pitched the red-stained scalpel on to the octagonal table; and instantly both doctors flung themselves upon me, making hasty and ill-conceived efforts to remedy the disaster. "Ice!" said Mowbray, gasping. But I knew that I was killed, though my body still clung to me.

I will not describe their belated endeavours to save me, though I perceived every detail. My perceptions were sharper and swifter than they had ever been in life; my thoughts rushed through my mind with incredible swiftness, but with perfect definition. I can only compare their crowded clarity to the effects of a reasonable dose of opium. In a moment it would all be over, and I should be free. I knew I was immortal, but what would happen I did not know. Should I drift off presently, like a puff of smoke from a gun, in some kind of half-material body, an attenuated version of my material self? Should I find myself suddenly among the innumerable hosts of the dead, and know the world about me for the phantas-magoria it had always seemed? Should I drift to some spiritualistic *séance*, and there make foolish, incomprehensible attempts to affect a purblind medium? It was a state of unemotional curiosity, of colourless expectation. And then I realized a growing stress upon me, a feeling as though some huge human magnet was drawing me upward out of my body. The stress grew and grew. I seemed an atom for which monstrous forces were fighting. For one brief, terrible moment sensation came back to me. That feeling of falling headlong which comes in nightmares, that feeling a thousand times intensified, that and a black horror swept across my thoughts in a torrent. Then the two doctors, the naked body with its cut side, the little room, swept away from under me and vanished, as a speck of foam vanishes down an eddy.

I was in mid-air. Far below was the West End of London, receding rapidly,—for I seemed to be flying swiftly upward,—and as it receded, passing westward like a panorama. I could see, through the faint haze of smoke, the innumerable roofs chimney-set, the narrow roadways, stippled with people and conveyances, the little specks of squares, and the church steeples like thorns sticking out of the fabric. But it spun away as the earth rotated on its axis, and in a few seconds (as it seemed) I was over the scattered clumps of town about Ealing, the little Thames a thread of blue to the south, and the Chiltern Hills and the North Downs coming up like the rim of a basin, far away and faint with haze. Up I rushed. And at first I had not the faintest conception what this headlong rush upward could mean.

Every moment the circle of scenery beneath me grew wider and wider, and the details of town and field, of hill and valley, got more and more hazy and pale and indistinct, a luminous grey was mingled more and more with the blue of the hills and the green of the open meadows; and a little patch of cloud, low and far to the west, shone ever more dazzlingly white. Above, as the veil of atmosphere between myself and outer space grew thinner, the sky, which had been a fair springtime blue at first, grew deeper and richer in colour, passing steadily through the intervening shades, until presently it was as dark as the blue sky of midnight, and presently as black as the blackness of a frosty starlight, and at last as black as no blackness I had ever beheld. And first one star, and then many, and at last an innumerable host broke out upon the sky: more stars than anyone has ever seen from the face of the earth. For the blueness of the sky is the light of the sun and stars sifted and spread abroad blindingly: there is diffused light even in the darkest skies of winter, and we do not see the stars by day only because of the dazzling irradiation of the sun. But now I saw things—I know not how; assuredly with no mortal eyes—and that defect of bedazzlement blinded me no longer. The sun was incredibly strange and wonderful. The body of it was a disc of blinding white light: not yellowish, as it seems to those who live upon the earth, but livid white, all streaked with scarlet streaks and rimmed about with a fringe of writhing tongues of red fire. And shooting half-way across the heavens from either side of it and brighter than the Milky Way, were two pinions of silver white, making it look more like those winged globes I have seen in Egyptian sculpture than anything else I can remember upon earth. These I knew for the solar corona, though I had never seen anything of it but a picture during the days of my earthly life.

When my attention came back to the earth again, I saw that it had fallen very far away from me. Field and town were long since indistinguishable, and all the varied hues of the country were merging into a uniform bright grey, broken only by the brilliant white of the clouds that lay scattered in flocculent masses over Ireland and the west of England. For now I could see the outlines of the north of France and Ireland, and all this Island of Britain, save where Scotland passed over the horizon to the north, or where the coast was blurred or obliterated by cloud. The sea was a dull grey, and darker than the land; and the whole panorama was rotating slowly towards the east.

All this had happened so swiftly that until I was some thousand miles or so from the earth I had no thought for myself. But now I perceived I had neither hands nor feet, neither parts nor organs, and that I felt neither alarm nor pain. All about me I perceived that the vacancy (for I had already left the air behind) was cold beyond the imagination of man; but it troubled me not. The sun's rays shot through the void, powerless to light or heat until they should strike on matter in their course. I saw things with a serene self-forgetfulness, even as if I were God. And down below there, rushing away from me,—countless miles in a second,—where a little dark spot on the grey marked the position of London, two doctors were struggling to restore life to the poor hacked and outworn shell I had abandoned. I felt then such release, such serenity as I can compare to no mortal delight I have ever known.

It was only after I had perceived all these things that the meaning of that headlong rush of the earth grew into comprehension. Yet it was so simple, so obvious, that I was amazed at my never anticipating the thing that was happening to me. I had suddenly been cut adrift from matter: all that was material of me was there upon earth, whirling away through space, held to the earth by gravitation, partaking of the earth-inertia, moving in its wreath of epicycles round the sun, and with the sun and the planets on their vast march through space. But the immaterial has no inertia, feels nothing of the pull of matter for matter: where it parts from its garment of flesh, there it remains (so far as space concerns it any longer) immovable in space. *I* was not leaving the earth: the earth was leaving *me*, and not only the earth but the whole solar system was streaming past. And about me in space, invisible to me, scattered in the wake of the earth upon its journey, there must be an innumerable multitude of souls, stripped like myself of the material, stripped like myself of the passions of the individual and the generous emotions of the gregarious brute, naked intelligences, things of new-born wonder and thought, marvelling at the strange release that had suddenly come on them!

As I receded faster and faster from the strange white sun in the black heavens, and from the broad and shining earth upon which my being had begun, I seemed to grow in some incredible manner vast: vast as regards this world I had left, vast as regards the moments and periods of a human life. Very soon I saw the full circle of the earth, slightly gibbous, like the moon when she nears her full, but very large; and the silvery shape of America was now in the noonday blaze wherein (as it seemed) little England had been basking but a few minutes ago. At first the earth was large, and shone in the heavens, filling a great part of them; but every moment she grew smaller and more distant. As she shrank, the broad moon in its third quarter crept into view over the rim of her disc. I looked for the constellations. Only that part of Aries directly behind the sun and the Lion, which the earth covered, were hidden. I recognized the tortuous, tattered band of the Milky Way with Vega very bright between sun and earth; and Sirius and Orion shone splendid against the unfathomable blackness in the opposite quarter of the heavens. The Pole Star was overhead, and the Great Bear hung over the circle of the earth. And away beneath and beyond the shining corona of the sun were strange groupings of stars I had never seen in my life—notably a dagger-shaped group that I knew for the Southern Cross. All these were no larger than when they had shone on earth, but the little stars that one scarce sees shone now against the setting of black vacancy as brightly as the first-magnitudes had done, while the larger worlds were points of indescribable glory and colour. Aldebaran was a spot of blood-red fire, and Sirius condensed to one point the light of innumerable sapphires. And they shone steadily: they did not scintillate, they were calmly glorious. My impressions had an adamantine hardness and brightness: there was no blurring softness, no atmosphere, nothing but infinite darkness set with the myriads of these acute and brilliant points and specks of light. Presently, when I looked again, the little earth seemed no bigger than the sun, and it dwindled and turned as I looked, until in a second's space (as it seemed to me), it was halved; and so it went on swiftly dwindling. Far away in the opposite direction, a little pinkish pin's head of light, shining steadily, was the planet Mars. I swam motionless in vacancy, and, without a trace of terror or astonishment, watched the speck of cosmic dust we call the world fall away from me.

Presently it dawned upon me that my sense of duration had changed; that my mind was moving not faster but infinitely slower, that between each separate impression there was a period of many days. The moon spun once round the earth as I noted this; and I perceived clearly the motion of Mars in his orbit. Moreover, it appeared as if the time between thought and thought grew steadily greater, until at last a thousand years was but a moment in my perception.

At first the constellations had shone motionless against the black background of infinite space; but presently it seemed as though the group of stars about Hercules and the Scorpion was contracting, while Orion and Aldebaran and their neighbours were scattering apart. Flashing suddenly out of the darkness there came a flying multitude of particles of rock, glittering like dust-specks in a sunbeam, and encompassed in a faintly luminous cloud. They swirled all about me, and vanished again in a twinkling far behind. And then I saw that a bright spot of light, that shone a little to one side of my path, was growing very rapidly larger, and perceived that it was the planet Saturn rushing towards me. Larger and larger it grew, swallowing up the heavens behind it, and hiding every moment a fresh multitude of stars. I perceived its flattened, whirling body, its disc-like belt, and seven of its little satellites. It grew and grew, till it towered enormous; and then I plunged amid a streaming multitude of clashing stones and dancing dust-particles and gas-eddies, and saw for a moment the mighty triple belt like three concentric arches of moonlight above me, its shadow black on the boiling tumult below. These things happened in one-tenth of the time it takes to tell them. The planet went by like a flash of lightning; for a few seconds it blotted out the sun, and there and then became a mere black, dwindling, winged patch against the light. The earth, the mother mote of my being, I could no longer see.

So with a stately swiftness, in the profoundest silence, the solar system fell from me as it had been a garment, until the sun was a mere star amid the multitude of stars, with its eddy of planet-specks lost in the confused glittering of the remoter light. I was no longer a denizen of the solar system: I had come to the outer Universe, I seemed to grasp and comprehend the whole world of matter. Ever more swiftly the stars closed in about the spot where Antares and Vega had vanished in a phosphorescent haze, until that part of the sky had the semblance of a whirling mass of nebulae, and ever before me yawned vaster gaps of vacant blackness, and the stars shone fewer and fewer. It seemed as if I moved towards a point between Orion's belt and sword; and the void about that region opened vaster and vaster every second, an incredible gulf of nothingness into which I was falling. Faster and ever faster the universe rushed by, a hurry of whirling motes at last, speeding silently into the void. Stars glowing brighter and brighter, with their circling planets catching the light in a ghostly fashion as I neared them, shone out and vanished again into inexistence; faint comets, clusters of meteorites, winking specks of matter, eddying light-points, whizzed past, some perhaps a hundred millions of miles or so from me at most, few nearer, travelling with unimaginable rapidity, shooting constellations, momentary darts of fire, through that black, enormous night. More than anything else it was like a dusty draught, sunbeam-lit. Broader and wider and deeper grew the starless space, the vacant Beyond, into which I was being drawn. At last a quarter of the heavens was black and blank, and the whole headlong rush of stellar universe closed in behind me like a veil of light that is gathered together. It drove away from me like a monstrous jack-o'-lantern driven by the wind. I had come out into the wilderness of space. Ever the vacant blackness grew broader until the hosts of the stars seemed only like a swarm of fiery specks hurrying away from me, inconceivably remote, and the darkness, the nothingness and emptiness, was about me on every side. Soon the little universe of matter, the cage of points in which I had begun to be, was dwindling, now to a whirling disc of luminous glittering, and now to one minute disc of hazy light. In a little while it would shrink to a point, and at last would vanish altogether.

Suddenly feeling came back to me—feeling in the shape of overwhelming terror; such a dread of those dark vastitudes as no words can describe, a passionate resurgence of sympathy and social desire. Were there other souls, invisible to me as I to them, about me in the blackness? or was I indeed, even as I felt, alone? Had I passed out of being into something that was neither being nor not-being? The covering of the body, the covering of matter, had been torn from me, and the hallucinations of companionship and security. Everything was black and silent. I had ceased to be. I was nothing. There was nothing, save only that infinitesimal dot of light that dwindled in the gulf. I strained myself to hear and see, and for a while there was naught but infinite silence, intolerable darkness, horror, and despair.

Then I saw that about the spot of light into which the whole world of matter had shrunk there was a faint glow. And in a band on either side of that the darkness was not absolute. I watched it for ages, as it seemed to me, and through the long waiting the haze grew imperceptibly more distinct. And then about the band appeared an irregular cloud of the faintest, palest brown. I felt a passionate impatience; but the things grew brighter so slowly that they scarce seemed to change. What was unfolding itself? What was this strange reddish dawn in the interminable night of space?

The cloud's shape was grotesque. It seemed to be looped along its lower side into four projecting masses, and, above, it ended in a straight line. What phantom was it? I felt assured I had seen that figure before; but I could not think what, nor where, nor when it was. Then the realization rushed upon me. *It was a clenched Hand.* I was alone in space, alone with this huge, shadowy Hand, upon which the whole Universe of Matter lay like an unconsidered speck of dust. It seemed as though I watched it through vast periods of time. On the forefinger glittered a ring; and the universe from which I had come was but a spot of light upon the ring's curvature. And the thing that the hand gripped had the likeness of a black rod. Through a long eternity I watched this Hand, with the ring and the rod, marvelling and fearing and waiting helplessly on what might follow. It seemed as though nothing could follow: that I should watch for ever, seeing only the Hand and the thing it held, and understanding nothing of its import. Was the whole universe but a refracting speck upon some greater Being? Were our worlds but the atoms of another universe, and those again of another, and so on through an endless progression? And what was I? Was I indeed immaterial? A vague persuasion of a body gathering about me came into my suspense. The abysmal darkness about the Hand filled with impalpable suggestions, with uncertain, fluctuating shapes.

Then, suddenly, came a sound, like the sound of a tolling bell: faint, as if infinitely far; muffled, as though heard through thick swathings of darkness: a deep, vibrating resonance, with vast gulfs of silence between each stroke. And the Hand appeared to tighten on the rod. And I saw far above the Hand, towards the apex of the darkness, a circle of dim phosphorescence, a ghostly sphere whence these sounds came throbbing; and at the last stroke the Hand vanished, for the hour had come, and I heard a noise of many waters. But the black rod remained as a great band across the sky. And then a voice, which seemed to run to the uttermost parts of space, spoke, saying, "There will be no more pain."

At that an almost intolerable gladness and radiance rushed in upon me, and I saw the circle shining white and bright, and the rod black and shining, and many things else distinct and clear. And the circle was the face of the clock, and the rod the rail of my bed. Haddon was standing at the foot, against the rail, with a small pair of scissors on his fingers; and the hands of my clock on the mantel over his shoulder were clasped together over the hour of twelve. Mowbray was washing something in a basin at the octagonal table, and at my side I felt a subdued feeling that could scarce be spoken of as pain.

The operation had not killed me. And I perceived, suddenly, that the dull melancholy of half a year was lifted from my mind.

LAURA (1914)

Hector Hugh Munro (Saki)

Hector Hugo Munro (1870–1916), better known under his pen
name Saki, was a writer whose frequently macabre stories sati-
rized Edwardian society. Authors such as Noël Coward and P. G.
Wodehouse among many others took inspiration from Munro,
admiring the way in which he used humour to describe a situation
that was, on the surface, deeply disturbing. A particularly common
theme in Munro's work is the comparison between the shifty and
hypocritical manoeuvrings of Edwardian England with the brutal
life-and-death struggles taking place in nature. Munro's life was often
marred by tragedy. His mother died when he was only two years old
and he was brought up by his grandmother and two maiden aunts,
Charlotte and Augusta, a strict upbringing that formed the back-
ground to arguably his most famous story 'Sredni Vashtar'. Munro
was 43 when World War I began. Officially over the age to enlist he
joined up all the same and served with distinction. He was killed at
the Battle of Ancre in November 1916.

'Laura' appeared in the collection *Beasts and Super-Beasts* in 1914,
the title being a parody of George Bernard Shaw's *Man and Superman*.
The story is a brilliantly funny tale infused with the macabre. The
central character, as the story begins, believes she has only a few
days to live and yet she appears totally unconcerned, confident in
the belief she will be reincarnated.

"You are not really dying, are you?" asked Amanda.

"I have the doctor's permission to live till Tuesday," said Laura.

"But today is Saturday; this is serious!" gasped Amanda.

"I don't know about it being serious; it is certainly Saturday," said Laura.

"Death is always serious," said Amanda.

"I never said I was going to die. I am presumably going to leave off being Laura, but I shall go on being something. An animal of some kind, I suppose. You see, when one hasn't been very good in the life one has just lived, one reincarnates in some lower organism. And I haven't been very good, when one comes to think of it. I've been petty and mean and vindictive and all that sort of thing when circumstances have seemed to warrant it."

"Circumstances never warrant that sort of thing," said Amanda hastily.

"If you don't mind my saying so," observed Laura, "Egbert is a circumstance that would warrant any amount of that sort of thing. You're married to him—that's different; you've sworn to love, honour, and endure him: I haven't."

"I don't see what's wrong with Egbert," protested Amanda.

"Oh, I daresay the wrongness has been on my part," admitted Laura dispassionately; "he has merely been the extenuating circumstance. He made a thin, peevish kind of fuss, for instance, when I took the collie puppies from the farm out for a run the other day."

"They chased his young broods of speckled Sussex and drove two sitting hens off their nests, besides running all over the flower beds. You know how devoted he is to his poultry and garden."

"Anyhow, he needn't have gone on about it for the entire evening and then have said, 'Let's say no more about it' just when I was beginning to enjoy the discussion. That's where one of my petty vindictive revenges came in," added Laura with an unrepentant chuckle; "I turned the entire family of speckled Sussex into his seedling shed the day after the puppy episode."

"How could you?" exclaimed Amanda.

"It came quite easy," said Laura; "two of the hens pretended to be laying at the time, but I was firm."

"And we thought it was an accident!"

"You see," resumed Laura, "I really *have* some grounds for supposing that my next incarnation will be in a lower organism. I shall be an animal of some kind. On the other hand, I haven't been a bad sort in my way, so I think I may count on being a nice animal, something elegant and lively, with a love of fun. An otter, perhaps."

"I can't imagine you as an otter," said Amanda.

"Well, I don't suppose you can imagine me as an angel, if it comes to that," said Laura.

Amanda was silent. She couldn't.

"Personally I think an otter life would be rather enjoyable," continued Laura; "salmon to eat all the year round, and the satisfaction of being able to fetch the trout in their own homes without having to wait for hours till they condescend to rise to the fly you've been dangling before them; and an elegant svelte figure—"

"Think of the otter hounds," interposed Amanda; "how dreadful to be hunted and harried and finally worried to death!"

"Rather fun with half the neighbourhood looking on, and anyhow not worse than this Saturday-to-Tuesday business of dying by inches; and then I should go on into something else. If I had been a moderately good otter I suppose I should get back into human shape of some sort; probably something rather primitive—a little brown, unclothed Nubian boy, I should think."

"I wish you would be serious," sighed Amanda; "you really ought to be if you're only going to live till Tuesday."

As a matter of fact Laura died on Monday.

"So dreadfully upsetting," Amanda complained to her uncle-in-law, Sir Lulworth Quayne. "I've asked quite a lot of people down for golf and fishing, and the rhododendrons are just looking their best."

"Laura always was inconsiderate," said Sir Lulworth; "she was born during Goodwood week, with an Ambassador staying in the house who hated babies."

"She had the maddest kind of ideas," said Amanda; "do you know if there was any insanity in her family?"

"Insanity? No, I never heard of any. Her father lives in West Kensington, but I believe he's sane on all other subjects."

"She had an idea that she was going to be reincarnated as an otter," said Amanda.

"One meets with those ideas of reincarnation so frequently, even in the West," said Sir Lulworth, "that one can hardly set them down as being mad. And Laura was such an unaccountable person in this life that I should not like to lay down definite rules as to what she might be doing in an after state."

"You think she really might have passed into some animal form?" asked Amanda. She was one of those who shape their opinions rather readily from the standpoint of those around them.

Just then Egbert entered the breakfast-room, wearing an air of bereavement that Laura's demise would have been insufficient, in itself, to account for.

"Four of my speckled Sussex have been killed," he exclaimed; "the very four that were to go to the show on Friday. One of them was dragged away and eaten right in the middle of that new carnation bed that I've been to such trouble and expense over. My best flower bed and my best fowls singled out for destruction; it almost seems as if the brute that did the deed had special knowledge how to be as devastating as possible in a short space of time."

"Was it a fox, do you think?" asked Amanda.

"Sounds more like a polecat," said Sir Lulworth.

"No," said Egbert, "there were marks of webbed feet all over the place, and we followed the tracks down to the stream at the bottom of the garden; evidently an otter."

Amanda looked quickly and furtively across at Sir Lulworth.

Egbert was too agitated to eat any breakfast, and went out to superintend the strengthening of the poultry yard defences.

"I think she might at least have waited till the funeral was over," said Amanda in a scandalized voice.

"It's her own funeral, you know," said Sir Lulworth; "it's a nice point in etiquette how far one ought to show respect to one's own mortal remains."

Disregard for mortuary convention was carried to further lengths next day; during the absence of the family at the funeral ceremony the remaining survivors of the speckled Sussex were massacred. The marauder's line of retreat seemed to have embraced most of the flower beds on the lawn, but the strawberry beds in the lower garden had also suffered.

"I shall get the otter hounds to come here at the earliest possible moment," said Egbert savagely.

"On no account! You can't dream of such a thing!" exclaimed Amanda. "I mean, it wouldn't do, so soon after a funeral in the house."

"It's a case of necessity," said Egbert; "once an otter takes to that sort of thing it won't stop."

"Perhaps it will go elsewhere now there are no more fowls left," suggested Amanda.

"One would think you wanted to shield the beast," said Egbert.

"There's been so little water in the stream lately," objected Amanda; "it seems hardly sporting to hunt an animal when it has so little chance of taking refuge anywhere."

"Good gracious!" fumed Egbert, "I'm not thinking about sport. I want to have the animal killed as soon as possible."

Even Amanda's opposition weakened when, during church time on the following Sunday, the otter made its way into the house, raided half a salmon from the larder and worried it into scaly fragments on the Persian rug in Egbert's studio.

"We shall have it hiding under our beds and biting pieces out of our feet before long," said Egbert, and from what Amanda knew of this particular otter she felt that the possibility was not a remote one.

On the evening preceding the day fixed for the hunt Amanda spent a solitary hour walking by the banks of the stream, making what she imagined to be hound noises. It was charitably supposed by those who overheard her performance, that she was practising for farmyard imitations at the forthcoming village entertainment.

It was her friend and neighbour, Aurora Burret, who brought her news of the day's sport.

"Pity you weren't out; we had quite a good day. We found at once, in the pool just below your garden."

"Did you—kill?" asked Amanda.

"Rather. A fine she-otter. Your husband got rather badly bitten in trying to 'tail it.' Poor beast, I felt quite sorry for it, it had such a human look in its eyes when it was killed. You'll call me silly, but do you know who the look reminded me of? My dear woman, what is the matter?"

When Amanda had recovered to a certain extent from her attack of nervous prostration Egbert took her to the Nile Valley to recuperate. Change of scene speedily brought about the desired recovery of health and mental balance. The escapades of an adventurous otter in search of a variation of diet were viewed in their proper light. Amanda's normally placid temperament reasserted itself. Even a hurricane of shouted curses, coming from her husband's dressing-room, in her husband's voice, but hardly in his usual vocabulary, failed to disturb her serenity as she made a leisurely toilet one evening in a Cairo hotel.

"What is the matter? What has happened?" she asked in amused curiosity.

"The little beast has thrown all my clean shirts into the bath! Wait till I catch you, you little—"

"What little beast?" asked Amanda, suppressing a desire to laugh; Egbert's language was so hopelessly inadequate to express his outraged feelings.

"A little beast of a naked brown Nubian boy," spluttered Egbert.

And now Amanda is seriously ill.

WHERE THEIR FIRE
IS NOT QUENCHED (1923)

May Sinclair

Mary Amelia St Clair, better known under her pseudonym May Sinclair (1863–1946), was a novelist, poet, translator, philosopher and critic. She was also an active suffragist and a member of the Woman Writers' Suffragist League. Her friends included Thomas Hardy, Henry James, H. G. Wells and Rebecca West. During her life she wrote twenty-three novels and numerous short stories, two philosophical treatises, several collections of poetry and a biography of the Brontës. Sinclair was also a significant modernist writer, employing stream-of-consciousness narration in many of her later novels. Although undeservedly neglected for far too long academic interest in her work is increasing and her books—which combine social and psychological insight with great technical artistry—are ripe for rediscovery.

'Where Their Fire is not Quenched'—the title is taken from the Gospel of Mark and refers to the everlasting fires of hell—looks at love, sexuality, death and the supernatural. In my opinion it offers one of the most disturbing depictions of eternal hell imaginable.

T HERE WAS NOBODY IN THE ORCHARD. HARRIOTT LEIGH WENT out, carefully, through the iron gate into the field. She had made the latch slip into its notch without a sound.

The path slanted widely up the field from the orchard gate to the stile under the elder-tree. George Waring waited for her there.

Years afterwards, when she thought of George Waring she smelt the sweet, hot wine-scent of the elder flowers. Years afterwards, when she smelt elder flowers she saw George Waring, with his beautiful, gentle face, like a poet's or a musician's, his black-blue eyes, and sleek, olive-brown hair. He was a naval lieutenant.

Yesterday he had asked her to marry him and she had consented. But her father hadn't, and she had come to tell him that and say good-bye before he left her. His ship was to sail the next day.

He was eager and excited. He couldn't believe that anything could stop their happiness, that anything he didn't want to happen could happen.

"Well?" he said.

"He's a perfect beast, George. He won't let us. He says we're too young."

"I was twenty last August," he said, aggrieved.

"And I shall be seventeen in September."

"And this is June. We're quite old, really. How long does he mean us to wait?"

"Three years."

"Three years before we can be engaged even—why, we might be dead."

She put her arms round him to make him feel safe. They kissed;

and the sweet, hot wine-scent of the elder flowers mixed with their kisses. They stood, pressed close together, under the elder-tree.

Across the yellow fields of charlock they heard the village clock strike seven. Up in the house a gong clanged.

"Darling, I must go," she said.

"Oh, stay—stay *five* minutes."

He pressed her close. It lasted five minutes, and five more. Then he was running fast down the road to the station, while Harriott went along the field-path, slowly, struggling with her tears.

"He'll be back in three months," she said. "I can live through three months."

But he never came back. There was something wrong with the engines of his ship, the *Alexandra*. Three weeks later she went down in the Mediterranean, and George with her.

Harriott said she didn't care how soon she died now. She was quite sure it would be soon, because she couldn't live without him.

Five years passed.

The two lines of beech-trees stretched on and on, the whole length of the Park, a broad green drive between. When you came to the middle they branched off right and left in the form of a cross, and at the end of the right arm there was a white stucco pavilion with pillars and a three-cornered pediment like a Greek temple. At the end of the left arm, the west entrance to the Park, were double gates and a side door.

Harriott, on her stone seat at the back of the pavilion, could see Stephen Philpotts the very minute he came through the side door.

He had asked her to wait for him there. It was the place he always chose to read his poems aloud in. The poems were a pretext. She knew what he was going to say. And she knew what she would answer.

There were elder-bushes in flower at the back of the pavilion, and Harriott thought of George Waring. She told herself that George was nearer to her now than he could ever have been, living. If she married Stephen she would not be unfaithful, because she loved him with another part of herself. It was not as though Stephen were taking George's place. She loved Stephen with her soul, in an unearthly way.

But her body quivered like a stretched wire when the door opened and the young man came towards her down the drive under the beech-trees.

She loved him; she loved his slenderness, his darkness and sallow whiteness, his black eyes lighting up with the intellectual flame, the way his black hair swept back from his forehead, the way he walked, tip-toe, as if his feet were lifted with wings.

He sat down beside her. She could see his hands tremble. She felt that her moment was coming; it had come.

"I wanted to see you alone because there's something I must say to you. I don't quite know how to begin…"

Her lips parted. She panted lightly.

"You've heard me speak of Sybill Foster?"

Her voice came stammering, "N-no, Stephen. Did you?"

"Well, I didn't mean to, till I knew it was all right. I only heard yesterday."

"Heard what?"

"Why, that she'll have me. Oh, Harriott—do you know what it's like to be terribly happy?"

She knew. She had known just now, the moment before he told her. She sat there, stone-cold and stiff, listening to his raptures; listening to her own voice saying she was glad.

Ten years passed.

*

Harriott Leigh sat waiting in the drawing-room of a small house in Maida Vale. She had lived there ever since her father's death two years before.

She was restless. She kept on looking at the clock to see if it was four, the hour that Oscar Wade had appointed. She was not sure that he would come, after she had sent him away yesterday.

She now asked herself, why, when she had sent him away yesterday, she had let him come today. Her motives were not altogether clear. If she really meant what she had said, then she oughtn't to let him come to her again. Never again.

She had shown him plainly what she meant. She could see herself, sitting very straight in her chair, uplifted by a passionate integrity, while he stood before her, hanging his head, ashamed and beaten; she could feel again the throb in her voice as she kept on saying that she couldn't, she couldn't; he must see that she couldn't; that no, nothing would make her change her mind; she couldn't forget he had a wife; that he must think of Muriel.

To which he had answered savagely, "I needn't. That's all over. We only live together for the look of the thing."

And she, serenely, with great dignity, "And for the look of the thing, Oscar, we must leave off seeing each other. Please go."

"Do you mean it?"

"Yes. We must never see each other again."

And he had gone then, ashamed and beaten.

She could see him, squaring his broad shoulders to meet the blow. And she was sorry for him. She told herself she had been unnecessarily hard. Why shouldn't they see each other again, now he understood where they must draw the line? Until yesterday the line had never been very clearly drawn. Today she meant to ask him to forget what he had said to her. Once it was forgotten they could go on being friends as if nothing had happened.

It was four o'clock. Half-past. Five. She had finished tea and given him up when, between the half-hour and six o'clock, he came.

He came as he had come a dozen times, with his measured, deliberate, thoughtful tread, carrying himself well braced, with a sort of held-in arrogance, his great shoulders heaving. He was a man of about forty, broad and tall, lean-flanked and short-necked, his straight, handsome features showing small and even in the big square face and in the flush that swamped it. The close-clipped reddish-brown moustache bristled forwards from the pushed-out upper lip. His small, flat eyes shone, reddish-brown, eager and animal.

She liked to think of him when he was not there, but always at the first sight of him she felt a slight shock. Physically, he was very far from her admired ideal. So different from George Waring and Stephen Philpotts.

He sat down, facing her.

There was an embarrassed silence, broken by Oscar Wade.

"Well, Harriott, you said I could come." He seemed to be throwing the responsibility on her.

"So I suppose you've forgiven me," he said.

"Oh, yes, Oscar, I've forgiven you."

He said she'd better show it by coming to dine with him somewhere that evening.

She could give no reason to herself for going. She simply went.

He took her to a restaurant in Soho. Oscar Wade dined well, even extravagantly, giving each dish its importance. She liked his extravagance. He had none of the mean virtues.

It was over. His flushed, embarrassed silence told her what he was thinking. But when he had seen her home he left her at her garden gate. He had thought better of it.

She was not sure whether she were glad or sorry. She had had her moment of righteous exaltation and she had enjoyed it. But there was no joy in the weeks that followed it. She had given up Oscar Wade because she didn't want him very much; and now she wanted him furiously, perversely, because she had given him up. Though he had no resemblance to her ideal, she couldn't live without him.

She dined with him again and again, till she knew Schnebler's Restaurant by heart, the white panelled walls picked out with gold; the white pillars, and the curling gold fronds of their capitals; the Turkey carpets, blue and crimson, soft under her feet; the thick crimson velvet cushions that clung to her skirts; the glitter of silver and glass on the innumerable white circles of the tables. And the faces of the diners, red, white, pink, brown, grey and sallow, distorted and excited; the curled mouths that twisted as they ate; the convoluted electric bulbs pointing, pointing down at them, under the red, crinkled shades. All shimmering in a thick air that the red light stained as wine stains water.

And Oscar's face, flushed with his dinner. Always, when he leaned back from the table and brooded in silence, she knew what he was thinking. His heavy eyelids would lift; she would find his eyes fixed on hers, wondering, considering.

She knew now what the end would be. She thought of George Waring, and Stephen Philpotts, and of her life cheated. She hadn't chosen Oscar, she hadn't really wanted him; but now he had forced himself on her she couldn't afford to let him go. Since George died no man had loved her, no other man ever would. And she was sorry for him when she thought of him going from her, beaten and ashamed.

She was certain, before he was, of the end. Only she didn't know when and where and how it would come. That was what Oscar knew.

It came at the close of one of their evenings when they had dined in a private sitting-room. He said he couldn't stand the heat and noise of the public restaurant.

She went before him, up a steep, red-carpeted stair to a white door on the second landing.

From time to time they repeated the furtive, hidden adventure. Sometimes she met him in the room above Schnebler's. Sometimes, when her maid was out, she received him at her house in Maida Vale. But that was dangerous, not to be risked too often.

Oscar declared himself unspeakably happy. Harriott was not quite sure. This was love, the thing she had never had, that she had dreamed of, hungered and thirsted for; but now she had it she was not satisfied. Always she looked for something just beyond it, some mystic, heavenly rapture, always beginning to come, that never came. There was something about Oscar that repelled her. But because she had taken him for her lover, she couldn't bring herself to admit that it was a certain coarseness. She looked another way and pretended it wasn't there. To justify herself, she fixed her mind on his good qualities, his generosity, his strength, the way he had built up his engineering business. She made him take her over his works and show her his great dynamos. She made him lend her the books he read. But always, when she tried to talk to him, he let her see that *that* wasn't what she was there for.

"My dear girl, we haven't time," he said. "It's waste of our priceless moments."

She persisted. "There's something wrong about it all if we can't talk to each other."

He was irritated. "Women never seem to consider that a man can get all the talk he wants from other men. What's wrong is our meeting in this unsatisfactory way. We ought to live together. It's the only sane thing. I would, only I don't want to break up Muriel's home and make her miserable."

"I thought you said she wouldn't care."

"My dear, she cares for her home and her position and the children. You forget the children."

Yes. She had forgotten the children. She had forgotten Muriel. She had left off thinking of Oscar as a man with a wife and children and a home.

He had a plan. His mother-in-law was coming to stay with Muriel in October and he would get away. He would go to Paris, and Harriott should come to him there. He could say he went on business. No need to lie about it; he *had* business in Paris.

He engaged rooms in an hotel in the Rue de Rivoli. They spent two weeks there.

For three days Oscar was madly in love with Harriott and Harriott with him. As she lay awake she would turn on the light and look at him as he slept at her side. Sleep made him beautiful and innocent, it laid a fine smooth tissue over his coarseness; it made his mouth gentle; it entirely hid his eyes.

In six days reaction had set in. At the end of the tenth day Harriott, returning with Oscar from Montmartre, burst into a fit of crying. When questioned she answered wildly that the Hôtel Saint Pierre was too hideously ugly; it was getting on her nerves. Mercifully, Oscar explained her state as fatigue following excitement. She tried hard to believe that she was miserable because her love was purer and more spiritual than Oscar's; but all the time she knew perfectly well she had cried from pure boredom. She was in love with Oscar and Oscar bored her. Oscar was in love with her and she bored him. At close quarters, day in and day out, each was revealed to the other as an incredible bore.

At the end of the second week she began to doubt whether she had ever been really in love with him.

Her passion returned for a little while after they got back to London. Freed from the unnatural strain which Paris had put on them, they persuaded themselves that their romantic temperaments were better fitted to the old life of casual adventure.

Then, gradually, the sense of danger began to wake in them. They lived in perpetual fear, face to face with all the chances of discovery. They tormented themselves and each other by imagining possibilities that they would never have considered in their first fine moments. It was as if they were beginning to ask themselves if it were, after all, worth while running such awful risks, for all they got out of it. Oscar still swore that if he had been free he would have married her.

He pointed out that his intentions, at any rate, were regular. But she asked herself: Would I marry *him*? Marriage would be the Hôtel Saint Pierre all over again, without any possibility of escape. But, if she wouldn't marry him, was she in love with him? That was the test. Perhaps it was a good thing he wasn't free. Then she told herself that these doubts were morbid, and that the question wouldn't arise.

One evening Oscar called to see her. He had come to tell her that Muriel was ill.

"Seriously ill?"

"I'm afraid so. It's pleurisy. May turn to pneumonia. We shall know one way or another in the next few days."

A terrible fear seized upon Harriott. Muriel might die of her pleurisy; and if Muriel died, she would have to marry Oscar. He was looking at her queerly, as if he knew what she was thinking, and she could see that the same thought had occurred to him and that he was frightened too.

Muriel got well again; but their danger had enlightened them. Muriel's life was now inconceivably precious to them both; she stood between them and that permanent union which they dreaded, and yet would not have the courage to refuse.

After enlightenment the rupture.

It came from Oscar, one evening when he sat with her in her drawing-room.

"Harriott," he said, "do you know I'm thinking seriously of settling down?"

"How do you mean, settling down?"

"Patching it up with Muriel, poor girl… Has it never occurred to you that this little affair of ours can't go on for ever?"

"You don't want it to go on?"

"I don't want to have any humbug about it. For God's sake, let's be straight. If it's done, it's done. Let's end it decently."

"I see. You want to get rid of me."

"That's a beastly way of putting it."

"Is there any way that isn't beastly? The whole thing's beastly. I should have thought you'd have stuck to it now you've made it what you wanted. When I haven't an ideal, I haven't a single illusion, when you've destroyed everything you didn't want."

"What didn't I want?"

"The clean, beautiful part of it. The part I wanted."

"My part at least was real. It was cleaner and more beautiful than all that putrid stuff you wrapped it up in. You were a hypocrite, Harriott, and I wasn't. You're a hypocrite now if you say you weren't happy with me."

"I was never really happy. Never for one moment. There was always something I missed. Something you didn't give me. Perhaps you couldn't."

"No. I wasn't spiritual enough," he sneered.

"You were not. And you made me what you were."

"Oh, I noticed that you were always very spiritual *after* you'd got what you wanted."

"What I wanted?" she cried. "Oh, my God!"

"If you ever knew what you wanted."

"What—I—wanted," she repeated, drawing out her bitterness.

"Come," he said, "why not be honest? Face facts. I was awfully gone on you. You were awfully gone on me—once. We got tired of each other and it's over. But at least you might own we had a good time while it lasted."

"A good time?"

"Good enough for me."

"For you, because for you love only means one thing. Everything that's high and noble in it you dragged down to that. Till there's nothing left for us but that. *That's* what you made of love."

Twenty years passed.

It was Oscar who died first, three years after the rupture. He did it suddenly one evening, falling down in a fit of apoplexy.

His death was an immense relief to Harriott. Perfect security had been impossible as long as he was alive. But now there wasn't a living soul who knew her secret.

Still, in the first moment of shock Harriott told herself that Oscar dead would be nearer to her than ever. She forgot how little she had wanted him to be near her, alive. And long before the twenty years had passed she had contrived to persuade herself that he had never been near to her at all. It was incredible that she had ever known such a person as Oscar Wade. As for their affair, she couldn't think of Harriott Leigh as the sort of woman to whom such a thing could happen. Schnebler's and the Hôtel Saint Pierre ceased to figure among prominent images of her past. Her memories, if she had allowed herself to remember, would have clashed disagreeably with the reputation for sanctity which she had now acquired.

For Harriott at fifty-two was the friend and helper of the Reverend Clement Farmer, Vicar of St. Mary the Virgin's, Maida Vale. She worked as a deaconess in his parish, wearing the uniform of a deaconess, the semi-religious gown, the cloak, the bonnet and veil, the cross and rosary, the holy smile. She was also secretary to the Maida Vale and Kilburn Home for Fallen Girls.

Her moments of excitement came when Clement Farmer, the lean, austere likeness of Stephen Philpotts, in his cassock and lace-bordered surplice, issued from the vestry, when he mounted the pulpit, when he stood before the altar rails and lifted up his arms in the Benediction; her moments of ecstasy when she received the Sacrament from his hands. And she had moments of calm happiness when his study door closed on their communion. All these moments were saturated with a solemn holiness.

And they were insignificant compared with the moment of her dying.

She lay dozing in her white bed under the black crucifix with the ivory Christ. The basins and medicine bottles had been cleared from the table by her pillow; it was spread for the last rites. The priest moved quietly about the room, arranging the candles, the Prayer Book and the Holy Sacrament. Then he drew a chair to her bedside and watched with her, waiting for her to come up out of her doze.

She woke suddenly. Her eyes were fixed upon him. She had a flash of lucidity. She was dying, and her dying made her supremely important to Clement Farmer.

"Are you ready?" he asked.

"Not yet. I think I'm afraid. Make me not afraid." He rose and lit the two candles on the altar. He took down the crucifix from the wall and stood it against the foot-rail of the bed.

She sighed. That was not what she had wanted.

"You will not be afraid now," he said.

"I'm not afraid of the hereafter. I suppose you get used to it. Only it may be terrible just at first."

"Our first state will depend very much on what we are thinking of at our last hour."

"There'll be my—confession," she said.

"And after it you will receive the Sacrament. Then you will have your mind fixed firmly upon God and your Redeemer... Do you feel able to make your confession now, Sister? Everything is ready."

Her mind went back over her past and found Oscar Wade there. She wondered: Should she confess to him about Oscar Wade? One moment she thought it was possible; the next she knew that she couldn't. She could not. It wasn't necessary. For twenty years he had not been part of her life. No. She wouldn't confess about Oscar Wade. She had been guilty of other sins.

She made a careful selection.

"I have cared too much for the beauty of this world... I have failed in charity to my poor girls. Because of my intense repugnance to their sin... I have thought, often, about—people I love, when I should have been thinking about God."

After that she received the Sacrament.

"Now," he said, "there is nothing to be afraid of."

"I won't be afraid if—if you would hold my hand."

He held it. And she lay still a long time, with her eyes shut. Then he heard her murmuring something. He stooped close.

"This—is—dying. I thought it would be horrible. And it's bliss... Bliss."

The priest's hand slackened, as if at the bidding of some wonder. She gave a weak cry.

"Oh—don't let me go."

His grasp tightened.

"Try," he said, "to think about God. Keep on looking at the crucifix."

"If I look," she whispered, "you won't let go my hand?"

"I will not let you go."

He held it till it was wrenched from him in the last agony.

★

She lingered for some hours in the room where these things had happened.

Its aspect was familiar and yet unfamiliar and slightly repugnant to her. The altar, the crucifix, the lighted candles, suggested some tremendous and awful experience the details of which she was not able to recall. She seemed to remember that they had been connected in some way with the sheeted body on the bed; but the nature of the connection was not clear, and she did not associate the dead body with herself. When the nurse came in and laid it out, she saw that it was the body of a middle-aged woman. Her own living body was that of a young woman of about thirty-two.

Her mind had no past and no future, no sharp-edged, coherent memories, and no idea of anything to be done next.

Then, suddenly, the room began to come apart before her eyes, to split into shafts of floor and furniture and ceiling that shifted and were thrown by their commotion into different planes. They leaned slanting at every possible angle; they crossed and overlaid each other with a transparent mingling of dislocated perspectives, like reflections fallen on an interior seen behind glass.

The bed and the sheeted body slid away somewhere out of sight. She was standing by the door that still remained in position.

She opened it and found herself in the street, outside a building of yellowish-grey brick and freestone, with a tall slated spire. Her mind came together with a palpable click of recognition. This object was the Church of St. Mary the Virgin, Maida Vale. She could hear the droning of the organ. She opened the door and slipped in.

She had gone back into a definite space and time and recovered a certain limited section of coherent memory. She remembered the rows of pitch-pine benches, with their Gothic peaks and mouldings; the stone-coloured walls and pillars with their chocolate stencilling; the hanging rings of lights along the aisles of the nave; the high altar with its lighted candles, and the polished brass cross, twinkling. These things were somehow permanent and real, adjusted to the image that now took possession of her.

She knew what she had come there for. The service was over. The choir had gone from the chancel; the sacristan moved before the altar putting out the candles. She walked up the middle aisle to a seat that she knew under the pulpit. She knelt down and covered her face with her hands. Peeping sideways through her fingers, she could see the door of the vestry on her left at the end of the north aisle. She watched it steadily.

Up in the organ loft the organist drew out the Recessional, slowly and softly, to its end in the two solemn, vibrating chords.

The vestry door opened and Clement Farmer came out, dressed in his black cassock. He passed before her, close, close, outside the bench where she knelt. He paused at the opening. He was waiting for her. There was something he had to say.

She stood up and went towards him. He still waited. He didn't move to make way for her. She came close, closer than she had ever come to him, so close that his features grew indistinct. She bent her head back peering, short-sightedly, and found herself looking into Oscar Wade's face.

He stood still, horribly still, and close, barring her passage.

She drew back; his heaving shoulders followed her. He leaned forward, covering her with his eyes. She opened her mouth to scream and no sound came.

She was afraid to move lest he should move with her. The heaving of his shoulders terrified her.

One by one the lights in the side aisles were going out. The lights in the middle aisle would go next. They had gone. If she didn't get away she would be shut up with him there in the appalling darkness.

She turned and moved towards the north aisle, groping, steadying herself by the book ledge.

When she looked back Oscar Wade was not there.

Then she remembered that Oscar Wade was dead. Therefore what she had seen was not Oscar; it was his ghost. He was dead; dead seventeen years ago. She was safe from him for ever.

When she came out on to the steps of the church she saw that the road it stood in had changed. It was not the road she remembered. The pavement on this side was raised slightly and covered in. It ran under a succession of arches. It was a long gallery walled with glittering shop windows on one side; on the other a line of tall grey columns divided it from the street.

She was going along the arcades of the Rue de Rivoli. Ahead of her she could see the edge of an immense grey pillar jutting out. That was the porch of the Hôtel Saint Pierre. The revolving glass doors swung forward to receive her; she crossed the grey, sultry vestibule under the pillared arches. She knew it. She knew the porter's shining, wine-coloured mahogany pen on her left, and the shining, wine-coloured mahogany barrier of the clerk's bureau on her right; she made straight for the great grey-carpeted staircase; she climbed the endless flights that turned round and round the caged-in shaft of the well, past the latticed doors of the lift, and came up on to a landing that she knew, and into the long, ash-grey, foreign corridor lit by a dull window at one end.

It was there that the horror of the place came on her. She had no longer any memory of St. Mary's Church, so that she was unaware of her backward course through time. All space and time were here.

She remembered she had to go to the left, the left.

But there was something there; where the corridor turned by the window; at the end of all the corridors. If she went the other way she would escape it.

The corridor stopped there. A blank wall. She was driven back past the stairhead to the left.

At the corner, by the window, she turned down another long ash-grey corridor on her right, and to the right again where the night-light sputtered on the table-flap, at the turn.

This third corridor was dark and secret and depraved. She knew the soiled walls and the warped door at the end. There was a sharp-pointed streak of light at the top. She could see the number on it now, 107.

Something had happened there. If she went in, it would happen again.

Oscar Wade was in the room waiting for her behind the closed door. She felt him moving about in there. She leaned forward, her ear to the key-hole, and listened. She could hear the measured, deliberate, thoughtful footsteps. They were coming from the bed to the door.

She turned and ran; her knees gave way under her; she sank and ran on, down the long grey corridors and the stairs, quick and blind, a hunted beast seeking for cover, hearing his feet coming after her.

The revolving doors caught her and pushed her out into the street.

The strange quality of her state was this, that it had no time. She remembered dimly that there had once been a thing called time; but she had forgotten altogether what it was like. She was aware of things happening and about to happen; she fixed them by the place they occupied, and measured their duration by the space she went through.

So now she thought: If I could only go back and get to the place where it hadn't happened.

To get back farther—

She was walking now on a white road that went between broad grass borders. To the right and left were the long raking lines of the hills, curve after curve, shimmering in a thin mist.

The road dropped to the green valley. It mounted the humped bridge over the river. Beyond it she saw the twin gables of the grey house pricked up over the high grey garden wall. The tall iron gate stood in front of it between the ball-topped stone pillars.

And now she was in a large, low-ceilinged room with drawn blinds. She was standing before the wide double bed. It was her father's bed. The dead body, stretched out in the middle under the drawn white sheet, was her father's body.

The outline of the sheet sank from the peak of the upturned toes to the shin-bone, and from the high bridge of the nose to the chin.

She lifted the sheet and folded it back across the breast of the dead man. The face she saw then was Oscar Wade's face, stilled and smoothed in the innocence of sleep, the supreme innocence of death. She stared at it, fascinated, in a cold, pitiless joy.

Oscar was dead.

She remembered how he used to lie like that beside her in the room in the Hôtel Saint Pierre, on his back with his hands folded on his waist, his mouth half-open, his big chest rising and falling. If he was dead, it would never happen again. She would be safe.

The dead face frightened her, and she was about to cover it up again when she was aware of a light heaving, a rhythmical rise and fall. As she drew the sheet up tighter, the hands under it began to struggle convulsively, the broad ends of the fingers appeared above the edge, clutching it to keep it down. The mouth opened; the eyes opened; the whole face stared back at her in a look of agony and horror.

Then the body drew itself forwards from the hips and sat up, its eyes peering into her eyes; he and she remained for an instant motionless, each held there by the other's fear.

Suddenly she broke away, turned and ran, out of the room, out of the house.

She stood at the gate, looking up and down the road, not knowing by which way she must go to escape Oscar. To the right, over the bridge, and up the hill and across the downs she would come to the arcades of the Rue de Rivoli and the dreadful grey corridors of the hotel. To the left the road went through the village.

If she could get further back she would be safe, out of Oscar's reach. Standing by her father's death-bed, she had been young, but not young enough. She must get back to the place where she was younger still, to the Park and the green drive under the beech-trees and the white pavilion at the cross. She knew how to find it. At the end of the village the high road ran right and left, east and west, under the Park walls; the south gate stood there at the top, looking down the narrow street.

She ran towards it through the village, past the long grey barns of Goodyer's farm, past the grocer's shop, past the yellow front and blue sign of the Queen's Head, past the post office, with its one black window blinking under its vine, past the church and the yew-trees in the churchyard, to where the south gate made a delicate black pattern on the green grass.

These things appeared insubstantial, drawn back behind a sheet of air that shimmered over them like thin glass. They opened out, floated past and away from her; and instead of the high road and park walls she saw a London street of dingy white façades, and instead of the south gate the swinging glass doors of Schnebler's Restaurant.

The glass doors swung open and she passed into the restaurant. The scene beat on her with the hard impact of reality: the white and gold panels, the white pillars and their curling gold capitals, the white circles of the tables, glittering, the flushed faces of the diners, moving mechanically.

She was driven forward by some irresistible compulsion to a table in the corner, where a man sat alone. The table napkin he was using hid his mouth, and jaw, and chest; and she was not sure of the upper part of the face above the straight-drawn edge. It dropped, and she saw Oscar Wade's face. She came to him, dragged, without power to resist; she sat down beside him, and he leaned to her over the table; she could feel the warmth of his red, congested face; the smell of wine floated towards her on his thick whisper.

"I knew you would come."

She ate and drank with him in silence, nibbling and sipping slowly, staving off the abominable moment it would end in.

At last they got up and faced each other. His long bulk stood before her, above her; she could almost feel the vibration of its power.

"Come," he said, "come."

And she went before him, slowly, slipping out through the maze of the tables, hearing behind her Oscar's measured, deliberate, thoughtful tread. The steep, red-carpeted staircase rose up before her.

She swerved from it, but he turned her back.

"You know the way," he said.

At the top of the flight she found the white door of the room she knew. She knew the long windows guarded by drawn muslin blinds; the gilt looking-glass over the chimney-piece that reflected Oscar's head and shoulders grotesquely, between two white porcelain babies with bulbous limbs and garlanded loins, she knew the sprawling stain on the drab carpet by the table, the shabby, infamous couch behind the screen.

They moved about the room, turning and turning in it like beasts in a cage, uneasy, inimical, avoiding each other.

At last they stood still, he at the window, she at the door, the length of the room between.

"It's no good your getting away like that," he said. "There couldn't be any other end to it—to what we did."

"But that *was* ended."

"Ended there, but not here."

"Ended for ever. We've done with it for ever."

"We haven't. We've got to begin again. And go on. And go on."

"Oh, no. No. Anything but that."

"There isn't anything else."

"We can't. We can't. Don't you remember how it bored us?"

"Remember? Do you suppose I'd touch you if I could help it?… That's what we're here for. We must. We must."

"No. No. I shall get away—now."

She turned to the door to open it.

"You can't," he said. "The door's locked."

"Oscar—what did you do that for?"

"We always did it. Don't you remember?"

She turned to the door again and shook it; she beat on it with her hands.

"It's no use, Harriott. If you got out now you'd only have to come back again. You might stave it off for an hour or so, but what's that in an immortality?"

"Immortality?"

"That's what we're in for."

"Time enough to talk about immortality when we're dead… Ah—"

They were being drawn towards each other across the room, moving slowly, like figures in some monstrous and appalling dance, their heads thrown back over their shoulders, their faces turned from the horrible approach. Their arms rose slowly, heavy with intolerable reluctance; they stretched them out towards each other, aching as if they held up an overpowering weight. Their feet dragged and were drawn.

Suddenly her knees sank under her; she shut her eyes; all her being went down before him in darkness and terror.

It was over. She had got away, she was going back, back, to the green drive of the Park, between the beech-trees, where Oscar had never been, where he would never find her. When she passed through the south gate her memory became suddenly young and clean. She forgot the Rue de Rivoli and the Hôtel Saint Pierre; she forgot Schnebler's Restaurant and the room at the top of the stairs. She was back in her youth. She was Harriott Leigh going to wait for Stephen Philpotts in the pavilion opposite the west gate. She could feel herself, a slender figure moving fast over the grass between the lines of the great beech-trees. The freshness of her youth was upon her.

She came to the heart of the drive, where it branched right and left in the form of a cross. At the end of the right arm the white Greek temple, with its pediment and pillars, gleamed against the wood.

She was sitting on their seat at the back of the pavilion, watching the side door that Stephen would come in by.

The door was pushed open; he came towards her, light and young, skimming between the beech-trees with his eager, tip-toeing stride. She rose up to meet him. She gave a cry.

"Stephen!"

It had been Stephen. She had seen him coming. But the man who stood before her between the pillars of the pavilion was Oscar Wade.

And now she was walking along the field-path that slanted from the orchard door to the stile; further and further back, to where young George Waring waited for her under the elder-tree. The smell of the elder flowers came to her over the field. She could feel on her lips and in all her body the sweet, innocent excitement of her youth.

"George, oh, George!"

As she went along the field-path she had seen him. But the man who stood waiting for her under the elder-tree was Oscar Wade.

"I told you it's no use getting away, Harriott. Every path brings you back to me. You'll find me at every turn."

"But how did you get *here*?"

"As I got into the pavilion. As I got into your father's room, on to his death-bed. Because I *was* there. I am in all your memories."

"My memories are innocent. How could you take my father's place, and Stephen's, and George Waring's? You?"

"Because I did take them."

"Never. My love for *them* was innocent."

"Your love for me was part of it. You think the past affects the future. Has it never struck you that the future may affect the past? In your innocence there was the beginning of your sin. You *were* what you *were to be*."

"I shall get away," she said.

"And this time I shall go with you."

The stile, the elder-tree, and the field floated away from her. She was going under the beech-trees down the park drive towards the south gate and the village, slinking close to the right-hand row of trees. She was aware that Oscar Wade was going with her under the left-hand row, keeping even with her, step by step, and tree by tree. And presently there was grey pavement under her feet and a row of grey pillars on her right hand. They were walking side by side down the Rue de Rivoli towards the hotel.

They were sitting together now on the edge of the dingy white bed. Their arms hung by their sides, heavy and limp, their heads drooped, averted. Their passion weighed on them with the unbearable, unescapable boredom of immortality.

"Oscar—how long will it last?"

"I can't tell you. I don't know whether *this* is one moment of eternity, or the eternity of one moment."

"It must end some time," she said. "Life doesn't go on for ever. We shall die."

"Die? We *have* died. Don't you know what this is? Don't you know where you are? This is death. We're dead, Harriott. We're in hell."

"Yes. There can't be anything worse than this."

"This isn't the worst. We're not quite dead yet, as long as we've life in us to turn and run and get away from each other; as long as we can escape into our memories. But when you've got back to the farthest memory of all and there's nothing beyond it—when there's no memory but this—

"In the last hell we shall not run away any longer; we shall find no more roads, no more passages, no more open doors. We shall have no need to look for each other.

"In the last death we shall be shut up in this room, behind that locked door, together. We shall lie here together, for ever and ever, joined so fast that even God can't put us asunder. We shall be one flesh and one spirit, one sin repeated for ever and ever; spirit loathing flesh, flesh loathing spirit; you and I loathing each other."

"Why, why?" she cried.

"Because that's all that's left us. That's what you made of love."

The darkness came down swamping; it blotted out the room. She was walking along a garden-path between high borders of phlox and larkspur and lupin. They were taller than she was, their flowers swayed and nodded above her head. She tugged at the tall stems and had no strength to break them. She was a little thing.

She said to herself then that she was safe. She had gone back so far that she was a child again; she had the blank innocence of childhood.

To be a child, to go small under the heads of the lupins, to be blank and innocent, without memory, was to be safe.

The walk led her out through a yew hedge on to a bright green lawn. In the middle of the lawn there was a shallow round pond in a ring of rockery cushioned with small flowers, yellow and white and purple. Goldfish swam in the olive-brown water. She would be safe when she saw the goldfish swimming towards her. The old one with the white scales would come up first, pushing up his nose, making bubbles in the water.

At the bottom of the lawn there was a privet hedge cut by a broad path that went through the orchard. She knew what she would find there; her mother was in the orchard. She would lift her up in her arms to play with the hard, red balls of the apples that hung from the tree. She had got back to the farthest memory of all; there was nothing beyond it.

There would be an iron gate in the wall of the orchard. It would lead into a field.

Something was different here, something that frightened her. An ash-grey door instead of an iron gate.

She pushed it open and came into the last corridor of the Hôtel Saint Pierre.

KECKSIES (1923)

Marjorie Bowen

Margaret Gabrielle Vere Long, née Campbell, much better known under her pseudonym Marjorie Bowen (1885–1952), was the author of novels, short stories, popular history and biography. She was born on Hayling Island in Hampshire and studied at the Slade School of Fine Art. Her first novel, *The Viper of Milan* (1906), which she began writing at the age of sixteen caused a sensation. With its passages of violence, it was rejected by several publishers who deemed its content inappropriate in a narrative written by a young woman. Her 1909 novel *Black Magic*, about a medieval witch, similarly caused eyebrows to be raised. Under another pseudonym, 'Joseph Shearing', Bowen wrote several mystery novels, based on true-life crimes, which achieved considerable popularity, especially in America. The novelist Graham Greene, writing soon after Bowen's death, cited her as a major influence on his own literary career.

'Kecksies' is a delightful Gothic tale, one in which all the atmospheric trappings of a quintessential ghost story are present. First collected in *Seeing Life! And Other Stories* (1923) the tale tells of two upper-class gentlemen who find themselves caught in a storm and take shelter in the house of Goody Boyle. Unfortunately, Boyle already has a guest in her house—the body of a recently deceased man who had a bitter dispute with one of the visiting gentlemen.

TWO YOUNG ESQUIRES WERE RIDING FROM CANTERBURY, JOLLY and drunk, they shouted and trolled and rolled in their saddles as they followed the winding road across the downs.

A dim sky was overhead and shut in the wide expanse of open country that one side stretched to the sea and the other to the Kentish Weald.

The primroses grew in thick posies in the ditches, the hedges were full of fresh hawthorn green, the new grey leaves of eglantine and honeysuckle, the long boughs of ash with the hard black buds, the wand-like shoots of sallow willow hung with catkins and the smaller red tassels of the nut and birch; little the two young men heeded of any of these things for they were in their own country that was thrice familiar; but Nick Bateup blinked across to the distant purple hills and cursed the gathering rain.

"Ten miles more of the open," he muttered, "and a great storm blackening upon us."

Young Crediton who was more full of wine laughed drowsily.

"We'll lie at a cottage on the way, Nick—think you I've never a tenant who'll let me share board and bed?"

He maundered into singing,

> "There's a light in the old mill,
>   Where the witch weaves her charms,
> But dark is the chamber
>   Where you sleep in my arms.
> Now came you by magic, by trick or by spell
>   I have you and hold you,
> And love you right well!"

The clouds overtook them like an advancing army; the wayside green looked livid under the purplish threat of the heavens and the birds were all still and silent.

"Split me if I'll be soaked," muttered young Bateup. "Knock up one of these boors of thine, Ned—but damn me if I see as much as hut or barn!"

"We come to Banells farm soon, or have we passed it?" answered the other confusedly. "What's the pother? A bold bird as thou art and scared of a drop of rain?"

"My lungs are not as lusty as thine," replied Bateup, who was indeed of a delicate build and more carefully dressed in great coat and muffler.

"But thy throat is as wide!" laughed Crediton, "and God help you, you are shawled like an old woman—and as drunk as a Spanish parrot.

> "Tra la la, my sweeting,
>   Tra la la, my May,
> If now I miss the meeting
>   I'll come some other day."

His companion took no notice of this nonsense, but with as much keenness as his muddled faculties would allow, was looking out for some shelter, for he retained sufficient perception to enable him to mark the violence of the approaching storm and the loneliness of the vast stretch of country where the only human habitations appeared to be some few poor cottages far distant in the fields.

He lost his good humour and as the first drops of stinging cold rain began to fall, he cursed freely, using the terms common to the pot houses where he had intoxicated himself on the way from Canterbury.

Urging their tired horses they came on to the top of the little hill they ascended; immediately before them was the silver ashen skeleton of a blasted oak, polished like worn bone standing over a small pool of stagnant water (for there had been little rain and much east wind) where a few shivering ewes crouched together from the oncoming storm.

Just beyond this, rising out of the bare field, was a humble cottage of black timber and white plaster and a deep thatched roof.

For the rest the crest of the hill was covered by a hazel copse and then dipped lonely again to the clouded lower levels that now began to slope into the marsh.

"This will shelter us, Nick," cried Crediton.

"'Tis a foul place and the boors have a foul reputation," objected the lord of the Manor. "There are those who swear to seeing the devil's own fize leer from Goody Boyle's windows—but anything to please, thee and thy weak chest."

They staggered from their horses, knocked open the rotting gate and leading the beasts across the hard dry grazing field, knocked with their whips at the tiny door of the cottage.

The grey sheep under the grey tree looked at them and bleated faintly; the rain began to fall like straight yet broken darts out of the sombre clouds.

The door was opened by a woman very neatly dressed, with large scrubbed hands, who looked at them with fear and displeasure; for if her reputation was bad, theirs was no better; the lord of the Manor was a known roysterer and wild liver and spent his idleness in rakish expeditions with Sir Nicholas Bateup from Bodiam, who was easily squandering a fine property.

Neither were believed to be free of bloodshed, and as for honour they were as stripped of that as the blasted tree by the lonely pool was stripped of leaves.

Besides they were both, now, as usual, drunk.

"We want shelter, Goody Boyle," cried Crediton, pushing his way in as he threw her his reins. "Get the horses into the barn."

The woman could not deny the man who could make her homeless in a second; she shouted hoarsely an inarticulate name and a loutish boy came and took the horses, while the two young men stumbled into the cottage which they filled and dwarfed with their splendour.

Edward Crediton had been a fine young man and though he was marred with insolence and excess he still made a magnificent appearance, with his full blunt features, his warm colouring, the fair hair rolled and curled and all his bravery of blue broad cloth, buckskin breeches, foreign lace, top boots, French sword and gold rings and watch chains.

Sir Nicholas Bateup was darker and more effeminate, having a cast of weakness in his constitution that betrayed itself in his face; but his dress was splendid to the point of foppishness and his manners even more arrogant and imposing.

Of the two he had the more evil repute; he was unwed and, therefore, there was no check upon his mischief, whereas Crediton had a young wife whom he loved after his fashion and who checked some of his doings and softened others and stayed very faithful to him and adored him still after five years of a wretched marriage, as is the manner of some women.

The rain came down with slashing severity; the little cottage panes were blotted with water.

Goody Boyle put logs on the fire and urged them with the bellows.

It was a gaunt white room with nothing in it but a few wooden stools, a table and an eel catcher's prong.

On the table were two large fair wax candles.

"What are these for, Goody?" asked Crediton.

"For the dead, sir."

"You've dead in the house?" cried Sir Nicholas, who was leaning by the fire-place and warming his hands. "What do you want with dead men in the house, you trollop?"

"It is no dead of mine, my lord," answered the woman with evil civility, "but one who took shelter here and died."

"A curst witch!" roared Crediton. "You hear that, Nick! Came here—died—and now you'll put spells on us, you ugly slut—"

"No spells of mine," answered the woman quietly, rubbing her large clean hands together. "He had been long ailing and died here of an ague."

"And who sent the ague?" asked Crediton with drunken gravity. "And who sent him here?"

"Perhaps the same hand that sent us," laughed Sir Nicholas. "Where is your corpse, Goody?"

"In the next room—I have but two."

"And two too many—you need but a bundle of faggots and a tuft of tow to light it—an arrant witch, a confest witch," muttered Crediton; he staggered up from the stool. "Where is your corpse? I've a mind to see if he looks as if he died a natural death."

"Will you not ask first who it is?" asked the woman unlatching the inner door.

"Why should I care?"

"Who is it?" asked Sir Nicholas, who had the clearer wits, drunk or sober.

"Richard Horne," said Goody Boyle.

Ned Crediton looked at her with the eyes of a sober man.

"Richard Horne," said Sir Nicholas. "So he is dead at last—your wife will be glad of that, Ned."

Crediton gave a sullen laugh.

"I'd broken him—she wasn't afraid any longer of a lost wretch cast out to die of ague on the marsh."

But Sir Nicholas had heard differently; he had been told, even by Ned himself, how Anne Crediton shivered before the terror of Richard Horne's pursuit, and would wake up in the dark crying out for fear of him like a lost child; for he had wooed her before her marriage and persisted in loving her afterwards with mad boldness and insolent confidence, so that justice had been set on him and he had been banished to the marsh, a ruined man.

"Well, sirs," said Goody Boyle in her thin voice that had the pinched accent of other parts, "my lady can sleep of nights now—for Robert Horne will never disturb her again."

"Do you think he ever troubled us?" asked Crediton with a coarse oath. "I flung him out like an adder that had writhed across the threshold—"

"A wonder he did not put a murrain on thee, Ned. He had fearful ways and a deep knowledge of unholy things."

"A warlock. God help us," added the woman.

"The devil's proved an ill master then," laughed Crediton. "He could not help Richard Horne into Anne's favour—nor prevent him lying in a cold bed in the flower of his age."

"The devil," smiled Sir Nicholas, "was over busy, Ned, helping *you* to the lady's favour and a warm bed. You were the dearer disciple."

"Oh, good lords, will you talk less wildly with a lost man's corpse in the house and his soul riding the storm without?" begged Goody Boyle; and she latched again the inner door.

Murk filled the cottage now, waves of shadow flowed over the landscape without the rain-blotted window and drowned the valley; in the bitter field the melancholy ewes huddled beneath the blasted oak beside the bare pool the stagnant surface of which was now broken by the quick rain drops; a low thunder grumbled from the horizon and all the young greenery looked livid in the ghastly light of heaven.

"I'll see him," said Ned Crediton, swaggering. "I'll look at this gay gallant in his last smock—so that I can swear to Anne he has taken his amorous smile to the earth worms—surely."

"Look as you like," answered Sir Nicholas, "glut your eyes with looking—"

"But you'll remember, sirs, that he was a queer man and died queerly and there was no parson or priest to take the edge off his going, or challenge the fiends who stood at his head and feet."

"Saw you the fiends?" asked Ned curiously.

"Question not what I saw," muttered the woman. "You'll have your own familiars, Esquire Crediton."

She unlatched the inner door again and Ned passed in, bowing low on the threshold.

"Good day, Robert Horne," he jeered. "We parted in anger, but my debts are paid now and I greet you well."

The dead man lay on a pallet bed with a coarse white sheet over him that showed his shape but roughly; the window was by his head and looked blankly onto the rain-bitten fields and dismal sky; the light was cold and colourless on the white sheet and the miserable room.

Sir Nicholas lounged in the doorway; he feared no death but his own, and that he set so far away it was but a dim dread.

"Look and see if it is Robert Horne," he urged, "or if the beldame lies."

And Crediton turned down the sheet.

"'Tis Robert Horne," he said.

The dead man had his chin uptilted, his features sharp and horrible in the setting of the spilled fair hair on the coarse pillow. Ned Crediton triumphed over him, making lewd jests of love and death, and sneering at this great gallant who had been crazed for love and driven by desire and who now lay impotent.

And Sir Nicholas in the doorway listened and laughed and had his own wicked jeers to add; for both of them had haled Robert Horne as a man who had defied them.

But Goody Boyle stole away with her fingers in her ears.

When these two were weary of their insults they replaced the flap of the sheet over the dead face and returned to the outer room.

And Ned asked for drink, declaring that Goody Boyle was a known smuggler and had cellars of rare stuff.

So the lout brought up glasses of cognac and a bottle of French wine, and these two drank grossly, sitting over the fire; and Goody Boyle made excuse for the drink by saying that Robert Horne had given her two gold pieces before he died (not thin pared coins but thick and heavy) for his funeral and the entertainment of those who should come to his burying.

"What mourners could he hope for?" laughed Ned Crediton. "The crow and the beetle and the death watch spider!"

But Goody Boyle told him that Robert Horne had made friends while he had lived an outcast on the marshes; they were no doubt queer and even monstrous people but they were coming tonight to sit with Robert Horne before he was put in the ground.

"And who, Goody, have warned this devil's congregation of the death of Robert Horne?" asked Sir Nicholas.

She answered him—that Robert Horne was not ill an hour or a day but for a long space struggled with fits of the marsh fever, and in between these bouts of the ague he went abroad like a well man, and his friends would come up and see him and the messenger who came up to enquire after him was Tora, the Egyptian girl who walked with her bosom full of violets.

The storm was in full fury now, muttering low and sullen round the cottage with great power of beating rain.

"Robert Horne was slow in dying," said Sir Nicholas. "Of what did he speak in those days?"

"Of a woman, good sir."

"Of my wife!" cried Ned.

Goody Boyle shook her head with a look of stupidity.

"I know nothing of that. Though for certain he called her Anne, sweet Anne, and swore he would possess her yet—in so many words and very roundly."

"But he died baulked," said Ned swaying on his stool, "and he'll rot outside holy ground."

"They'll lay him in Deadman's field, which is full of old bones none can plough and no sheep will graze," answered the woman, "and I must set out to see lame Jonas who promised to have the grave ready—but maybe the rain has hindered him."

She looked at them shrewdly as she added,

"That is, gentles, if you care to remain alone with the body of Robert Horne."

"I think of him as a dead dog," replied Ned Crediton.

And when the woman had gone, he, being loosened with the French brandy, suggested a gross jest. "Why should Robert Horne have all this honour, even from rogues and Egyptians? Let us fool them—throwing his corpse out into the byre, and I will lie under the sheet and presently sit up and fright them all, with the thought it is the devil!"

Sir Nicholas warmly cheered this proposal and they lurched into the inner chamber which was dark enough now by reason of a great Northern cloud that blocked the light from the window.

They pulled the sheet off Robert Horne and found him wrapped in another that was furled up under his chin, and so they carried him to the back door and peered through the storm for some secret place where they might throw him.

And Ned Crediton saw a dark bed of rank hemlock and cried,

"Cast him into the kecksies," that being the rustic name for the weed.

So they flung the dead man into the hemlocks which were scarce high enough to cover him, and to hide the whiteness of the sheet, broke off boughs from the hazel copse and put over him, and went back laughing to the cottage, and there kept a watch out from the front window and when they saw Goody Boyle toiling along through the rain, Ned took off his hat and coat and sword and folded them away under the bed, then Sir Nicholas wrapped him in the under sheet, so that he was shrouded to the chin, and he lay on the pillow, and drew the other sheet over him.

"If thou sleepst do not snore," said Sir Nicholas, and went back to the fire and lit his long clay full of virginian tobacco.

When Goody Boyle entered with her wet shawl over her head, she had two ragged creatures behind her who stared malevolently at the fine gentleman with his bright clothes and dark curls lolling by the fire and watching the smoke rings rise from his pipe.

"Esquire Crediton has ridden for home," he said, "but I am not minded to risk the ague."

And he sipped more brandy and laughed at them, and they muttering, for they knew his fame, went into the death chamber and crouched round the couch where Sir Nicholas had just laid Ned Crediton under the sheet.

And presently others came up, Egyptians, eel catchers and the like, outcasts and vagrants who crept in to watch by the corpse.

Sir Nicholas presently rolled after them to see the horror and shriekings for grace there would be when the dead man threw aside his shroud and sat up.

But the vigil went on till the night closed in and the two wax candles were lit, and still Ned Crediton gave no sign, nor did he snore or heave beneath the sheet, and Sir Nicholas became impatient, for the rain was over and he was weary of the foul air and the grotesque company.

"The fool," he thought (for he kept his wits well even in his cups) "has gone into a drunken sleep and forgot the joke."

So he pushed his way to the bed and turned down the sheet, whispering,

"This jest will grow stale with keeping."

But the words withered on his lips for he looked into the face of a dead man. At the cry he gave they all came babbling about him and he told them of the trick that had been put upon them.

"But there's devil's work here," he ended. "For here is the body back again—or less Ned Crediton dead and frozen into a likeness of the other—" and he flung the sheet end quickly over the pinched face and fair hair.

"And what did ye do with Robert Horne, outrageous dare fiend that ye be?" demanded an old vagrant; and the young lord passed the ill words and answered with whitened lips.

"We cast him into yon bed of kecksies."

And they all beat out into the night, the lout with a lantern.

And there was nothing at all in the bed of kecksies... and Ned Crediton's horse was gone from the stable.

"He was drunk," said Sir Nicholas, "and forgot his part—and fled that moment I was in the outer room."

"And in that minute did he carry Robert Horne in alone and wrap him up so neatly?" queried Goody Boyle.

"We'll go in," said another hag, "and strip the body and see which man it be—"

But Sir Nicholas was in the saddle.

"Let be," he cried wildly, "there's been gruesome work enough for tonight—it's Robert Horne you have there—let be—I'll back to Crediton Manor—"

And he rode his horse out of the field, then more quickly down the darkling road for the fumes of the brandy were out of his brain and he saw clearly and dreaded many things.

At the cross roads when the ghastly moon had suddenly struck free of the retreating clouds he saw Ned Crediton ahead of him riding sharply, and he called out:

"Eh, Ned, what have you made of this jest? This way it is but a mangled folly."

"What matter now for jest or earnest?" answered the other. "I ride home at last."

Sir Nicholas kept pace with him; he was hatless and wore a shabby cloak that was twisted about him with the wind of his riding.

"Why did not you take your own garments?" asked Sir Nicholas. "Belike that rag you've snatched up belonged to Robert Horne—"

"If Crediton could steal his shroud, he can steal his cloak," replied Ned, and his companion said no more, thinking him wrought into a frenzy with the brandy and the evil nature of the joke.

The moon shone clear and cold with a faint stain like old blood in the halo, and the trees, bending in a seaward wind, cast the recent rain that loaded them heavily to the ground, as the two rode into the gates of Crediton Manor.

The hour was later than even Sir Nicholas knew (time had been blurred for him since the coming of the storm), and there was no light save a dim lamp in an upper window.

Ned Crediton dropped out of the saddle, not waiting for the mounting block, and rang the iron bell till it clattered through the house like a madman's fury.

"Why, Ned, why this panic home-coming?" asked Sir Nicholas; but the other answered him not, but rang again.

There were footsteps within and the rattle of chains, and a voice asked from the side window:

"Who goes there?"

And Crediton dragged at the bell and screamed:

"I! The master!"

The door was opened and an old servant stood there, pale in his bedgown.

Ned Crediton passed him and stood by the newel-post, like a man spent, yet alert.

"Send someone for the horses," said Nick Bateup, "for your master is crazy drunk—I tell you, Mathews, he has seen Robert Horne dead tonight—"

Crediton laughed; the long rays of the lamplight showed him pale, haggard, distorted with tumbled fair hair and a torn shirt under the mantle, and at his waist a ragged bunch of hemlock thrust into his sash.

"A posy of kecksies for Anne," he said; the sleepy servants who were already up, began to come into the hall, looked at him with dismay.

"I'll lie here tonight," said Sir Nicholas; "bring me lights into the parlour. I've no mind to sleep."

He took off his hat and fingered his sword and glanced uneasily at the figure by the newel-post with the posy of kecksies.

Another figure appeared at the head of the stairs, Anne Crediton holding her candle, wearing a grey lute-string robe and a lace cap with long ribbons that hung on to her bosom; she peered over the baluster and some of the hot wax from her taper fell on to the oak treads.

"I've a beau pot for you, Anne," said Crediton, looking up and holding out the hemlocks. "I've long been dispossessed, Anne, but I've come home at last."

She drew back without a word and her light flickered away across the landing; Crediton went up after her and they heard a door shut.

In the parlour the embers had been blown to flames and fresh logs put on, and Sir Nicholas warmed his cold hands and told old Mathews, in a sober manner for him, the story of the jest they had striven to put on Goody Boyle and the queer, monstrous people from the marsh, and the monstrous ending of it, and the strangeness of Ned Crediton; it was not his usual humour to discourse with serv- ants or to discuss his vagrant debaucheries with any, but tonight he seemed to need company and endeavoured to retain the old man, who was not reluctant to stay, though usually he hated to see the dark face and bright clothes of Nick Bateup before the hearth of Crediton Manor.

And as these two talked, disconnectedly, as if they would fill the gap of any silence that might fall in the quiet house, there came the wail of a woman, desperate yet sunken.

"It is Mistress Crediton," said Mathews with a downcast look.

"He ill-uses her?"

"God help us, he will use buckles and straps to her, Sir Nicholas."

A quivering shriek came brokenly down the stairs and seemed to form the word "mercy."

Sir Nicholas was an evil man who died unrepentant; but he was not of a temper to relish raw cruelty or crude brutalities to women; he would break their souls but never their bodies.

So he went to the door and listened, and old Mathews had never liked him so well as now when he saw the look on the thin dark face.

For the third time she shrieked and they marvelled that any human being could hold their breath so long; yet it was muffled as if someone held a hand over her mouth.

The sweat stood on the old man's forehead.

"I've never before known her complain, sir," he whispered. "She is a very dog to her lord and takes her whip mutely—"

"I know, I know—she adores his hand when it caresses or when it strikes—but tonight—if I know anything of a woman's accents, that is a note of abhorrence—"

He ran up the stairs, the old man panting after him with the snatched up lantern.

"Which is her chamber?"

"Here, Sir Nicholas."

The young man struck on the heavy oak panels with the hilt of his sword.

"Madam—Madam Crediton, why are you so ill at ease?"

She moaned from within.

"Open to me, I'll call some of your women—come out—"

Their blood curdled to hear her wails.

"Damn you to hell," cried Sir Nicholas in a fury. "Come out, Ned Crediton, or I'll have the door down and run you through."

The answer was a little break of maniac laughter.

"She has run mad or he," cried Mathews, backing from the room. "And surely there is another clamour at the door—"

Again the bell clanged and there were voices and tumult at the door; Mathews went and opened, and Sir Nicholas, looking down the stairs, saw in the moonlight a dirty farm cart, a sweating horse and some of the patched and rusty crew who had been keeping vigil in Goody Boyle's cottage.

"We've brought Esquire Crediton home," said one; and the others lifted a body from the cart and carried it through the murky moonlight.

Sir Nicholas came downstairs, for old Mathews could do nothing but cry for mercy.

"It was Edward Crediton," repeated the eel catcher, shuffling into the hall, "clothed all but his coat and hat, and that was under the bed—there be his watches and chains, his seals and the papers in his pockets—and for his visage now there is no mistaking it."

They had laid the body on the table where it had so often sat and larked and ate and drunk and cursed; Sir Nicholas gazed, holding up the lantern.

Edward Crediton—never any doubt of that now, though his face was distorted as by the anguish of a sudden and ugly death.

"We never found Robert Horne," muttered one of the mourners, trailing his foul muddy rags nearer the fire, and thrusting his crooked hands to the blaze.

And Mathews fell on his knees and tried to pray, but could think of no words.

"Who is upstairs?" demanded Sir Nicholas in a terrible voice. "Who is with that wretched woman?"

And he stared at the body of her husband.

Mathews, who had loved her as a little child, began gibbering and moaning.

"Did he not say he'd have her? And did not yon fool change places with him? Oh God, oh God, and has he not come to take his place—"

"But Robert Horne was *dead*. I saw him dead," stammered Sir Nicholas, and set the lantern down for his hand shook so the flame waved in gusts.

"Eh," shrieked old Mathews, grovelling on his hands and knees in his bedgown. "Might not the devil have lent his body back for his own pitchy purposes?"

They looked at him a little, seeing he was suddenly crazed; then Sir Nicholas ran up the stairs with the others at his heels and thundered with his sword, and kicked and shouted outside Anne Crediton's chamber door.

All the foul, muddy, earthy crew cowered on the stairs and chittered together, and in the parlour before the embers old Mathews crouched huddled and whimpered.

The bedroom door opened and Robert Horne came out and stood and smiled at them, and the young man in his fury fell back and his sword rattled from his hand to the floor.

Robert Horne was a white death, nude to the waist and from there swathed in grave clothes; under the tattered dark cloak he had ridden in was his shroud knotted round his neck; his naked chest gleamed with ghastly dews, and under the waxen polish of his sunken face the decayed blood showed in discoloured patches; he went down the stairs and they hid their faces while his foul whiteness passed.

Sir Nicholas stumbled into the bedchamber. The moonlight showed Anne Crediton tumbled on the bed, dead and staring with the posy of kecksies on her bare breast, and her mouth hung open and her hands clutching at the curtains.

The mourners rode back and picked up Robert Horne's body whence it had returned from the kecksie patch and buried it in unholy ground with great respect, *as one to whom the devil had given his great desire.*

A LITTLE PLACE OFF
THE EDGWARE ROAD (1939)

Graham Greene

Graham Greene (1904–91) achieved that rarest and most enviable of feats for any novelist—namely a career in which popular success and critical acclaim went hand in hand. Greene was undoubtedly one of the most significant authors of the 20th century and in novels such as *Brighton Rock* (1938), *The Power and the Glory* (1940) and *The End of the Affair* (1951) he explored some of the darkest corners of the human condition. Indeed, the term 'Greeneland' entered the language to describe not only the hot, arid and down-at-heel settings for many of his novels but also to describe the bruised and defeated state of mind of many of his characters.

The supernatural occasionally intrudes into Greene's fiction, perhaps most memorably in the novel *The End of the Affair* where miracles do, possibly, occur during the narrative. 'A Little Place off the Edgware Road' is rather different though in that the events here are much more unpleasant. The story has the feel of a genuine nightmare. Greene was a great admirer of the novelist Henry James and, although in a very different style, this particular story like James' *The Turn of the Screw* is as much to do with what happens inside the mind, as with what happens in the outside world.

CRAVEN CAME UP PAST THE ACHILLES STATUE IN THE THIN summer rain. It was only just after lighting-up time, but already the cars were lined up all the way to the Marble Arch, and the sharp acquisitive faces peered out ready for a good time with anything possible which came along. Craven went bitterly by with the collar of his mackintosh tight round his throat: it was one of his bad days.

All the way up the Park he was reminded of passion, but you needed money for love. All that a poor man could get was lust. Love needed a good suit, a car, a flat somewhere, or a good hotel. It needed to be wrapped in cellophane. He was aware all the time of the stringy tie beneath the mackintosh, and the frayed sleeves: he carried his body about with him like something he hated. (There were moments of happiness in the British Museum reading-room, but the body called him back.) He bore, as his only sentiment, the memory of ugly deeds committed on park chairs. People talked as if the body died too soon—that wasn't the trouble, to Craven, at all. The body kept alive—and through the glittering tinselly rain, on his way to a rostrum, passed a little man in a black suit carrying a banner, "The Body shall rise again." He remembered a dream he had three times woken trembling from: he had been alone in the huge dark cavernous burying ground of all the world. Every grave was connected to another under the ground: the globe was honeycombed for the sake of the dead, and on each occasion of dreaming he had discovered anew the horrifying fact that the body doesn't decay. There are no worms and dissolution. Under the ground the world was littered with masses of dead flesh ready to rise again with their warts and boils and eruptions. He had lain in bed and remembered—as "tidings of great joy"—that the body after all was corrupt.

He came up into the Edgware Road walking fast—the Guardsmen were out in couples, great languid elongated beasts—the bodies like worms in their tight trousers. He hated them, and hated his hatred because he knew what it was, envy. He was aware that every one of them had a better body than himself: indigestion creased his stomach: he felt sure that his breath was foul—but who could he ask? Sometimes he secretly touched himself here and there with scent: it was one of his ugliest secrets. Why should he be asked to believe in the resurrection of this body he wanted to forget? Sometimes he prayed at night (a hint of religious belief was lodged in his breast like a worm in a nut) that *his* body at any rate should never rise again.

He knew all the side streets round the Edgware Road only too well: when a mood was on, he simply walked until he tired, squinting at his own image in the windows of Salmon & Gluckstein and the A.B.C.s. So he noticed at once the posters outside the disused theatre in Culpar Road. They were not unusual, for sometimes Barclays Bank Dramatic Society would hire the place for an evening—or an obscure film would be trade-shown there. The theatre had been built in 1920 by an optimist who thought the cheapness of the site would more than counter-balance its disadvantage of lying a mile outside the conventional theatre zone. But no play had ever succeeded, and it was soon left to gather rat-holes and spider-webs. The covering of the seats was never renewed, and all that ever happened to the place was the temporary false life of an amateur play or a trade show.

Craven stopped and read—there were still optimists it appeared, even in 1939, for nobody but the blindest optimist could hope to make money out of the place as "The Home of the Silent Film". The first season of "primitives" was announced (a high-brow phrase): there would never be a second. Well, the seats were cheap, and it was perhaps worth a shilling to him, now that he was tired, to get in somewhere out of the rain. Craven bought a ticket and went in to the darkness of the stalls.

In the dead darkness a piano tinkled something monotonously recalling Mendelssohn: he sat down in a gangway seat, and could immediately feel the emptiness all round him. No, there would never be another season. On the screen a large woman in a kind of toga wrung her hands, then wobbled with curious jerky movements towards a couch. There she sat and stared out like a sheep-dog distractedly through her loose and black and stringy hair. Sometimes she seemed to dissolve altogether into dots and flashes and wiggly lines. A sub-title said, "Pompilia betrayed by her beloved Augustus seeks an end to her troubles."

Craven began at last to see—a dim waste of stalls. There were not twenty people in the place—a few couples whispering with their heads touching, and a number of lonely men like himself wearing the same uniform of the cheap mackintosh. They lay about at intervals like corpses—and again Craven's obsession returned: the tooth-ache of horror. He thought miserably—I am going mad: other people don't feel like this. Even a disused theatre reminded him of those interminable caverns where the bodies were waiting for resurrection.

"A slave to his passion Augustus calls for yet more wine."

A gross middle-aged Teutonic actor lay on an elbow with his arm round a large woman in a shift. The Spring Song tinkled ineptly on, and the screen flickered like indigestion. Somebody felt his way through the darkness, scrabbling past Craven's knees—a small man: Craven experienced the unpleasant feeling of a large beard brushing his mouth. Then there was a long sigh as the newcomer found the next chair, and on the screen events had moved with such rapidity that Pompilia had already stabbed herself—or so Craven supposed—and lay still and buxom among her weeping slaves.

A low breathless voice sighed out close to Craven's ear: "What's happened? Is she asleep?"

"No. Dead."

"Murdered?" the voice asked with a keen interest.

"I don't think so. Stabbed herself."

Nobody said "Hush": nobody was enough interested to object to a voice: they drooped among the empty chairs in attitudes of weary inattention.

The film wasn't nearly over yet: there were children somehow to be considered: was it all going on to a second generation? But the small bearded man in the next seat seemed to be interested only in Pompilia's death. The fact that he had come in at that moment apparently fascinated him. Craven heard the word "coincidence" twice, and he went on talking to himself about it in low out-of-breath tones. "Absurd when you come to think of it," and then "no blood at all". Craven didn't listen: he sat with his hands clasped between his knees, facing the fact as he had faced it so often before, that he was in danger of going mad. He had to pull himself up, take a holiday, see a doctor (God knew what infection moved in his veins). He became aware that his bearded neighbour had addressed him directly. "What?" he asked impatiently, "what did you say?"

"There would be more blood than you can imagine."

"What are you talking about?"

When the man spoke to him, he sprayed him with damp breath. There was a little bubble in his speech like an impediment. He said, "When you murder a man…"

"This was a woman," Craven said impatiently.

"That wouldn't make any difference."

"And it's got nothing to do with murder anyway."

"That doesn't signify." They seemed to have got into an absurd and meaningless wrangle in the dark.

"I know, you see," the little bearded man said in a tone of enormous conceit.

"Know what?"

"About such things," he said with guarded ambiguity.

Craven turned and tried to see him clearly. Was he mad? Was this a warning of what he might become—babbling incomprehensibly to strangers in cinemas? He thought, By God, no, trying to see: I'll be sane yet. I *will* be sane. He could make out nothing but a small black hump of body. The man was talking to himself again. He said, "Talk. Such talk. They'll say it was all for fifty pounds. But that's a lie. Reasons and reasons. They always take the first reason. Never look behind. Thirty years of reasons. Such simpletons," he added again in that tone of breathless and unbounded conceit. So this was madness. So long as he could realize that, he must be sane himself—relatively speaking. Not so sane perhaps as the seekers in the park or the Guardsmen in the Edgware Road, but saner than this. It was like a message of encouragement as the piano tinkled on.

Then again the little man turned and sprayed him. "Killed herself, you say? But who's to know that? It's not a mere question of what hand holds the knife." He laid a hand suddenly and confidingly on Craven's: it was damp and sticky: Craven said with horror as a possible meaning came to him: "What are you talking about?"

"I know," the little man said. "A man in my position gets to know almost everything."

"What is your position?" Craven said, feeling the sticky hand on his, trying to make up his mind whether he was being hysterical or not—after all, there were a dozen explanations—it might be treacle.

"A pretty desperate one *you'd* say." Sometimes the voice almost died in the throat altogether. Something incomprehensible had happened on the screen—take your eyes from these early pictures for a moment and the plot had proceeded on at such a pace… Only the actors moved slowly and jerkily. A young woman in a night-dress seemed to be weeping in the arms of a Roman centurion: Craven hadn't seen either of them before. *"I am not afraid of death, Lucius—in your arms."*

The little man began to titter—knowingly. He was talking to himself again. It would have been easy to ignore him altogether if it had not been for those sticky hands which he now removed: he seemed to be fumbling at the seat in front of him. His head had a habit of lolling suddenly sideways—like an idiot child's. He said distinctly and irrelevantly: "Bayswater Tragedy."

"What was that?" Craven said sharply. He had seen those words on a poster before he entered the park.

"What?"

"About the tragedy."

"To think they call Cullen Mews Bayswater." Suddenly the little man began to cough—turning his face towards Craven and coughing right at him: it was like vindictiveness. The voice said brokenly, "Let me see. My umbrella." He was getting up.

"You didn't have an umbrella."

"My umbrella," he repeated. "My—" and seemed to lose the word altogether. He went scrabbling out past Craven's knees.

Craven let him go, but before he had reached the billowy dusty curtains of the Exit the screen went blank and bright—the film had broken, and somebody immediately turned up one dirt-choked chandelier above the circle. It shone down just enough for Craven to see the smear on his hands. This wasn't hysteria: this was a fact. He wasn't mad: he had sat next a madman who in some mews—what was the name Colon, Collin… Craven jumped up and made his own way out: the black curtain flapped in his mouth. But he was too late: the man had gone and there were three turnings to choose from.

He chose instead a telephone-box and dialled with an odd sense for him of sanity and decision 999.

It didn't take two minutes to get the right department. They were interested and very kind. Yes, there had been a murder in a mews—Cullen Mews. A man's neck had been cut from ear to ear with a bread knife—a horrid crime. He began to tell them how he had sat next the murderer in a cinema: it couldn't be anyone else: there was blood now on his hands—and he remembered with repulsion as he spoke the damp beard. There must have been a terrible lot of blood. But the voice from the Yard interrupted him. "Oh no," it was saying, "we have the murderer—no doubt of it at all. It's the body that's disappeared."

Craven put down the receiver. He said to himself aloud, "Why should this happen to *me*? Why to *me*?" He was back in the horror of his dream—the squalid darkening street outside was only one of the innumerable tunnels connecting grave to grave where the imperishable bodies lay. He said, "It was a dream, a dream," and leaning forward he saw in the mirror above the telephone his own face sprinkled by tiny drops of blood like dew from a scent-spray. He began to scream, "I won't go mad. I won't go mad. I'm sane. I won't go mad." Presently a little crowd began to collect, and soon a policeman came.

YOUR TINY HAND IS FROZEN (1966)

Robert Aickman

Robert Aickman (1914–81) was a writer and conservationist. He co-founded the Inland Waterways Association which worked to preserve and repair England's waterways. He was also born into a family with a rich literary heritage. Aickman was the grandson of the prolific Victorian novelist Richard Marsh, whose occult thriller *The Beetle* (1897) initially outsold Bram Stoker's novel *Dracula* which appeared in the same year. As a writer Aickman is best known for his short stories. Many authors have been able to write a good ghost story but very few, if any, have been as good as Aickman at writing tales which are disturbing, unsettling and so enigmatically, indecipherably strange.

'Your Tiny Hand is Frozen' tells of a young man, Edmund St Jude, who becomes increasingly disturbed by a series of phone calls. Like many of the protagonists in Aickman's stories Edmund is aloof, rather unpopular and out of his depth when it comes to the women in his life. As events progress Edmund's grip on reality becomes distinctly tenuous. The ending, when it comes, is horrifying.

IT WAS ON THE THIRD NIGHT THAT THE TROUBLE WITH THE telephone started. Edmund St Jude had been a light sleeper for years; but the previous day had been occupied with steady and unwonted domestic tasks, and when the telephone began to ring he was slumbering heavily and dreaming vividly. For some time, indeed, it was in his dream that the bell rang: then he found that he was sitting crouched in bed, shuddering a little, and totally uncertain how far the dream had ended. Moonlight drifted in through the glass mansard of the studio north light, but the telephone, being on a low table immediately beneath the sill, was in darkness. In the absence of other sounds to muffle or compete, the peals of the bell were thrown back and forth from wall to wall, icy and imperative.

Clutching his personality, jeopardized by the dream, about him, Edmund resolved not to answer. At that hour it could only be a wrong number... or a friend of Teddie's, he suddenly thought. The bell continued to ring. What time was it? His beautiful hunter, symbol of his former life, lay on a chair by the bed. It was twenty-five minutes past five. That the caller could be for Teddie seemed improbable. The bell continued to ring.

In the end, Edmund, who was an amiable man, always yielded to importunity. He crawled out into the autumnal November moonlight and lifted the instrument from its black bed. His aunt, with whom he had previously resided for a number of years, had contrived to retain an instrument of the earlier candlestick pattern; to which Edmund's reflexes were accordingly accustomed, especially in the middle of the night. He fumbled slightly, almost dropping this newer contraption. Now the silence was as disconcerting as the former noise.

"Hullo."

There was no answering sound of any kind.

"Hullo."

After a silence of seconds, there was a loud sharp click. It was as if the caller had counted one, two, three, and then, as if by premeditation, rung off.

"*Hullo*," said Edmund futilely. But nothing happened. It was not an hour for the operator forthwith to ask what number he wanted.

Edmund replaced the telephone and sped back to bed. He slept again, but now lightly and brokenly, as he usually did.

The episode amounted to little, and Edmund, had he been permitted, would probably soon have forgotten it, especially among the many other nuisances of which his new life seemed largely composed. But during the next few weeks the incident was repeated again and again. Almost always it happened if not during the hours of daylight, which now were daily shrinking, then at least during the hours when Edmund was up and about; although there were further night alarms on at least two occasions.

One of these night calls was especially curious. The telephone rang almost immediately after Edmund had got into bed. Suspecting, with a sinking of his already low spirits, that it was one of the unaccountable calls, but knowing that for him there was no escape in letting the bell go on ringing (two minutes and fifty seconds had proved his maximum period of endurance to date, counted out upon the second-hand of his hunter), he at once switched on the weak bedside light, rose, and answered.

"Hullo."

There was the usual silence.

"Hullo."

Not for the first time, he was permitted to speak thrice.

"Hullo."

There came the click; and then a sound which was new. Edmund heard it before he put back the telephone, but that it came after and not before the dismissive click he was sure. It was a sound which could be nothing but a light short laugh. It seemed to mock his certainly derisory plight. It upset him very much. But no such quirk, additional to the mischief of the calls themselves, occurred again.

There appeared no method or regularity about the calls. Several days would pass without one; then there would be three in twenty-four hours. The apparent chanciness of the calls played its part in for long dissuading Edmund, who always delayed such approaches, from communicating with the Exchange. He was also deterred by the extreme rarity of his other calls, received or initiated. He felt that this put him in a weak position to complain, and would make his complaint seem ridiculous. The whole telephone installation was only a survival from Teddie's occupancy, and it was one of several with which he would have dispensed.

Another was a habit which seemed common to many of Teddie's friends of calling without previous announcement. The callers con-sisted of rather commonplace young women, obviously in great need of a good gossip, and of well-set-up young men with the wrong kind of haircut and few overt stigmata of imagination. Edmund, who could afford few friends of his own, had known few of Teddie's. He was now much surprised by the implications with regard to Teddie's nature and character which these stray visitors conveyed. As he was engaged to marry Teddie, he was also somewhat concerned.

On one occasion, when Edmund was standing at the studio door trying to ward off a large youth who said his name was Toby, the telephone rang. It proved to be one of the mysterious calls, but by the time Edmund had heard the usual click and had replaced the instru-ment, he perceived that his visitor had followed him into the studio.

"Nothing wrong, I hope?"

With each successive call, Edmund was becoming fractionally more irritated, and also perturbed; so that the young man's question was as unwelcome as his presence.

"Nothing," said Edmund stonily. Then he thought. He was beginning to need a confidant. "Nothing *wrong*," he continued. "But perhaps something unusual. The telephone rings. I answer it. And then the person at the other end rings off. That's all. But it happens again and again."

"Nothing unusual about that," said Toby, failing to grasp the essence of the matter. "We all get it." His manner was insensitive and insufferable. "Now tell me, St Jude." He was also over-familiar. "How long has Teddie had T.B.? I never knew she had it at all."

"No one knew," replied Edmund. "But I'm sorry. I was working. I must get on, you know. I'll tell Teddie you called."

"O.K." Toby had evidently given Edmund up. He shrugged his bulging shoulders and departed without further comment. Edmund had to shut the door behind him.

Annoyance with Toby seemed to imbue Edmund with the small increment of aggression required for him to complain to the Exchange.

"It must have happened more than thirty times now," he concluded. "I mean since I arrived here, about three weeks ago."

"Are you the subscriber?" asked the Exchange.

"No, Miss Taylor-Smith's the subscriber. But I'm her sub-tenant."

"Have we been notified?"

"I don't think so. The arrangement's only temporary."

"Please send us full particulars or we may have to discontinue the service."

"I'll write to you. But these calls—"

"I'm sorry, but if you don't tell us when there's a new subscriber—"

"That's nothing to do with it."

"If you'll complete a new Application Form, we'll go into the matter further."

The odd thing was that after that the calls ceased. Edmund never wrote to the Exchange. His inclination was to ask for the telephone to be removed from the studio as soon as possible, but he reflected that this might be unfair to Teddie, as it was understood that telephones were by most people both sought after and hard to obtain, and Teddie probably needed one in order that she might communicate with the parents of her sitters. So Edmund did nothing. None the less the call which came when Toby was there was the last unexplained call Edmund received for a long time.

It was when Christmas approached that the climate of unsuccess in which Edmund nowadays passed too much of his life became annually most intolerable. Every year since the sale of the family's ancient manors and estates had so nearly extinguished his income, he had participated in his aunt's sober Christmas celebrations, if only because she so clearly counted upon him to do so. Now, however, he seemed to have a measure of choice. It was unfortunate that the family débâcle and his past feeling of obligation to his aunt had combined to terminate the previous modest influx of Christmas invitations; but at least he once more had premises where, to the extent his means permitted, he himself could offer hospitality.

Not that the position was unequivocal. He was, after all, only a superior caretaker, with love the consideration in place of cash; and the atmosphere of the studio remained Teddie's entirely. He looked carefully round, before making a list of friends who might join him for Christmas Dinner, bringing, if possible, some festive contributions of their own. Lacking the presence of Teddie to indicate that they were but stock-in-trade (the expression was hers), the pictures of children which covered all the walls made a scheme of decoration that was oppressively insipid. Conspicuously embarrassing were the two biggest works: one a much enlarged reproduction of Reynolds's "The Age of Innocence", specially photo-printed with the maximum fidelity accessible to science, and intended both as lure to parents and as reassurance that Teddie's muse had strict principles; the other Teddie's own "Children of Mr and Mrs Preston Brook". This work had been shown, upon Mr Brook's instructions, at a number of exhibitions; after which Mr Brook, a successful manufacturer of vegetable sundries, had so far failed to take possession of his property. The picture hung above the electric heater, and still bore a name-plate, with "Edwina Taylor-Smith M.S.P.C." in prominent capitals. Edmund could still hear Teddie saying "Edwina. It's a noise like a slowly squeaking wheel."

Twenty-five minutes later Edmund had made little progress with his list. Most of his acquaintances were too rich, too distant, or too obviously provided already with better fare than his. Almost all were married; commonly to spouses who were either unknown or unsuitable. With many he had lost all touch. There were three or four men who were possible, being generally situated much as he was; but Edmund was shocked and disheartened by the specific demonstration that women, other than Teddie, had almost disappeared from his life. None the less a start had to be made if he was not to spend Christmas in solitude. Edmund lifted the telephone and dialled the number of his friend Tadpole, who had been at Oriel with him.

He could hear the bell begin to ring immediately. It continued ringing. Reluctant to acknowledge the evaporation of his first essay, he allowed it to ring long after the time had expired when his friend, who lived in chambers, could be expected to answer. He began to think of the exigent ringing which had marked the unexplained calls he himself had been receiving until about a month before; when the noise stopped and a voice spoke. By then the rhythmic thrumming of the bell in his ear had slightly hypnotized Edmund, and the voice made him start. Still, it seemed to him an unknown voice. And it said something quite unintelligible to him.

"I beg your pardon?"

Again the voice said something unintelligible, but this time longer. Edmund could hear only a rather high-pitched gabbling.

"I wanted to speak to Mr Pusey. Is he in?"

The reply seemed to be two short, sharp sentences, but Edmund could not distinguish a single word. It occurred to him even that the sounds might not be vocal, but might come from the telephone system itself.

"I'd better ring off and try again," said Edmund, unsure that he was not merely speaking to himself.

There was a much softer gabbling, which diminished into silence.

Edmund rang off.

After a minute or two, he tried again. This time the bell simply rang, and went on ringing. Palpably though depressingly, Tadpole was out.

Edmund made three more calls. One of his friends was spending Christmas in Paris; one would have to let him know later (Edmund was certain that he was hoping for something better to offer itself); and one, like Tadpole, did not reply. Edmund decided to write to the remaining names on his list. If only he could write "Evelyn Laye will be there, so we'll be sure of some good talk!"

During the following seven days, Edmund used the telephone more than was his wont. He began to ring up everyone he had met, however casually, during the previous year. Probably because his contact with them had been so casual, none of them seemed to want to spend Christmas with him. In the course of one of these, usually brief, calls, the somewhat uneasy conversation was at one point intruded upon by a repetition in the background of the indistinct gabbling talk.

"Can you hear that sound?" asked Edmund, interrupting his acquaintance's meagre trickle of explanation.

"What sound, old boy?"

"Like someone talking gibberish."

"Some woman on a cross-line, I expect."

"You think it's a woman?"

"How do I know, old boy? But look here, as I was saying, Nell and I—but, of course, you've not met Nell—we always go to stay with her people up in Galloway—"

By the end of the week, his friend who had wavered decided against him. Something better had duly appeared. Of those Edmund had written to, one had replied pleading a previous commitment by return of post. The others had not replied at all. Upon Edmund descended a colourless suffocating fog of loneliness.

Suddenly, in his despair, Edmund thought of Queenie. Queenie was a girl of whom he had seen much when, twenty years before, he had first lived in London. Even at that period, though fortified with a private income which sufficed, he had been commonly unsuccessful in reaching the hearts of the girls who really appealed to him; and in retrospect he perceived that Queenie had much in common with Teddie. He had been fond of her, and she had been more than fond of him. In those days Edmund's remarkable linguistic aptitude had served to make smooth the highways of the continent, instead of as now merely bringing him an undependable stipend as a translator; and Queenie had travelled many of the highways with him. She was well formed, and had been carefully nurtured (her baptismal name was Estelle; Queenie had attached itself to her at Newnham, reflection, perhaps, of something within her); and Edmund might

well in the end have married her, had not ruin supervened. In fact
she had married a man much older than herself, who had almost
immediately afterwards fallen into invalidism. During the previous
summer, in Victoria Street, Edmund had walked into an old friend
of Queenie's named Sefton, a civil servant. They had not met for
many years, and their only common subject of conversation was
Queenie. Sefton told Edmund that Queenie's husband was now
dead, and Edmund wrote down her new address and telephone
number.

That number he now dialled for the first time.

"Who is it?" There had been no sound of ringing. The enquiry
seemed to come immediately Edmund had dialled the last figure. The
voice sounded warm and eager. It surpassed Edmund's recollection.

"You'll be surprised. It's Edmund. How are you, Queenie?"

"Edmund! Edmund St Jude?" It was delightful. There was real
joy in her voice.

"I am glad you sound pleased. I wasn't sure…"

"You don't know how lonely I've been. No one knows." Her voice
had a slight throb in it which was charming, and also new.

Edmund's own recent experiences made it impossible for him
to offer easy commiseration. Instead he offered specific aid. "I want
you to dine with me on Christmas Day."

"Are you giving a party?"

"I meant to originally. But I've thought better of it. Just the two
of us, Queenie. If you will."

She said nothing. Edmund could hear a light intermittent humming on the wire, like the sound of a very distant multitude. He
spoke again. "Please come, Queenie. I'm living in a friend's studio,
and—"

She had apparently been gathering resolution, because now she
burst out, "I'm not Queenie."

Edmund's heart would have fallen further than it did, had it not already premonished him.

"Then I should certainly apologize."

"For asking me to Christmas Dinner?"

"Yes."

"To dinner, perhaps. Surely *Christmas* Dinner's entirely different?"

The implication was perhaps too blatant, but Edmund was desperate, and, blatant or not, she sounded pleasant.

"In that case, will you come? Perhaps you would accompany Queenie, if she's not otherwise engaged?"

"Queenie *is* otherwise engaged."

"Oh." Edmund was not sure whether to feel disappointed. "In that case—"

"I'd love to. But I can't."

"Are you engaged too?"

"Not engaged. I just can't." There was something a little hysterical about the way she made this plain statement. The humming sound had stopped. No less hysterically she added, "I'm very sorry... Please don't ring off."

"I'm sorry too," said Edmund.

"Don't ring off," she said again. "I really am sorry."

"Prove it by coming some other time," suggested Edmund. "What about tomorrow night?"

"You've never seen me. You don't know what I look like."

"I can hear you," replied Edmund, smiling into the telephone. "Your voice speaks for you." He hoped it did.

She made no reply, but suddenly began to sob. There was no doubt about it. Edmund could hear each separate gulping intake of breath. It seemed an unusually good line.

"Well, come some time," said Edmund, embarrassed and slightly raising his voice.

"I may never be able to."

It seemed unwise to probe. But Edmund thought that she would continue and explain.

"You've been so kind to me. May I ring you up again?"

"Of course." Edmund gave her his number, but she seemed too overwrought particularly to take note of it.

"You'll really let me?" Her gratitude was embarrassing, but somehow not ridiculous.

"I might even ring *you*," Edmund said gallantly.

"No. Just let *me*."

"What about Christmas Day?"

"Oh *yes*." She sounded like a schoolgirl.

The humming had resumed.

"And what about Queenie?"

She said something which he could not distinguish.

"Sorry. This humming noise."

It was now quite loud. He realized that she was gone.

The afternoon post brought a still further rejection of Edmund's hospitality. Face to face with the unpleasing prospect of spending Christmas Day entirely alone, he again dialled the number which Sefton had given him. He reflected that Queenie might have returned by now, or that he might at least find out where she was from her curious friend. This time the bell began to ring at once. It continued to ring. Edmund let it ring for an interminable time before he capitulated. Then he rang up Sefton at his Ministry.

"I haven't actually seen her myself since her husband became so bad. In fact I can't have seen her for more than three years. To tell you the truth, I only got her address off another mutual friend. I meant to look her up, but you know what happens."

"She doesn't answer the telephone."

"Christmas, I expect. You know what it is. Sorry I can't help, but if you'll excuse me, I must go to a meeting."

Civil servants at least have "meetings", thought Edmund. The pink and blue children on the walls smiled at his plight, winsomely, cheekily, plethorically, according to character. Edmund settled to translating the first chapter of a Dutch work on the technological revolution of our time.

Christmas Day was the first of the many days which Edmund spent waiting for the telephone to ring. The morning post had brought a woolly scarf from his aunt (she had gone to the trouble of procuring one in his College colours), two Christmas cards, and a cablegram from Teddie: "LOVELY XMAS HERE ALL LAID ON STOP HAPPIEST GREETINGS DARLING STOP CAN'T WAIT FOR CHRISTMAS NEXT YEAR." After that there was nothing except to attend upon the horrid little bell.

The fact that Edmund was far from sure that it would ring at all made the waiting much worse. He had several times attempted to telephone Queenie's number, but there was never a reply. The worst thing of all was the dreary knowledge that he who had dined tête-à-tête with Fritzi Massary, and been accounted a man of insight and judgment in certain high affairs, was now wholly preoccupied with and dependent upon the favours of an unknown with whom he had upon one single occasion exchanged some unintended remarks upon the telephone. He was fond of Teddie, but no more; and the thousands of miles which separated her from him tended also, to his real regret, to obliterate her as a living image in his thoughts. The unrest which the voice on the telephone had certainly created within him seemed to prove both the tenuousness of poor Teddie's hold on him and the general aridity of his days. It was absurd and out of proportion, but certainly true that the unknown, and the doubt whether he would hear from her again, had affected his nerves and further diminished his already sketchy appetite. On Christmas Day systematic translation seemed impossible. Edmund found it difficult to settle to occupation of any kind, and constantly caught his attention wandering into the evolution of persuasive verbal gambits. Before it was time for lunch, he was wondering whether his Christmas malaise would have been any worse if he had never heard from her at all.

She telephoned just when the fleeting and dreamlike December day had finally subsided into darkness. Although their conversation was disturbed by various cracklings and rumblings on the line, Edmund was astonished to notice, when it was over, that it had continued for at least half an hour. During this period, Edmund and she seemed to discover several points of sympathy. For example, when she said that her name was Nera Condamine, Edmund became certain that she belonged to the ancient and distinguished family of that name, and that she had descended in the world as he had. She took a critical and informed but appreciative interest in his remarks upon the eighteenth-century English poets, about whom he was an authority, and who entered the conversation when he quoted topically from Thomson's "The Seasons". Above all, Edmund felt, they had loneliness in common: each of them (he deprecatingly, she eagerly) seemed to throw out feelers of interrogation at which the other clutched. Only questions which were direct and personal she refused to answer: where she lived or why she must remain inaccessible. At the first sign of persistence on Edmund's part, she became hysterical.

"Please don't ask me. Please. Please."

"Naturally I understand if you'd rather not tell me. I only thought—"

"I'll have to ring off if you ask me."

"Then I'll certainly not ask you."

In the end, however, she did let fall one minor fact.

"Of course I understand that very well," she said. "Because I'm a painter."

"Do I know your work?" asked Edmund. All the children on the walls looked interrogative.

"I only paint for myself. There used to be others, but now there's only me." The telephone croaked in mournful confirmation. Edmund dared not ask what had happened to the others.

By the end of their talk, in fact, a curious change had taken place. Originally it had been Nera, as Edmund at her request had begun to call her, who had repeatedly besought him not to ring off; now the fear lest they stop talking seemed to be primarily his. He perceived the change before he could think about it and account for it. On the whole, by the end of their talk, he was delighted with her.

"I'm glad we have made one another's acquaintance." (He had almost said "found one another".) "You have transformed Christmas Day for me."

"We have a lot to say yet," she replied lightly. "But we've both time to burn."

There was a click; without a farewell she was gone; and the Exchange was speaking: "What number do you want?"

"That same number again," replied Edmund with unusual resourcefulness.

"What number was it?" asked the Exchange, not without petulance.

"I'm afraid I don't know. Can't you please trace it? I'd be most obliged if you could."

"Sorry you've been troubled," replied the Exchange.

Edmund looked at the electric clock, then sat for a long time staring at the small square electric heater. Thinking it over, he was unable to determine very clearly what indeed they had said to each other which had consumed so much time. There had been the eighteenth-century English poets (it was remarkable indeed to make a casual acquaintance who knew Addison's "Cato"); but otherwise there seemed to have been little but an interchange of remarks which barely amounted to conversation, because his preoccupation had been curiosity, hers a seemingly almost desperate reaching out for a response, for friendship. Edmund was not one of the many men whose response to an emotional need is inversely proportionate to the degree of that need. On the contrary, he tended by temperament to fall in with any demand made upon him. For this among other reasons, he now felt that, despite the queer circumstances, a new and important factor had entered his life. He had certainly been swept and ready...

At this time the oddness of the circumstances seemed to Edmund to come within the probable boundaries of such familiar concepts as "discretion", "gaining time", or even "coquetry". It was not until a later call that Nera's mysterious elusiveness began significantly to perturb him. Because during this particular conversation, in the course of which she took a clearer initiative than before, she stated, most unmistakably, that she loved him; and he, instead of proceeding as if he thought her remark was meant partly or mainly in jest, replied almost seriously: "I think I love you too." And when after that, and after sundry strange endearments between these lovers who had never set eyes upon one another and who often found themselves at cross purposes on the telephone, she still refused to say where she lived, Edmund was naturally aghast. He was able to notice, however, that whereas previously his more direct approaches had made her hysterical, she now refused him quite tranquilly.

"Am I then never to see you?" he cried.

"I haven't said that."

"But when?"

"Wait until you can't live without me."

Edmund checked himself from replying to that.

"Can I ring you?"

"No. No. No. But I'll ring you."

"When?"

"Whenever I can, darling. Trust me."

After that there was nothing for Edmund to do but translate from the Dutch, buy his food, and wait for the telephone. The call which had brought about such a striking alteration in the terms of his association with Nera had taken place on the Sunday after Christmas, but on Christmas Day she had not forewarned him, and now she had virtually stated her inability in future ever to do so. None the less, Edmund had something of emotional content to think about and to fill his life: for despairing inertia he had substituted dreams of desire; and for listlessness, eager and unresting expectancy. But there was something else. Edmund could never forget that he had not looked upon the being who so agitated his mind and heart; and never was able altogether to disregard the peril possibly implicit in her reluctance to let him look upon her. Simple sameness of days, therefore, had now for him been replaced by a difficult and intense inner combat.

When next he heard from Nera, however, she so enchanted him with tender words and a previously undisclosed richness of expression that the conflict within him began thereafter to abate, and the telephone more and more to become a simple instrument of bliss, like the soup kitchen to the outcast, or the syringe to the drug-addict. When the first defences of convention and restraint had been penetrated, it was surprisingly easy to be intimate into the telephone, very intimate indeed…

Inevitably Edmund's various employers began to complain of late deliveries. In one case a decline in standard was also alleged; which was ominous, because Edmund knew that few publishers and editors can afford to care much about the quality of a translation. The complaint probably implied some different, unnamed complaint in the background. On the other hand, Edmund now spent less time and money shopping; although previously he had contrived to continue gratifying some few of his more refined and expensive tastes, he now fed more and more on bread, potatoes, and the wholly flavourless "luncheon meat" which a shop in the next street seemed always to conjure up in Ali Baba-like quantities.

Always it was impossible to tell when Nera would ring next. She might ring at any hour of the twenty-four, although in the main she seemed to favour the early evening or the early hours of the morning. Edmund would sit all day waiting for her, unable to work or eat; then after she had telephoned at six or seven o'clock, find himself so nervously exhausted by the wasted hours that still he was unable to settle himself and concentrate. And things were, of course, made worse at such times by the complete uncertainty as to when he would hear from her again. For a long time a bad sleeper, he now hardly slept at all; so that when the bell rang at three or four in the morning, he was already taut and wakeful, and rose to answer like an opium-eater going to his brew and knowing as he goes that he is making worse tension for himself in the future.

A minor nuisance was the shortness of the flex. Unlike most women, Teddie had not provided for the telephone to stand by her bed. It stood at the other end of the studio, under the big window, and therefore nearly on the floor. The most inconvenient place possible, Edmund had thought soon after he took possession; especially in that the hanging of Teddie's pictures made it difficult to reposition the bed.

On one occasion Nera suggested an application for a longer flex.

"Don't suppose they'd give me one."

"I got a longer flex years ago. Do try, darling."

But Edmund did nothing. One reason was that he feared lest Nera ring up while the flex purveyor was in the studio, so that his end of one of their strange indispensable conversations would be overheard and questioned. A worse possibility was that the fitting of the flex might involve the temporary disconnection of the telephone, so that he might miss a call altogether. He was at all times haunted by the possibility that if he were to miss one of Nera's calls, there might never be another one.

He found it impossible to communicate to her such fears as these. He had tried never to let her know even that he waited for hours, in fact all day and all night, for her calls, but sought to leave with her the presumption that it was by happy accident alone that so far she had always found him in. For whereas his attendance was incessant, her calls were remarkably undependable, and, all things considered, not particularly frequent. It was, in fact, this irregularity and infrequency which especially made Edmund shrink from disclosing his servitude to the little black instrument. Against Nera's refusal of information surely essential, he maintained this fiction of freedom.

Somewhere about the end of February began the intrusion of the Chromium Supergloss Corporation. For some reason the telephone began to ring several times a day (on some days as much as twelve or fifteen times), and when Edmund lifted the receiver it was almost always to discover the caller was dialling for the Corporation. Often when he ventured out in quest of his unappetizing food, he would hear his telephone ringing from the bottom of the staircase to the studios. The studios were on the fourth floor of the block, with flats below; and had it been a still higher block, Edmund would not have been there, for he much feared heights. He would race up the eight flights of stone steps, his heart beating even more from warring emotions than from the ill-alimented exertion, collapse on the floor under the big window, and find only a customer for the Corporation, peevish at having reached the wrong number. These numerous strangers, Edmund noticed, regularly, when they got that far in their demands, asked for Extension 281. Edmund felt that this extension must be a busy one, but he knew that the Corporation was a large and multifunctional organization, as was confirmed by the fact that calls for it (commonly still for Extension 281) not infrequently reached him after office hours, and indeed throughout the night.

The incessant "wrong number" calls tended to convert Edmund from a passive into an active servitor of the telephone. After some weeks of it, he did write a strong letter to the Supervisor; and, ten days later, received a courteous acknowledgment, printed in a carefully chosen type-face, and with a handwritten postscript, difficult to read but apparently conveying an assurance that his complaint was "under investigation". The calls continued as before. This development in Edmund's relationship with the telephone helped to conceal from him for some time that Nera's calls were becoming slowly but markedly fewer than ever. One morning he noticed that there were buds on the plane trees beneath the studio window, and realized that, although the telephone bell seemed seldom to stop ringing, he had not heard from Nera for a week. Instantly his concentration upon the telephone leapt to and remained at a new intensity. As the tender tide of spring trickled round the grey rocks of London, Edmund became a man eviscerated and absorbed by the squat black monster tethered by its stubby flex.

As soon as possible, he challenged Nera. "Wrong number" calls had been coming in all that day, varied by one call which was not a wrong number but informed Edmund that he would not be wanted to translate the Italian book on the eighteenth century in England after all. Nera came through at 11.25 p.m. precisely. She was as alluring as ever; roses in Edmund's horizonless desert. Never in retrospect could he at all determine what it was about those bare words of hers, intensified by no accessory charm beyond her attractive voice, which so moved him that he had become as one of Odysseus's sailors. Now he remonstrated and begged.

At first she made light of her remissness and little of Edmund's trouble. He noticed, however, that she did not, as she had originally seemed to do, claim that she had been *unable* to telephone. Convinced that she was tiring of their inadequate and unsatisfying association, he found himself pleading desperately.

"I can't live without you." The rags and bones of his pride had hitherto prevented him from admitting so much as long as she persisted without explanation in standing so far off.

"Oh," she said. "Then it's time for me to come and see you." Her voice was soft as grass new sprung from the seed.

This fulfilment of her previous vague promise was the last thing that Edmund had expected. He looked round the room for his reflection, but Teddie had managed to smash the mirror on the day she left, and Edmund had not replaced it.

"Yes," he said in a low voice. "Any time. When?"

"Very soon. Wait for me. Goodbye."

After that Nera stopped telephoning Edmund altogether; but the telephone itself began to behave more and more strangely. The calls for the Corporation came as frequently as before; but now there were other calls which were wholly inexplicable. Believing that Nera would surely ring him up to tell him when she was coming, Edmund became more frightened than ever lest he miss a single one of them. He renewed efforts, suspended as unavailing during the first week of his tenancy, to arrange for food to be delivered at his door, but with no more success than then. Now, moreover, his money was fast running out, and the reservoir was by no means being replenished. He tried to arrange credit with the shop in the next street, but was no more successful than when he tried to persuade them to deliver. Edmund had never been apt with shop assistants, and now he felt that he was being eyed with positive hatred. There was a long London heat-wave, premature, opaque, and damp; through which Edmund sat seeing almost nobody, eating almost nothing, and no longer waiting for, but increasingly ministering to the telephone.

Sometimes now he would lift the receiver and hear only a crescendo of terrifying abuse and curses; at other times, groans and screams, as of the dying or the damned. Sometimes unknown voices would conduct hectoring or wheedling conversations with him; and when he questioned them upon the number they wanted, persist that they wanted his. If he rang off, they would often ring again; threatening, or breaking down. Sometimes there was a cat's-cradle of confused noises, in part, it seemed to Edmund, mechanical, in part simply disembodied and without significance. Several times there was laughter on the line; and once an enormous voice which plunged through Edmund's head, then diminished before plunging again. It was like overhearing an immense ram as it battered its way through mighty resistances and defences. It was even more frightening than the confused noises.

One day the studio bell rang. It was the first occasion for weeks. Edmund, supposing that the shop in the next street might have changed its mind, opened the door. It was Teddie's friend, Toby.

"Didn't recognize you, St Jude. It's that beard…"

He was inside the studio before Edmund could stop him.

"Sorry to butt in when you're not dressed."

He looked round for Edmund to offer him a cigarette.

"When's Teddie coming back? Do you hear from her?" He barely attempted even the surface of politeness.

"I see that you do." He picked up a heap of air mail envelopes which stood on Teddie's Benares table.

"Unopened, by God." Toby was staring at Edmund. He was now by the window. Edmund was at the door willing him to go.

The telephone rang.

Toby lifted the receiver.

"Miss Taylor-Smith's studio."

Edmund was upon him, fighting like a starving animal.

"What the hell—"

Toby's free arm wheeled round, pushed rather than struck: and Edmund was on the floor.

"It's a bloke called Sefton." Toby was holding out the receiver. He seemed to bear no malice, but instead of going, he seated himself in Teddie's big armchair and found a cigarette of his own.

Sefton was speaking. "I say, is everything all right?"

"Of course." Edmund was picking himself up.

"Then in that case I can only say there's something wrong with your line. I've been trying to get you for days. I should report it to the Supervisor."

"I'm sorry."

"It's all right. But I've got some bad news. Did you know that Queenie's dead?"

"No, I didn't. When did it happen?"

"I've only just heard about it. From another mutual friend, you know. But it seems she died about six months ago. Same trouble as her husband, I understand. It must have been about the time we last met. Strange how small the world is. I just thought I'd let you know, in case you hadn't heard."

"Thank you," said Edmund. "I suppose you don't know who's now got her telephone number?"

"I don't," said Sefton. "If it matters, I should ask the Exchange."

Toby didn't move when Edmund rang off. "Still having trouble with the telephone?" he asked, filling the stuffy air with cigarette smoke and crossing his legs. "It was going on when I came here before. Remember?"

"What makes you think—" began Edmund.

"I overheard your friend Sefton. I'm used to the telephone, you know. You're not."

Edmund was now waiting for it to ring again.

"Things mechanical are like the ladies," continued Toby. "You need to understand their ways. If you understand them, they'll do what you want from the start. If you don't, they've got you. And then God help you."

"Would you mind going?" said Edmund.

"I'll go," said Toby. "But first let me get the Supervisor for you." He rose, returned to the telephone, and dialled O. Edmund, wrought up because the line was again being occupied, would have liked to stop him, but could not see how.

"Get me the Supervisor."

There was a pause, but only a short one.

Toby gave the number. "There've been a lot of complaints about delays in getting through. Look into it, will you, and report back as soon as possible?"

Clearly the answer was deferential.

"That's all." He was about to ring off, but Edmund stopped him.

"I've got something to say myself."

"Hold on." Toby handed over the receiver.

"Would you mind leaving me?"

"O.K. I'll be back. About Teddie, you know." His glance was on the heap of unopened letters. "I happen to love that girl, St Jude." He went. This time he even shut the door.

"Hullo," said Edmund.

"Do you wish to make a complaint?" enquired the voice at the other end, fretful with waiting.

"No. I just want to know who's got a certain number." He mentioned the number which Sefton had given him, and which he would never forget.

"We're not supposed to give information like that," snapped the voice. "But hold on." Plainly some part of Toby's aura remained.

There was a long wait.

"That number's dead."

"I rang up. And someone answered."

"Oh, you often get an answer on a dead number."

"How can that be?"

"Dead person, I suppose." Whether or not this was meant for facetiousness was unsure because the voice then rang off. Toby would never have been so treated.

None the less, the telephone now ceased to ring, as had happened on the previous occasion when Edmund had grappled with the Exchange. Instead the studio was filled by day and night with a silent hot airlessness into which the children on the walls stared with assertive insignificance. There were no more callers, no more money, and, Edmund realized, no more letters from Teddie. After a week of silence, Edmund brought himself to tear open the last of the heap. The contents appalled him. Alarmed by his long-continued failure to write, Teddie was on her way home. She had left the New Mexico sanatorium in defiance of a united medical commination. Edmund looked at the date. Clearly she might arrive at any moment.

He dialled the familiar number. One or another kind of climax was inevitable. He could hear the telephone ringing, but faintly and distantly, as if at the end of a very long corridor. Then, although the bell continued dimly audible, he heard a voice.

"At last, darling, at last."

"Nera! Where have you been?"

"There are terrible difficulties. We have to find a channel, you know."

"We?" Edmund could still hear the bell, far off and minute. It was as if cushioned by a very thick fog.

"I've been trying to reach you, darling, ever since you came here. Didn't you know?" She laughed coquettishly. "But here I am! You can ring off."

As she spoke, the bell stopped ringing, and the line went quite silent.

"The line's gone dead."

"Already?" She seemed unconcerned.

"Where are you?"

"What frightful-looking children! Put back the receiver, darling. You said the line was dead." Edmund's arm slowly dropped, lowering the receiver to his waist, as he fell back against the window. "Where are you?"

"As the line's already dead, I suppose it doesn't matter whether you put back the receiver or not." The worst thing was that her voice still sounded exactly as it had sounded over the telephone; attractive though it was, it retained the effect of having been filtered through the Exchange. Edmund let fall the receiver. It crashed to the floor.

"For God's sake, where are you?"

"I'm *here*, darling." The voice, slightly dehumanized, seemed to come from no particular point. "You said you couldn't live without me."

"I can't see you." The breakfast-food faces of the children smiled brightly at him through the sunshine.

"Not yet, darling. You said you couldn't live without me."

"What do you mean?"

"Darling, you said you couldn't live without me." It was exactly like one of the telephone's standard locutions: "Sorry you've been troubled," or "Number please."

Edmund placed his hands before his eyes.

"Now there's no need to live without me. Don't you understand? Darling: just look behind you. Over your shoulder."

Edmund stood rigid.

"Just one look, darling."

Edmund was trembling all over with hunger and loneliness and terror.

"You must look, you know, darling." The puppet-like voice seemed nearer. "If you knew how hard it's been to reach you—"

Edmund was groping for his last charges of willpower.

"Now turn your head, darling."

There was a rat-tat-tat at the door. Edmund clenched his fists and leaped towards it. He was sobbing as he flung it open.

"Bread."

The shop in the next street had taken pity on him.

When Teddie arrived home, full of evil surmises, she duly found that Edmund was not only in hospital but on the danger-list. Immediately she put on her pinkest Transatlantic frock, and, accompanied by Toby, a note from whom, left in the studio against her arrival, had given her the news, went to visit him. She found him unbelievably thin, and his face a cadaverous dirty yellow: but immediately she approached, he clutched her hand and croaked, "I love you, Nera. Forgive me, Nera. Please please forgive me."

Teddie withdrew her hand. The nurse was looking at her penetratingly.

Toby shrugged, as if he had known all the time. "Name mean anything to you?"

"A little," said Teddie, and changed the subject. Edmund said nothing further, but lay glazed and panting.

"I think you'd better go now, Miss Taylor-Smith. You have your own health to take care of." Toby must have told her.

"He looks like a poet," said Teddie. "Will he get better?"

"Naturally we shall do all we can."

"No, Toby. It's quite impossible. She can't even paint. Not even as well as me." All the children smiled benignly, Toby did not care how well or badly Teddie painted.

"Nothing like that's impossible. Particularly not with a cove like St Jude."

"Well, *this* is impossible." She thought for a moment. "Look, Toby. If you still doubt me, I'll introduce you."

"O.K. by me. I'm only trying to save you from making a big mistake."

"She's always at home in the evening."

On the way to Nera Condamine's flat, which was in another part of London, he put his arm round her.

"Of course I know she was lonely."

"There you are."

"She used to ring me up at all hours. She always wanted me to ring her back. Where she worked. Some number or other—Extension 281."

"Now that does cut out St Jude. Never known a chap so scared of the telephone."

Teddie wriggled herself free for the moment. "I'm going to introduce you anyway. You were at the hospital, and this must be stopped."

"What's that on the floor?"

They had been standing for several minutes in the dim passage, unavailingly manipulating Miss Condamine's small brass knocker. The design was a jester's head.

"Telephone Directory," reported Toby. "A to D volume with her in it. Issued in July."

They looked at one another.

"They bring it round, you know. If there's no answer, they leave it."

Teddie raised the flap of the letter-box.

"Toby!" Now she clutched his arm.

Toby squared up to the door. "Shall I?"

Teddie was coughing. But she nodded emphatically. Both door and lock were cheap and nasty; and Toby was through in a minute. Inside the sun came mistily through the drawn magenta blinds. It was simpler to switch on the light.

The details it revealed were most horrible. Dressed in decaying party pyjamas of cerise satin, and regarded by several academic but aphrodisiac studies of the nude, lay on a chaise-longue the elderly body of Miss Condamine, a bread knife in one mouldering, but still well-shaped hand. With the knife she appeared for some reason to have amputated the telephone from the telephone system; but none the less the unusually long flex was wound tightly round her again and again and again from neck to ankles.

KISS ME AGAIN, STRANGER (1951)

Daphne du Maurier

Daphne du Maurier (1907–89) was one of English Literature's true originals. She combined elements of romance with an acute psychological perception and the darkest of Gothic themes to create something unique in British fiction. Du Maurier was born into an artistic family: her mother, Muriel Beaumont, was an actress and her father, Gerald du Maurier, was an influential actor and theatre manager. Her grandfather, George du Maurier, was a famous cartoonist and the author of three novels including *Trilby* (1894) which introduced the character of Svengali to the world. Her fiction, which includes the novels *Jamaica Inn* (1936), *Rebecca* (1938), *My Cousin Rachel* (1951) and *The House on the Strand* (1969), has a cinematic quality making her work extremely popular with film directors. Many of her short stories, including 'The Birds' and 'Don't Look Now', have also been adapted for the cinema.

Any number of Daphne du Maurier's short stories would have been at home in this anthology but in the end I chose 'Kiss me Again, Stranger'. Violence and death are encountered at every turn as the tale progresses and yet such was du Maurier's brilliance as a writer that one can't help but be carried along by the narrative. Du Maurier began her career writing short stories, tales in which the men are usually domineering and brutal while the women are very much in the shadows. By the time she came to write 'Kiss Me Again, Stranger' the tables had been turned. Now it is the men who are shabby and weak and the cemetery-loving femme fatale at the heart of the story definitely has the upper hand.

I LOOKED AROUND FOR A BIT, AFTER LEAVING THE ARMY AND before settling down, and then I found myself a job up Hampstead way, in a garage it was, at the bottom of Haverstock Hill near Chalk Farm, and it suited me fine. I'd always been one for tinkering with engines, and in REME that was my work and I was trained to it—it had always come easy to me, anything mechanical.

My idea of having a good time was to lie on my back in my greasy overalls under a car's belly, or a lorry's, with a spanner in my hand, working on some old bolt or screw, with the smell of oil about me, and someone starting up an engine, and the other chaps around clattering their tools and whistling. I never minded the smell or the dirt. As my old Mum used to say when I'd be that way as a kid, mucking about with a grease can, "It won't hurt him, it's clean dirt," and so it is, with engines.

The boss at the garage was a good fellow, easy-going, cheerful, and he saw I was keen on my work. He wasn't much of a mechanic himself, so he gave me the repair jobs, which was what I liked.

I didn't live with my old Mum—she was too far off, over Shepperton way, and I saw no point in spending half the day getting to and from my work. I like to be handy, have it on the spot, as it were. So I had a bedroom with a couple called Thompson, only about ten minutes' walk away from the garage. Nice people, they were. He was in the shoe business, cobbler I suppose he'd be called, and Mrs Thompson cooked the meals and kept the house for him over the shop. I used to eat with them, breakfast and supper— we always had a cooked supper—and being the only lodger I was treated as family.

I'm one for routine. I like to get on with my job, and then when the day's work's over settle down to a paper and a smoke and a bit of music on the wireless, variety or something of the sort, and then turn in early. I never had much use for girls, not even when I was doing my time in the army. I was out in the Middle East, too, Port Said and that.

No, I was happy enough living with the Thompsons, carrying on much the same day after day, until that one night, when it happened. Nothing's been the same since. Nor ever will be. I don't know...

The Thompsons had gone to see their married daughter up at Highgate. They asked me if I'd like to go along, but somehow I didn't fancy barging in, so instead of staying home alone after leaving the garage I went down to the picture palace, and taking a look at the poster saw it was cowboy and Indian stuff—there was a picture of a cowboy sticking a knife into the Indian's guts. I like that—proper baby I am for westerns—so I paid my one and twopence and went inside. I handed my slip of paper to the usherette and said, "Back row, please," because I like sitting far back and leaning my head against the board.

Well, then I saw her. They dress the girls up no end in some of these places, velvet tams and all, making them proper guys. They hadn't made a guy out of this one, though. She had copper hair, page-boy style I think they call it, and blue eyes, the kind that look short-sighted but see further than you think, and go dark by night, nearly black, and her mouth was sulky-looking, as if she was fed up, and it would take someone giving her the world to make her smile. She hadn't freckles, nor a milky skin, but warmer than that, more like a peach, and natural too. She was small and slim, and her velvet coat—blue it was—fitted her close, and the cap on the back of her head showed up her copper hair.

I bought a programme—not that I wanted one, but to delay going in through the curtain—and I said to her, "What's the picture like?"

She didn't look at me. She just went on staring into nothing, at the opposite wall. "The knifing's amateur," she said, "but you can always sleep."

I couldn't help laughing. I could see she was serious though. She wasn't trying to have me on or anything.

"That's no advertisement," I said. "What if the manager heard you?"

Then she looked at me. She turned those blue eyes in my direction, still fed-up they were, not interested, but there was something in them I'd not seen before, and I've never seen it since, a kind of laziness like someone waking from a long dream and glad to find you there. Cat's eyes have that gleam sometimes, when you stroke them, and they purr and curl themselves into a ball and let you do anything you want. She looked at me this way a moment, and there was a smile lurking somewhere behind her mouth if you gave it a chance, and tearing my slip of paper in half she said, "I'm not paid to advertise. I'm paid to look like this and lure you inside."

She drew aside the curtains and flashed her torch in the darkness. I couldn't see a thing. It was pitch black, like it always is at first until you get used to it and begin to make out the shapes of the other people sitting there, but there were two great heads on the screen and some chap saying to the other, "If you don't come clean I'll put a bullet through you," and somebody broke a pane of glass and a woman screamed.

"Looks all right to me," I said, and began groping for somewhere to sit.

She said, "This isn't the picture, it's the trailer for next week," and she flicked on her torch and showed me a seat in the back row, one away from the gangway.

I sat through the advertisements and the news reel, and then some chap came and played the organ, and the colours of the curtains over the screen went purple and gold and green—funny, I suppose they think they have to give you your money's worth—and looking around I saw the house was half empty—and I guessed the girl had been right, the big picture wasn't going to be much, and that's why nobody much was there.

Just before the hall went dark again she came sauntering down the aisle. She had a tray of ice-creams, but she didn't even bother to call them out and try and sell them. She could have been walking in her sleep, so when she went up the other aisle I beckoned to her.

"Got a sixpenny one?" I said.

She looked across at me. I might have been something dead under her feet, and then she must have recognized me, because that half-smile came back again, and the lazy look in the eye, and she walked round the back of the seats to me.

"Wafer or cornet?" she said.

I didn't want either, to tell the truth. I just wanted to buy something from her and keep her talking.

"Which do you recommend?" I asked.

She shrugged her shoulders. "Cornets last longer," she said, and put one in my hand before I had time to give her my choice.

"How about one for you too?" I said.

"No thanks," she said, "I saw them made."

And she walked off, and the place went dark, and there I was sitting with a great sixpenny cornet in my hand looking a fool. The damn thing slopped all over the edge of the holder, spilling on to my shirt, and I had to ram the frozen stuff into my mouth as quick as I could for fear it would all go on my knees, and I turned sideways, because someone came and sat in the empty seat beside the gangway.

I finished it at last, and cleaned myself up with my pocket handkerchief, and then concentrated on the story flashing across the screen. It was a western all right, carts lumbering over prairies, and a train full of bullion being held to ransom, and the heroine in breeches one moment and full evening dress the next. That's the way pictures should be, not a bit like real life at all; but as I watched the story I began to notice the whiff of scent in the air, and I didn't know what it was or where it came from, but it was there just the same. There was a man to the right of me, and on my left were two empty seats, and it certainly wasn't the people in front, and I couldn't keep turning round and sniffing.

I'm not a great one for liking scent. It's too often cheap and nasty, but this was different. There was nothing stale about it, or stuffy, or strong; it was like the flowers they sell up in the West End in the big flower shops before you get them on the barrows—three bob a bloom sort of touch, rich chaps buy them for actresses and such—and it was so darn good, the smell of it there, in that murky old picture palace full of cigarette smoke, that it nearly drove me mad.

At last I turned right round in my seat, and I spotted where it came from. It came from the girl, the usherette; she was leaning on the back board behind me, her arms folded across it.

"Don't fidget," she said. "You're wasting one and twopence. Watch the screen."

But not out loud, so that anyone could hear. In a whisper, for me alone. I couldn't help laughing to myself. The cheek of it! I knew where the scent came from now, and somehow it made me enjoy the picture more. It was as though she was beside me in one of the empty seats and we were looking at the story together.

When it was over, and the lights went on, I saw I'd sat through the last showing and it was nearly ten. Everyone was clearing off for the night. So I waited a bit, and then she came down with her torch and started squinting under the seats to see if anybody had dropped a glove or a purse, the way they do and only remember about afterwards when they get home, and she took no more notice of me than if I'd been a rag which no one would bother to pick up.

I stood up in the back row, alone—the house was clear now—and when she came to me she said, "Move over, you're blocking the gangway," and flashed about with her torch, but there was nothing there, only an empty packet of Player's which the cleaners would throw away in the morning. Then she straightened herself and looked me up and down, and taking off the ridiculous cap from the back of her head that suited her so well she fanned herself with it and said, "Sleeping here tonight?" and then went off, whistling under her breath, and disappeared through the curtains.

It was proper maddening. I'd never been taken so much with a girl in my life. I went into the vestibule after her, but she had gone through a door to the back, behind the box-office place, and the commissionaire chap was already getting the doors to and fixing them for the night. I went out and stood in the street and waited. I felt a bit of a fool, because the odds were that she would come out with a bunch of others, the way girls do. There was the one who had sold me my ticket, and I dare say there were other usherettes up in the balcony, and perhaps a cloak-room attendant too, and they'd all be giggling together, and I wouldn't have the nerve to go up to her.

In a few minutes, though, she came swinging out of the place alone. She had a mac on, belted, and her hands in her pockets, and she had no hat. She walked straight up the street, and she didn't look to right or left of her. I followed, scared that she would turn round and see me off, but she went on walking, fast and direct, staring straight in front of her, and as she moved her copper page-boy hair swung with her shoulders.

Presently she hesitated, then crossed over and stood waiting for a bus. There was a queue of four or five people, so she didn't see me join the queue, and when the bus came she climbed on to it, ahead of the others, and I climbed too, without the slightest notion where it was going, and I couldn't have cared less. Up the stairs she went with me after her, and settled herself in the back seat, yawning, and closed her eyes.

I sat myself down beside her, nervous as a kitten, the point being that I never did that sort of thing as a rule and expected a rocket, and when the conductor stumped up and asked for fares I said, "Two sixpennies, please," because I reckoned she would never be going the whole distance and this would be bound to cover her fare and mine too.

He raised his eyebrows—they like to think themselves smart, some of these fellows—and he said, "Look out for the bumps when the driver changes gear. He's only just passed his test." And he went down the stairs chuckling, telling himself he was no end of a wag, no doubt.

The sound of his voice woke the girl, and she looked at me out of her sleepy eyes, and looked too at the tickets in my hand—she must have seen by the colour they were sixpennies—and she smiled, the first real smile I had got out of her that evening, and said without any sort of surprise, "Hullo, stranger."

I took out a cigarette, to put myself at ease, and offered her one, but she wouldn't take it. She just closed her eyes again, to settle herself to sleep. Then, seeing there was no one else to notice up on the top deck, only an Air Force chap in the front slopped over a newspaper, I put out my hand and pulled her head down on my shoulder, and got my arm round her, snug and comfortable, thinking of course she'd throw it off and blast me to hell. She didn't though. She gave a sort of laugh to herself, and settled down like as if she might have been in an armchair, and she said, "It's not every night I get a free ride and a free pillow. Wake me at the bottom of the hill, before we get to the cemetery."

I didn't know what hill she meant, or what cemetery, but I wasn't going to wake her, not me. I had paid for two sixpennies, and I was darn well going to get value for my money.

So we sat there together, jogging along in the bus, very close and very pleasant, and I thought to myself that it was a lot more fun than sitting at home in the bed-sit reading the football news, or spending an evening up Highgate at Mr and Mrs Thompson's daughter's place.

Presently I got more daring, and let my head lean against hers, and tightened up my arm a bit, not too obvious-like, but nicely. Anyone coming up the stairs to the top deck would have taken us for a courting couple.

Then, after we had had about fourpenny-worth, I got anxious. The old bus wouldn't be turning round and going back again, when we reached the sixpenny limit; it would pack up for the night, we'd have come to the terminus. And there we'd be, the girl and I, stuck out somewhere at the back of beyond, with no return bus, and I'd got about six bob in my pocket and no more. Six bob would never pay for a taxi, not with a tip and all. Besides, there probably wouldn't be any taxis going.

What a fool I'd been not to come out with more money. It was silly, perhaps, to let it worry me, but I'd acted on impulse right from the start, and if only I'd known how the evening was going to turn out I'd have had my wallet filled. It wasn't often I went out with a girl, and I hate a fellow who can't do the thing in style. Proper slap-up do at a Corner House—they're good these days with that help-yourself service—and if she had a fancy for something stronger than coffee or orangeade, well, of course as late as this it wasn't much use, but nearer home I knew where to go. There was a pub where my boss went, and you paid for your gin and kept it there, and could go in and have a drink from your bottle when you felt like it. They have the same sort of racket at the posh night clubs up West, I'm told, but they make you pay through the nose for it.

Anyway, here I was riding a bus to the Lord knows where, with my girl beside me—I called her "my girl" just as if she really was and we were courting—and bless me if I had the money to take her home. I began to fidget about, from sheer nerves, and I fumbled in one pocket after another, in case by a piece of luck I should come across a half-crown, or even a ten-bob note I had forgotten all about, and I suppose I disturbed her with all this, because she suddenly pulled my ear and said, "Stop rocking the boat."

Well, I mean to say… It just got me. I can't explain why. She held my ear a moment before she pulled it, like as though she were feeling the skin and liked it, and then she just gave it a lazy tug. It's the kind of thing anyone would do to a child, and the way she said it, as if she had known me for years and we were out picnicking together, "Stop rocking the boat." Chummy, matey, yet better than either.

"Look here," I said, "I'm awfully sorry, I've been and done a darn silly thing. I took tickets to the terminus because I wanted to sit beside you, and when we get there we'll be turned out of the bus, and it will be miles from anywhere, and I've only got six bob in my pocket."

"You've got legs, haven't you?" she said.

"What d'you mean, I've got legs?"

"They're meant to walk on. Mine were," she answered.

Then I knew it didn't matter, and she wasn't angry either, and the evening was going to be all right. I cheered up in a second, and gave her a squeeze, just to show I appreciated her being such a sport—most girls would have torn me to shreds—and I said, "We haven't passed a cemetery, as far as I know. Does it matter very much?"

"Oh, there'll be others," she said. "I'm not particular."

I didn't know what to make of that. I thought she wanted to get out at the cemetery stopping point because it was her nearest stop for home, like the way you say, "Put me down at Woolworth's" if you live handy. I puzzled over it for a bit, and then I said, "How do you mean, there'll be others? It's not a thing you see often along a bus route."

"I was speaking in general terms," she answered. "Don't bother to talk, I like you silent best."

It wasn't a slap on the face, the way she said it. Fact was, I knew what she meant. Talking's all very pleasant with people like Mr and Mrs Thompson, over supper, and you say how the day has gone, and one of you reads a bit out of the paper, and the other says, "Fancy, there now," and so it goes on, in bits and pieces until one of you yawns, and somebody says, "Who's for bed?" Or it's nice enough with a chap like the boss, having a cuppa midmorning, or about three when there's nothing doing, "I'll tell you what I think, those blokes in the government are making a mess of things, no better than the last lot," and then we'll be interrupted with someone coming to fill up with petrol. And I like talking to my old Mum when I go and see her, which I don't do often enough, and she tells me how she spanked my bottom when I was a kid, and I sit on the kitchen table like I did then, and she bakes rock cakes and gives me peel, saying, "You always were one for peel." That's talk, that's conversation.

But I didn't want to talk to my girl. I just wanted to keep my arm round her the way I was doing, and rest my chin against her head, and that's what she meant when she said she liked me silent. I liked it too.

One last thing bothered me a bit, and that was whether I could kiss her before the bus stopped and we were turned out at the terminus. I mean, putting an arm round a girl is one thing, and kissing her is another. It takes a little time as a rule to warm up. You start off with a long evening ahead of you, and by the time you've been to a picture or a concert, and then had something to eat and to drink, well, you've got yourselves acquainted, and it's the usual thing to end up with a bit of kissing and a cuddle, the girls expect it. Truth to tell, I was never much of a one for kissing. There was a girl I walked out with back home, before I went into the army, and she was quite a good sort, I liked her. But her teeth were a bit prominent, and even if you shut your eyes and tried to forget who it was you were kissing, well, you knew it was her, and there was nothing to it. Good old Doris from next door. But the opposite kind are even worse, the ones that grab you and nearly eat you. You come across plenty of them, when you're in uniform. They're much too eager, and they muss you about, and you get the feeling they can't wait for a chap to get busy about them. I don't mind saying it used to make me sick. Put me dead off, and that's a fact. I suppose I was born fussy. I don't know.

But now, this evening in the bus, it was all quite different. I don't know what it was about the girl—the sleepy eyes, and the copper hair, and somehow not seeming to care if I was there yet liking me at the same time; I hadn't found anything like this before. So I said to myself, "Now, shall I risk it, or shall I wait?", and I knew, from the way the driver was going and the conductor was whistling below and saying "goodnight" to the people getting off, that the final stop couldn't be far away; and my heart began to thump under my coat, and my neck grew hot below the collar—darn silly, only a kiss you know, she couldn't kill me—and then... It was like diving off a spring-board. I thought, "Here goes," and I bent down, and turned her face to me, and lifted her chin with my hand, and kissed her good and proper.

Well, if I was poetical, I'd say what happened then was a revelation. But I'm not poetical, and I can only say that she kissed me back, and it lasted a long time, and it wasn't a bit like Doris.

Then the bus stopped with a jerk, and the conductor called out in a sing-song voice, "All out, please." Frankly, I could have wrung his neck.

She gave me a kick on the ankle. "Come on, move," she said, and I stumbled from my seat and racketed down the stairs, she following behind, and there we were, standing in a street. It was beginning to rain too, not badly but just enough to make you notice and want to turn up the collar of your coat, and we were right at the end of a great wide street, with deserted unlighted shops on either side, the end of the world it looked to me, and sure enough there was a hill over to the left, and at the bottom of the hill a cemetery. I could see the railings and the white tombstones behind, and it stretched a long way, nearly half-way up the hill. There were acres of it.

"God darn it," I said, "is this the place you meant?"

"Could be," she said, looking over her shoulder vaguely, and then she took my arm. "What about a cup of coffee first?" she said.

First...? I wondered if she meant before the long trudge home, or was this home? It didn't really matter. It wasn't much after eleven. And I could do with a cup of coffee, and a sandwich too. There was a stall across the road, and they hadn't shut up shop.

We walked over to it, and the driver was there too, and the conductor, and the Air Force fellow who had been up in front on the top deck. They were ordering cups of tea and sandwiches, and we had the same, only coffee. They cut them tasty at the stalls, the sandwiches, I've noticed it before, nothing stingy about it, good slices of ham between thick white bread, and the coffee is piping hot, full cups too, good value, and I thought to myself "Six bob will see this lot all right."

I noticed my girl looking at the Air Force chap, sort of thoughtful-like, as though she might have seen him before, and he looked at her too. I couldn't blame him for that. I didn't mind either; when you're out with a girl it gives you a kind of pride if other chaps notice her. And you couldn't miss this one. Not my girl.

Then she turned her back on him, deliberate, and leant with her elbows on the stall, sipping her hot coffee, and I stood beside her doing the same. We weren't stuck up or anything, we were pleasant and polite enough, saying good evening all round, but anyone could tell that we were together, the girl and I, we were on our own. I liked that. Funny, it did something to me inside, gave me a protective feeling. For all they knew we might have been a married couple on our way home.

They were chaffing a bit, the other three and the chap serving the sandwiches and tea, but we didn't join in.

"You want to watch out, in that uniform," said the conductor to the Air Force fellow, "or you'll end up like those others. It's late too, to be out on your own."

They all started laughing. I didn't quite see the point, but I supposed it was a joke.

"I've been awake a long time," said the Air Force fellow. "I know a bad lot when I see one."

"That's what the others said, I shouldn't wonder," remarked the driver, "and we know what happened to them. Makes you shudder. But why pick on the Air Force, that's what I want to know?"

"It's the colour of our uniform," said the fellow. "You can spot it in the dark."

They went on laughing in that way. I lighted up a cigarette, but my girl wouldn't have one.

"I blame the war for all that's gone wrong with the women," said the coffee-stall bloke, wiping a cup and hanging it up behind. "Turned a lot of them barmy, in my opinion. They don't know the difference between right or wrong."

"'Tisn't that, it's sport that's the trouble," said the conductor. "Develops their muscles and that, what weren't never meant to be developed. Take my two youngsters, f'r instance. The girl can knock the boy down any time, she's a proper little bully. Makes you think."

"That's right," agreed the driver, "equality of the sexes, they call it, don't they? It's the vote that did it. We ought never to have given them the vote."

"Garn," said the Air Force chap, "giving them the vote didn't turn the women barmy. They've always been the same, under the skin. The people out East know how to treat 'em. They keep 'em shut up, out there. That's the answer. Then you don't get any trouble."

"I don't know what my old woman would say if I tried to shut her up," said the driver. And they all started laughing again.

My girl plucked at my sleeve and I saw she had finished her coffee. She motioned with her head towards the street.

"Want to go home?" I said.

Silly, I somehow wanted the others to believe we were going home. She didn't answer. She just went striding off, her hands in the pockets of her mac. I said goodnight, and followed her, but not before I noticed the Air Force fellow staring after her over his cup of tea.

She walked off along the street, and it was still raining, dreary somehow, made you want to be sitting over a fire somewhere snug, and when she had crossed the street, and had come to the railings outside the cemetery she stopped, and looked up at me, and smiled.

"What now?" I said.

"Tombstones are flat," she said, "sometimes."

"What if they are?" I asked, bewildered-like.

"You can lie down on them," she said.

She turned and strolled along, looking at the railings, and then she came to one that was bent wide, and the next beside it broken, and she glanced up at me and smiled again.

"It's always the same," she said. "You're bound to find a gap if you look long enough."

She was through that gap in the railings as quick as a knife through butter. You could have knocked me flat.

"Here, hold on," I said, "I'm not as small as you."

But she was off and away, wandering among the graves. I got through the gap, puffing and blowing a bit, and then I looked around, and bless me if she wasn't lying on a long flat gravestone, with her arms under her head and her eyes closed.

Well, I wasn't expecting anything. I mean, it had been in my mind to see her home and that. Date her up for the next evening. Of course, seeing as it was late, we could have stopped a bit when we came to the doorway of her place. She needn't have gone in right away. But lying there on the gravestone wasn't hardly natural.

I sat down, and took her hand.

"You'll get wet lying there," I said. Feeble, but I didn't know what else to say.

"I'm used to that," she said.

She opened her eyes and looked at me. There was a street light not far away, outside the railings, so it wasn't all that dark, and anyway in spite of the rain the night wasn't pitch black, more murky somehow. I wish I knew how to tell about her eyes, but I'm not one for fancy talk. You know how a luminous watch shines in the dark. I've got one myself. When you wake up in the night, there it is on your wrist, like a friend. Somehow my girl's eyes shone like that, but they were lovely too. And they weren't lazy cat's eyes any more. They were loving and gentle, and they were sad, too, all at the same time.

"Used to lying in the rain?" I said.

"Brought up to it," she answered. "They gave us a name in the shelters. The dead-end kids, they used to call us, in the war days."

"Weren't you never evacuated?" I asked.

"Not me," she said. "I never could stop any place. I always came back."

"Parents living?"

"No. Both of them killed by the bomb that smashed my home."
She didn't speak tragic-like. Just ordinary.

"Bad luck," I said.

She didn't answer that one. And I sat there, holding her hand,
wanting to take her home.

"You been on your job some time, at the picture-house?" I asked.

"About three weeks," she said. "I don't stop anywhere long. I'll
be moving on again soon."

"Why's that?"

"Restless," she said.

She put up her hands suddenly and took my face and held it. It
was gentle the way she did it, not as you'd think.

"You've got a good kind face. I like it," she said to me.

It was queer. The way she said it made me feel daft and soft, not
sort of excited like I had been in the bus, and I thought to myself,
well, maybe this is it, I've found a girl at last I really want. But not
for an evening, casual. For going steady.

"Got a bloke?" I asked.

"No," she said.

"I mean, regular."

"No, never."

It was a funny line of talk to be having in a cemetery, and she
lying there like some figure carved on the old tombstone.

"I haven't got a girl either," I said. "Never think about it, the way
other chaps do. Faddy, I guess. And then I'm keen on my job. Work
in a garage, mechanic you know, repairs, anything that's going. Good
pay. I've saved a bit, besides what I send my old Mum. I live in digs.
Nice people, Mr and Mrs Thompson, and my boss at the garage is
a nice chap too. I've never been lonely, and I'm not lonely now. But
since I've seen you, it's made me think. You know, it's not going to
be the same any more."

She never interrupted once, and somehow it was like speaking my thoughts aloud.

"Going home to the Thompsons is all very pleasant and nice," I said, "and you couldn't wish for kinder people. Good grub too, and we chat a bit after supper, and listen to the wireless. But d'you know, what I want now is different. I want to come along and fetch you from the cinema, when the programme's over, and you'd be standing there by the curtains, seeing the people out, and you'd give me a bit of a wink to show me you'd be going through to change your clothes and I could wait for you. And then you'd come out into the street, like you did tonight, but you wouldn't go off on your own, you'd take my arm, and if you didn't want to wear your coat I'd carry it for you, or a parcel maybe, or whatever you had. Then we'd go off to the Corner House or some place for supper, handy. We'd have a table reserved—they'd know us, the waitresses and them; they'd keep back something special, just for us."

I could picture it too, clear as anything. The table with the ticket on "Reserved". The waitress nodding at us, "Got curried eggs tonight." And we going through to get our trays, and my girl acting like she didn't know me, and me laughing to myself.

"D'you see what I mean?" I said to her. "It's not just being friends, it's more than that."

I don't know if she heard. She lay there looking up at me, touching my ear and my chin in that funny, gentle way. You'd say she was sorry for me.

"I'd like to buy you things," I said, "flowers sometimes. It's nice to see a girl with a flower tucked in her dress, it looks clean and fresh. And for special occasions, birthdays, Christmas, and that, something you'd seen in a shop window, and wanted, but hadn't liked to go in and ask the price. A brooch perhaps, or a bracelet, something pretty. And I'd go in and get it when you weren't with me, and it'd cost much more than my week's pay, but I wouldn't mind."

I could see the expression on her face, opening the parcel. And she'd put it on, what I'd bought, and we'd go out together, and she'd be dressed up a bit for the purpose, nothing glaring I don't mean, but something that took the eye. You know, saucy.

"It's not fair to talk about getting married," I said, "not in these days, when everything's uncertain. A fellow doesn't mind the uncertainty, but it's hard on a girl. Cooped up in a couple of rooms maybe, and queueing and rations and all. They like their freedom, and being in a job, and not being tied down, the same as us. But it's nonsense the way they were talking back in the coffee stall just now. About girls not being the same as in old days, and the war to blame. As for the way they treat them out East—I've seen some of it. I suppose that fellow meant to be funny, they're all smart Alicks in the Air Force, but it was a silly line of talk, I thought."

She dropped her hands to her side and closed her eyes. It was getting quite wet there on the tombstone. I was worried for her, though she had her mac of course, but her legs and feet were damp in her thin stockings and shoes.

"You weren't ever in the Air Force, were you?" she said.

Queer. Her voice had gone quite hard. Sharp, and different. Like as if she was anxious about something, scared even.

"Not me," I said, "I served my time with REME. Proper lot they were. No swank, no nonsense. You know where you are with them."

"I'm glad," she said. "You're good and kind. I'm glad."

I wondered if she'd known some fellow in the RAF who had let her down. They're a wild crowd, the ones I've come across. And I remembered the way she'd looked at the boy drinking his tea at the stall. Reflective, somehow. As if she was thinking back. I couldn't expect her not to have been around a bit, with her looks, and then brought up to play about the shelters, without parents, like she said. But I didn't want to think of her being hurt by anyone.

"Why, what's wrong with them?" I said. "What's the RAF done to you?"

"They smashed my home," she said.

"That was the Germans, not our fellows."

"It's all the same, they're killers, aren't they?" she said.

I looked down at her, lying on the tombstone, and her voice wasn't hard any more, like when she'd asked me if I'd been in the Air Force, but it was tired, and sad, and oddly lonely, and it did something queer to my stomach, right in the pit of it, so that I wanted to do the darnd-est silliest thing and take her home with me, back to where I lived with Mr and Mrs Thompson, and say to Mrs Thompson—she was a kind old soul, she wouldn't mind—"Look, this is my girl. Look after her." Then I'd know she'd be safe, she'd be all right, nobody could do anything to hurt her. That was the thing I was afraid of suddenly, that someone would come along and hurt my girl.

I bent down and put my arms round her and lifted her up close.

"Listen," I said, "it's raining hard. I'm going to take you home. You'll catch your death, lying here on the wet stone."

"No," she said, her hands on my shoulders, "nobody ever sees me home. You're going back where you belong, alone."

"I won't leave you here," I said.

"Yes, that's what I want you to do. If you refuse I shall be angry. You wouldn't want that, would you?"

I stared at her, puzzled. And her face was queer in the murky old light there, whiter than before, but it was beautiful, Jesus Christ, it was beautiful. That's blasphemy. But I can't say it no other way.

"What do you want me to do?" I asked.

"I want you to go and leave me here, and not look back," she said, "like someone dreaming, sleep-walking, they call it. Go back walking through the rain. It will take you hours. It doesn't matter, you're young and strong and you've got long legs. Go back to your room, wherever it is, and get into bed, and go to sleep, and wake and have your breakfast in the morning, and go off to work, the same as you always do."

"What about you?"

"Never mind about me. Just go."

"Can I call for you at the cinema tomorrow night? Can it be like what I was telling you, you know… going steady?"

She didn't answer. She only smiled. She sat quite still, looking in my face, and then she closed her eyes and threw back her head and said, "Kiss me again, stranger."

I left her, like she said. I didn't look back. I climbed through the railings of the cemetery, out on to the road. No one seemed to be about, and the coffee stall by the bus stop had closed down, the boards were up.

I started walking the way the bus had brought us. The road was straight, going on for ever. A High Street it must have been. There were shops on either side, and it was right away north-east of London, nowhere I'd ever been before. I was proper lost, but it didn't seem to matter. I felt like a sleep-walker, just as she said.

I kept thinking of her all the time. There was nothing else, only her face in front of me as I walked. They had a word for it in the army, when a girl gets a fellow that way, so he can't see straight or hear right or know what he's doing; and I thought it a lot of cock, or it only happened to drunks, and now I knew it was true and it had happened to me. I wasn't going to worry any more about how she'd get home; she'd told me not to, and she must have lived handy, she'd never have ridden out so far else, though it was funny living such a way from her work. But maybe in time she'd tell me more, bit by bit. I wouldn't drag it from her. I had one thing fixed in my mind, and that was to pick her up the next evening from the picture palace. It was firm and set, and nothing would budge me from that. The hours in between would just be a blank for me until ten p.m. came round.

I went on walking in the rain, and presently a lorry came along and I thumbed a lift, and the driver took me a good part of the way before he had to turn left in the other direction, and so I got down and walked again, and it must have been close on three when I got home.

I would have felt bad, in an ordinary way, knocking up Mr Thompson to let me in, and it had never happened before either, but I was all lit up inside from loving my girl, and I didn't seem to mind. He came down at last and opened the door. I had to ring several times before he heard, and there he was, grey with sleep, poor old chap, his pyjamas all crumpled from the bed.

"Whatever happened to you?" he said. "We've been worried, the wife and me. We thought you'd been knocked down, run over. We came back here and found the house empty and your supper not touched."

"I went to the pictures," I said.

"The pictures?" He stared up at me, in the passage-way. "The pictures stop at ten o'clock."

"I know," I said, "I went walking after that. Sorry. Goodnight."

And I climbed up the stairs to my room, leaving the old chap muttering to himself and bolting the door, and I heard Mrs Thompson calling from her bedroom, "What is it? Is it him? Is he come home?"

I'd put them to trouble and to worry, and I ought to have gone in there and then and apologized, but I couldn't somehow, it wouldn't have come right; so I shut my door and threw off my clothes and got into bed, and it was like as if she was with me still, my girl, in the darkness.

They were a bit quiet at breakfast the next morning, Mr and Mrs Thompson. They didn't look at me. Mrs Thompson gave me my kipper without a word, and he went on looking at his newspaper.

I ate my breakfast, and then I said, "I hope you had a nice evening up at Highgate?" and Mrs Thompson, with her mouth a bit tight, she said, "Very pleasant, thank you, we were home by ten," and she gave a little sniff and poured Mr Thompson out another cup of tea.

We went on being quiet, no one saying a word, and then Mrs Thompson said, "Will you be in to supper this evening?" and I said, "No, I don't think so. I'm meeting a friend," and then I saw the old chap look at me over his spectacles.

"If you're going to be late," he said, "we'd best take the key for you."

Then he went on reading his paper. You could tell they were proper hurt that I didn't tell them anything, or say where I was going.

I went off to work, and we were busy at the garage that day, one job after the other came along, and any other time I wouldn't have minded. I liked a full day and often worked overtime, but today I wanted to get away before the shops closed; I hadn't thought about anything else since the idea came into my head.

It was getting on for half past four, and the boss came to me and said, "I promised the doctor he'd have his Austin this evening, I said you'd be through with it by seven-thirty. That's O.K., isn't it?"

My heart sank. I'd counted on getting off early, because of what I wanted to do. Then I thought quickly that if the boss let me off now, and I went out to the shop before it closed, and came back again to do the job on the Austin, it would be all right, so I said, "I don't mind working a bit of overtime, but I'd like to slip out now, for half an hour, if you're going to be here. There's something I want to buy before the shops shut."

He told me that suited him, so I took off my overalls and washed and got my coat and I went off to the line of shops down at the

bottom of Haverstock Hill. I knew the one I wanted. It was a jeweller's, where Mr Thompson used to take his clock to be repaired, and
it wasn't a place where they sold trash at all, but good stuff, solid
silver frames and that, and cutlery.

There were rings, of course, and a few fancy bangles, but I didn't
like the look of them. All the girls in the NAAFI used to wear bangles
with charms on them, quite common it was, and I went on staring
in at the window and then I spotted it, right at the back.

It was a brooch. Quite small, not much bigger than your thumb-
nail, but with a nice blue stone on it and a pin at the back, and it was
shaped like a heart. That was what got me, the shape. I stared at it a
bit, and there wasn't a ticket to it, which meant it would cost a bit,
but I went in and asked to have a look at it. The jeweller got it out
of the window for me, and he gave it a bit of a polish and turned it
this way and that, and I saw it pinned on my girl, showing up nice
on her frock or her jumper, and I knew this was it.

"I'll take it," I said, and then asked him the price.

I swallowed a bit when he told me, but I took out my wallet and
counted the notes, and he put the heart in a box wrapped up careful
with cotton wool, and made a neat package of it, tied with fancy
string. I knew I'd have to get an advance from the boss before I went
off work that evening, but he was a good chap and I was certain he'd
give it to me.

I stood outside the jeweller's, with the packet for my girl safe in
my breast pocket, and I heard the church clock strike a quarter to
five. There was time to slip down to the cinema and make sure she
understood about the date for the evening, and then I'd beat it fast
up the road and get back to the garage, and I'd have the Austin done
by the time the doctor wanted it.

When I got to the cinema my heart was beating like a sledgeham-
mer and I could hardly swallow. I kept picturing to myself how she'd

look, standing there by the curtains going in, with the velvet jacket and the cap on the back of her head.

There was a bit of a queue outside, and I saw they'd changed the programme. The poster of the western had gone, with the cowboy throwing a knife in the Indian's guts, and they had instead a lot of girls dancing, and some chap prancing in front of them with a walking-stick. It was a musical.

I went in, and didn't go near the box office but looked straight to the curtains, where she'd be. There was an usherette there all right, but it wasn't her. This was a great tall girl, who looked silly in the clothes, and she was trying to do two things at once—tear off the slips of tickets as the people went past, and hang on to her torch at the same time.

I waited a moment. Perhaps they'd switched over positions and my girl had gone up to the circle. When the last lot had got in through the curtains and there was a pause and she was free, I went up to her and I said, "Excuse me, do you know where I could have a word with the other young lady?"

She looked at me. "What other young lady?"

"The one who was here last night, with copper hair," I said. She looked at me closer then, suspicious-like.

"She hasn't shown up today," she said. "I'm taking her place."

"Not shown up?"

"No. And it's funny you should ask. You're not the only one. The police was here not long ago. They had a word with the manager, and the commissionaire too, and no one's said anything to me yet, but I think there's been trouble."

My heart beat different then. Not excited, bad. Like when someone's ill, took to hospital, sudden.

"The police?" I said. "What were they here for?"

"I told you, I don't know," she answered, "but it was something to do with her, and the manager went with them to the police station, and he hasn't come back yet. This way, please, circle on the left, stalls to the right."

I just stood there, not knowing what to do. It was like as if the floor had been knocked away from under me.

The tall girl tore another slip off a ticket and then she said to me, over her shoulder, "Was she a friend of yours?"

"Sort of," I said. I didn't know what to say.

"Well, if you ask me, she was queer in the head, and it wouldn't surprise me if she'd done away with herself and they'd found her dead. No, ice-creams served in the interval, after the news reel."

I went out and stood in the street. The queue was growing for the cheaper seats, and there were children too, talking, excited. I brushed past them and started walking up the street, and I felt sick inside, queer. Something had happened to my girl. I knew it now. That was why she had wanted to get rid of me last night, and for me not to see her home. She was going to do herself in, there in the cemetery. That's why she talked funny and looked so white, and now they'd found her, lying there on the gravestone by the railings.

If I hadn't gone away and left her she'd have been all right. If I'd stayed with her just five minutes longer, coaxing her, I'd have got her round to my way of thinking and seen her home, standing no nonsense, and she'd be at the picture palace now, showing the people to their seats.

It might be it wasn't as bad as what I feared. It might be she was found wandering, lost her memory and got picked up by the police and taken off, and then they found out where she worked and that, and now the police wanted to check up with the manager at the cinema to see if it was so. If I went down to the police station and asked them there, maybe they'd tell me what had happened, and I could say she was my girl, we were walking out, and it wouldn't matter if she didn't recognize me even, I'd stick to the story. I couldn't let down my boss, I had to get that job done on the Austin, but afterwards, when I'd finished, I could go down to the police station.

All the heart had gone out of me, and I went back to the garage hardly knowing what I was doing, and for the first time ever the smell of the place turned my stomach, the oil and the grease, and there was a chap roaring up his engine, before backing out his car, and a great cloud of smoke coming from his exhaust, filling the workshop with stink.

I went and got my overalls, and put them on, and fetched the tools, and started on the Austin, and all the time I was wondering what it was that had happened to my girl, if she was down at the police station, lost and lonely, or if she was lying somewhere... dead. I kept seeing her face all the time like it was last night.

It took me an hour and a half, not more, to get the Austin ready for the road, filled up with petrol and all, and I had her facing out-wards to the street for the owner to drive out, but I was all in by then, dead tired, and the sweat pouring down my face. I had a bit of a wash and put on my coat, and I felt the package in the breast pocket. I took it out and looked at it, done so neat with the fancy ribbon, and I put it back again, and I hadn't noticed the boss come in—I was standing with my back to the door.

"Did you get what you wanted?" he said, cheerful-like and smiling.

He was a good chap, never out of temper, and we got along well. "Yes," I said.

But I didn't want to talk about it. I told him the job was done and the Austin was ready to drive away. I went to the office with him so that he could note down the work done, and the overtime, and he offered me a fag from the packet lying on his desk beside the evening paper.

"I see Lady Luck won the three-thirty," he said. "I'm a couple of quid up this week."

He was entering my work in his ledger, to keep the pay-roll right.

"Good for you," I said.

"Only backed it for a place, like a clot," he said. "She was twenty-five to one. Still, it's all in the game."

I didn't answer. I'm not one for drinking, but I needed one bad, just then. I mopped my forehead with my handkerchief. I wished he'd get on with the figures, and say goodnight, and let me go.

"Another poor devil's had it," he said. "That's the third now in three weeks, ripped right up the guts, same as the others. He died in hospital this morning. Looks like there's a hoodoo on the RAF."

"What was it, flying jets?" I asked.

"Jets?" he said. "No, damn it, murder. Sliced up the belly, poor sod. Don't you ever read the papers? It's the third one in three weeks, done identical, all Air Force fellows, and each time they've found 'em near a graveyard or a cemetery. I was saying just now, to that chap who came in for petrol, it's not only men who go off their rockers and turn sex maniacs, but women too. They'll get this one all right though, you see. It says in the paper they've a line on her, and expect an arrest shortly. About time too, before another poor blighter cops it."

He shut up his ledger and stuck his pencil behind his ear.

"Like a drink?" he said. "I've got a bottle of gin in the cupboard."

"No," I said, "no, thanks very much. I've… I've got a date."

"That's right," he said, smiling, "enjoy yourself."

I walked down the street and bought an evening paper. It was like what he said about the murder. They had it on the front page. They said it must have happened about two a.m. Young fellow in the Air Force, in north-east London. He had managed to stagger to a call-box and get through to the police, and they found him there on the floor of the box when they arrived.

He made a statement in the ambulance before he died. He said a girl called to him, and he followed her, and he thought it was just a bit of love-making—he'd seen her with another fellow drinking coffee at a stall a little while before—and he thought she'd thrown this other fellow over and had taken a fancy to him, and then she got him, he said, right in the guts.

It said in the paper that he had given the police a full description of her, and it said also that the police would be glad if the man who had been seen with the girl earlier in the evening would come forward to help in identification.

I didn't want the paper any more. I threw it away. I walked about the streets till I was tired, and when I guessed Mr and Mrs Thompson had gone to bed I went home, and groped for the key they'd left on a piece of string hanging inside the letterbox, and I let myself in and went upstairs to my room.

Mrs Thompson had turned down the bed and put a thermos of tea for me, thoughtful-like, and the evening paper, the late edition.

They'd got her. About three o'clock in the afternoon. I didn't read the writing, nor the name nor anything. I sat down on my bed, and took up the paper, and there was my girl staring up at me from the front page.

Then I took the package from my coat and undid it, and threw away the wrapper and the fancy string, and sat there looking down at the little heart I held in my hand.

THE SCHOOL (1974)

Donald Barthelme

Donald Barthelme (1931–89) was an American short story writer
known for his playful, postmodernist style of fiction. He was born
in Philadelphia and studied journalism at the University of Houston.
During his career he wrote over one hundred short stories, many of
which first appeared in the *New Yorker*, and four novels. His stories
defy easy categorization, avoiding traditional plot structures and
instead relying on the steady accumulation of detail, much of which
initially appears unconnected.

'The School' is macabre and delightful in equal measure. The
story is awash with unfortunate deaths, each more tragic than the
last, but with a curious twist (or two) the narrative takes flight in
a totally different and unexpected direction. The end result is both
surreal and uplifting.

W ELL, WE HAD ALL THESE CHILDREN OUT PLANTING TREES, see, because we figured that… that was part of their education, to see how, you know, the root systems… and also the sense of responsibility, taking care of things, being individually responsible. You know what I mean. And the trees all died. They were orange trees. I don't know why they died, they just died. Something wrong with the soil possibly or maybe the stuff we got from the nursery wasn't the best. We complained about it. So we've got thirty kids there, each kid had his or her own little tree to plant, and we've got these thirty dead trees. All these kids looking at these little brown sticks, it was depressing.

It wouldn't have been so bad except that just a couple of weeks before the thing with the trees, the snakes all died. But I think that the snakes—well, the reason that the snakes kicked off was that… you remember, the boiler was shut off for four days because of the strike, and that was explicable. It was something you could explain to the kids because of the strike. I mean, none of their parents would let them cross the picket line and they knew there was a strike going on and what it meant. So when things got started up again and we found the snakes they weren't too disturbed.

With the herb gardens it was probably a case of overwatering, and at least now they know not to overwater. The children were very conscientious with the herb gardens and some of them probably… you know, slipped them a little extra water when we weren't looking. Or maybe… well, I don't like to think about sabotage, although it did occur to us. I mean, it was something that crossed our minds. We were thinking that way probably because before that the gerbils had died, and the white mice had died, and the salamander… well, now they know not to carry them around in plastic bags.

Of course we *expected* the tropical fish to die, that was no surprise. Those numbers, you look at them crooked and they're belly-up on the surface. But the lesson plan called for a tropical-fish input at that point; there was nothing we could do, it happens every year, you just have to hurry past it.

We weren't even supposed to have a puppy.

We weren't even supposed to have one, it was just a puppy the Murdoch girl found under a Gristede's truck one day and she was afraid the truck would run over it when the driver had finished making his delivery, so she stuck it in her knapsack and brought it to school with her. So we had this puppy. As soon as I saw the puppy I thought, Oh Christ, I bet it will live for about two weeks and then… And that's what it did. It wasn't supposed to be in the classroom at all, there's some kind of regulation about it, but you can't tell them they can't have a puppy when the puppy is already there, right in front of them, running around on the floor and yap yap yapping. They named it Edgar—that is, they named it after me. They had a lot of fun running after it and yelling, "Here, Edgar! Nice Edgar!" Then they'd laugh like hell. They enjoyed the ambiguity. I enjoyed it myself. I don't mind being kidded. They made a little house for it in the supply closet and all that. I don't know what it died of. Distemper, I guess. It probably hadn't had any shots. I got it out of there before the kids got to school. I checked the supply closet each morning, routinely, because I knew what was going to happen. I gave it to the custodian.

And then there was this Korean orphan that the class adopted through the Help the Children program, all the kids brought in a quarter a month, that was the idea. It was an unfortunate thing, the kid's name was Kim and maybe we adopted him too late or some-thing. The cause of death was not stated in the letter we got, they suggested we adopt another child instead and sent us some interesting case histories, but we didn't have the heart. The class took it pretty hard, they began (I think; nobody ever said anything to me directly) to feel that maybe there was something wrong with the school. But I don't think there's anything wrong with the school, particularly, I've seen better and I've seen worse. It was just a run of bad luck. We had an extraordinary number of parents passing away, for instance. There were I think two heart attacks and two suicides, one drowning, and four killed together in a car accident. One stroke. And we had the usual heavy mortality rate among the grandparents, or maybe it was heavier this year, it seemed so. And finally the tragedy.

The tragedy occurred when Matthew Wein and Tony Mavrogordo were playing over where they're excavating for the new federal office building. There were all these big wooden beams stacked, you know, at the edge of the excavation. There's a court case coming out of that, the parents are claiming that the beams were poorly stacked. I don't know what's true and what's not. It's been a strange year.

I forgot to mention Billy Brandt's father, who was knifed fatally when he grappled with a masked intruder in his home.

One day, we had a discussion in class. They asked me, where did they go? The trees, the salamander, the tropical fish, Edgar, the poppas and mommas, Matthew and Tony, where did they go? And I said, I don't know, I don't know. And they said, who knows? and I said, nobody knows. And they said, is death that which gives meaning to life? And I said, no, life is that which gives meaning to life. Then they said, but isn't death, considered as a fundamental datum, the means by which the taken-for-granted mundanity of the everyday may be transcended in the direction of—

I said, yes, maybe.

They said, we don't like it.

I said, that's sound.

They said, it's a bloody shame!

I said, it is.

They said, will you make love now with Helen (our teaching assistant) so that we can see how it is done? We know you like Helen.

I do like Helen but I said that I would not.

We've heard so much about it, they said, but we've never seen it.

I said I would be fired and that it was never, or almost never, done as a demonstration. Helen looked out of the window.

They said, please, please make love with Helen, we require an assertion of value, we are frightened.

I said that they shouldn't be frightened (although I am often frightened) and that there was value everywhere. Helen came and embraced me. I kissed her a few times on the brow. We held each other. The children were excited. Then there was a knock on the door, I opened the door, and the new gerbil walked in. The children cheered wildly.

DEATH BY SCRABBLE (2006)

Charlie Fish

Charlie Fish (1980–) is a short story writer and screenwriter. Born in Mount Kisco, New York, he now lives in South London.

'Death by Scrabble' is one of the funniest stories I have ever read and it feels right to end this anthology on a light note. Even so, as you read, you will find the story heading in some very dark directions. Scrabble always feels like a cerebral game, relying on an ability to combine a knowledge of vocabulary with an ability to work out all the possibilities for using those extra-point squares to the greatest effect. Surely this is a game made for the occasional gamble? Perhaps a game to be played for the highest stakes of all? As the story progresses, and as the tiles fall into place, just which of the competitors has the upper hand?

I T'S A HOT DAY AND I HATE MY WIFE.

We're playing Scrabble. That's how bad it is. I'm forty-two years old, it's a blistering hot Sunday afternoon and all I can think of to do with my life is play Scrabble.

I should be out, doing exercise, spending money, meeting people. I don't think I've spoken to anyone except my wife since Thursday morning. On Thursday morning I spoke to the milkman.

My letters are crap.

I play, appropriately, BEGIN. With the N on the little pink star. Twenty-two points.

I watch my wife's smug expression as she rearranges her letters. Clack, clack, clack. I hate her. If she wasn't around, I'd be doing something interesting right now. I'd be climbing Mount Kilimanjaro. I'd be starring in the latest Hollywood blockbuster. I'd be sailing the Vendée Globe on a sixty-foot clipper called New Horizons—I don't know, but I'd be doing something.

She plays JINXED, with the J on a double-letter score. Thirty points. She's beating me already. Maybe I should kill her.

If only I had a D, then I could play MURDER. That would be a sign. That would be permission.

I start chewing on my U. It's a bad habit, I know. All the letters are frayed. I play WARMER for twenty-two more points, mainly so I can keep chewing on my U.

As I'm picking new letters from the bag, I find myself thinking— the letters will tell me what to do. If they spell out KILL, or STAB, or her name, or anything, I'll do it right now. I'll finish her off.

My rack spells MIHZPA. Plus the U in my mouth. Damn.

The heat of the sun is pushing at me through the window. I can hear buzzing insects outside. I hope they're not bees. My cousin Harold swallowed a bee when he was nine, his throat swelled up and he died. I hope that if they are bees, they fly into my wife's throat.

She plays SWEATIER, using all her letters. Twenty-four points plus a fifty-point bonus. If it wasn't too hot to move I would strangle her right now.

I am getting sweatier. It needs to rain, to clear the air. As soon as that thought crosses my mind, I find a good word. HUMID on a double-word score, using the D of JINXED. The U makes a little splash of saliva when I put it down. Another twenty-two points. I hope she has lousy letters.

She tells me she has lousy letters. For some reason, I hate her more.

She plays FAN, with the F on a double letter, and gets up to fill the kettle and turn on the air conditioning.

It's the hottest day for ten years and my wife is turning on the kettle. This is why I hate my wife. I play ZAPS, with the Z doubled, and she gets a static shock off the air-conditioning unit. I find this remarkably satisfying.

She sits back down with a heavy sigh and starts fiddling with her letters again. Clack clack. Clack clack. I feel a terrible rage build up inside me. Some inner poison slowly spreading through my limbs, and when it gets to my fingertips I'm going to jump out of my chair, spilling the Scrabble tiles over the floor, and I'm going to start hitting her again and again and again.

The rage gets to my fingertips—and passes. My heart is beating. I'm sweating. I think my face actually twitches. Then I sigh, deeply, and sit back into my chair. The kettle starts whistling. As the whistle builds it makes me feel hotter.

She plays READY on a double word for eighteen points, then goes to pour herself a mug of tea. No I do not want one.

I steal a blank tile from the letter bag when she's not looking, and throw back a V from my rack. She gives me a suspicious look. She sits down with her tea, making a cup ring on the table, as I play an eight-letter word: CHEATING, using the A of READY. Sixty-four points, including the fifty-point bonus, which means I'm beating her now.

She asks me if I cheated.

I really, really hate her.

She plays IGNORE on the triple word for twenty-one points. The score is 153 to her, 155 to me.

The steam rising from her cup of tea makes me feel hotter. I try to make murderous words with the letters on my rack. If only there was some way for me to get rid of her.

I spot a chance to use all my letters. EXPLODES, using the X of JINXED. Seventy-two points. That'll show her.

As I put the last letter down, there is a deafening bang and the air-conditioning unit fails.

My heart is racing, but not from the shock of the bang. I don't believe it—but it can't be a coincidence. The letters made it happen. I played the word EXPLODES, and it happened—the air-conditioning unit exploded. And before, I played the word CHEATING when I cheated. And ZAP when my wife got the electric shock. The words are coming true. The letters are choosing their future. The whole game is—JINXED.

My wife plays SIGN for ten points.

I have to test this.

I have to play something and see if it happens. Something unlikely, to prove that the letters are making it happen. My rack is ABQYFWE. That doesn't leave me with a lot of options. I start frantically chewing on the B.

I play FLY, using the L of EXPLODES. I sit back and close my eyes, waiting for the sensation of rising up from my chair. Waiting to fly.

Stupid. I open my eyes, and there's a fly. Buzzing around above the Scrabble board, surfing the thermals from the tepid cup of tea. That proves nothing. The fly could have been there anyway.

I need to play something unambiguous. Something that cannot be misinterpreted. Something absolute and final.

My wife plays CAUTION, using a blank tile for the N. Eighteen points.

My rack is AQWEUK, plus the B in my mouth. I'm awed by the power of the letters, and frustrated that I can't wield it. Maybe I should cheat again, and pick out the letters I need to spell SLASH or SLAY.

Then it hits me. The perfect word. A powerful, dangerous, terrible word.

I play QUAKE for nineteen points.

I wonder if the strength of the quake will be proportionate to how many points it scored. I can feel the trembling energy of potential in my veins. I am commanding fate. I am manipulating destiny.

My wife plays DEATH for thirty-four points, just as the room starts to shake.

I gasp with surprise and vindication—and the B that I was chewing on gets lodged in my throat. I try to cough. My throat swells. I draw blood clawing at my neck. The earthquake builds to a climax.

I fall to the floor. My wife just sits there, watching.

BRITISH LIBRARY TALES OF THE WEIRD

*From the Depths & Other
Strange Tales of the Sea*
Edited by Mike Ashley

*Glimpses of the Unknown:
Lost Ghost Stories*
Edited by Mike Ashley

*Haunted Houses: Two
Novels by Charlotte Riddell*
Edited by Andrew Smith

*Spirits of the Season:
Christmas Hauntings*
Edited by Tanya Kirk

British Library Tales of the Weird collects a thrilling array of uncanny story-telling, from the realms of gothic, supernatural and horror fiction. With stories ranging from the 19th century to the present day, this series revives long-lost material from the Library's vaults to thrill again alongside beloved classics of the weird fiction genre.